*What kind of woman would marry
a man she only just met?
The kind with nothing to lose.*

Long ago, Evelyn Cross sacrificed her good name, her freedom, and any hope for love. Now, in the remote English countryside, she struggles to survive and avoid the scandal threatening to destroy all she holds dear . . . until a sinfully handsome viscount arrives on her doorstep, offering marriage, salvation, and tempting her with so much more . . .

*What kind of man would marry
a woman he only just met?
The kind bound by duty.*

Fresh from war, Spencer Lockhart returns home to claim his title and right the wrong his cousin perpetrated upon Evelyn Cross. In need of a wife, marrying her is a small price to pay for duty. But when he meets her, the fiery chit is not what he expects to find in a ruined lady. As desire flares hotly between them, honor is the last thing on his mind . . .

*What kind of man and woman would
marry when they've only just met?
The kind who could ignite a scandal
with just one touch.*

By Sophie Jordan

IN SCANDAL THEY WED
SINS OF A WICKED DUKE
SURRENDER TO ME
ONE NIGHT WITH YOU
TOO WICKED TO TAME
ONCE UPON A WEDDING NIGHT

Coming Soon

WICKED NIGHTS WITH A LOVER

Sophie Jordan

In SCANDAL THEY WED

AVON
An Imprint of HarperCollinsPublishers

AVON BOOKS
An Imprint of HarperCollins*Publishers*
10 East 53rd Street
New York, New York 10022-5299

Copyright © 2010 by Sharie Kohler
ISBN 978-0-06-157921-9
www.avonromance.com

First Avon Books paperback printing: April 2010

Avon Trademark Reg. U.S. Pat. Off. and in Other Countries, Marca Registrada, Hecho en U.S.A.
HarperCollins® is a registered trademark of HarperCollins Publishers.

Printed in the U.S.A.

10 9 8 7 6 5 4 3 2 1

For Jane Welborn:
Sometimes you meet a person and just know.
You were part of my heart before we ever met.

Acknowledgments

Each book has its different journey, each with its own joys and pains. I have several people to thank for taking this book's journey with me. To my editor, May Chen, for understanding and seeing so much in these pages . . . and being able to convey it all to me so that I can see it, too. Thank you! Maura Kye-Casella, for being the kind of agent who always calls, and leaves me smiling when I hang up.

Despite the hours that I sit alone typing at my keyboard, writing is never a solitary process. For those who have held my hand, brainstormed and saved me in one form or another through the writing of this book: Tera, Carlye, Lindsay, Vicki, Kate, Robyn, Ane, Jane and Ginny. I'm so lucky to have all of you in my life.

And to my wonderful husband and children—you are my life, and the life of every book I write.

Prologue

London, 1850

The screaming had stopped. A blessing and a curse.

Evie watched the wan, young girl collapse back upon the bed, shaking from her ordeal. She was free of the worst of the pain, but now the terrible eventuality that Evie had dreaded these past months was upon them.

An eerie silence held—the sort of silence one absorbs in the midst of a great storm, moments before nature recalls itself and breaks loose her full fury again.

Evie shivered, her skin rippling to gooseflesh. On her voyage home from Barbados, the ship had been struck with one such storm, and she recalled thinking the worst was over in the sudden fall of stillness. She'd been wrong. And she knew better than to think the storm had passed now—it was just beginning.

Seated at the edge of the bed, the midwife worked, chafing her large, square hands over the small bundle she held.

"Is it . . ." Linnie strained for a glimpse of her child.

At last, the babe released a lusty squall. At the glorious sound, Evie breathed her first even breath since her half sister began the arduous task of bringing her bastard into the world—had it been only yesterday? In all truth, it was Evie's first even breath since she'd been sacked and returned home to find her sister compromised.

Evie folded her sister's delicate fingers into her own, hoping she might inject strength into the slight girl.

For the worst was yet to come.

"You did so well." Evie pressed a quick kiss to Linnie's sweat-soaked brow.

Turning to the midwife, Evie saw that she struggled to lift her heavy girth from the bed. Grasping the woman's arm, Evie assisted her to her feet, wincing at the twinge in her side. Inhaling sharply, she fought the discomfort—fought harder the memory of how she had acquired the injury. Six months past and her employer's vicious attack that had prompted her dismissal still troubled her. Broken ribs, she was learning, took time to heal.

Shaking off the memory, bleakness entered her heart as the midwife handed the mewling bundle to her waiting stepmother. Dressed in a pink day gown with yellow trim, Georgianna was sorely out of place in the squalid surroundings of their rented room.

"She'll be fine then? I need her up and about as soon as possible." The tight lines on either side of Georgianna's mouth told Evie that she had not softened her stance.

The midwife shook her head in Linnie's direction. "It took a toll on 'er. Yer girl is small and the babe a big 'un."

Georgianna waved a hand in dismissal, still not glancing at her grandchild. "So long as she'll heal. We've plans for her."

Yes. Evie knew her stepmother's plans. She'd heard of little else since the day Linnie was born. Even as a child, she understood that her stepmother pinned all her hopes and dreams on her daughter. Linnie's beauty and grace would raise them from modest gentility to the privileged ranks of High Society. Needless to say, just as her plans failed to include Evie, they did not include a ruined daughter. Or bastard grandchild.

"I trust your discretion." Georgianna pulled a

pouch of coins from the folds of her skirts. "You may go now."

The midwife frowned, glancing darkly at Evie. "Ye've a lick of sense to ye. Send for me if the bleeding does not—"

"You've already given your instructions," Georgianna broke in. "Now go."

With a noisy sniff, the midwife gathered her things and opened the bedroom door. Papa stood in the hall outside. As the midwife strode past, he stepped inside. "Well. We've that over with then?"

As if it were no more than a messy chore.

"Here, Henry." Georgianna thrust the child into Papa's arms and gave her skirts a little shake, as if holding her grandchild had somehow spoiled her ensemble. "Take him. You remember the address, I trust."

Linnie sagged back against the bed, her weariness slurring her speech. "I have a son. . . ."

"It's of no account," her mother snapped before returning her gaze to Papa. "Henry, get rid of it."

It. A sick taste filled Evie's mouth.

"Drop him at the foundling home, and for God's sake, don't let anyone see your face."

"No," Linnie protested, fighting to rise on her elbows. "I want to keep—"

"Silence!" Georgianna's face mottled with rage. "We've already decided what's to be done. I won't have you ruin yourself, Linnie! Do you understand me?"

Linnie fell back, silent sobs shaking her body.

Evie's heart beat a hard, desperate rhythm in her chest as Papa turned to go. Her hands curled into fists, her nails cutting into her palms. This was *wrong*. She thought of Penwich—all the lonely, forgotten children. The cold winters. The food that never seemed enough . . . and they had not even been orphans, simply forgotten children. What would Linnie's child endure at a foundling home? Would he even survive?

Lurching forward, she grabbed her father's sleeve. "Papa, please. *Don't.*"

She had said those words before. When he'd sent her away to Penwich's. They had failed to sway him then.

Her father stiffened. She knew he resented being dragged into this. He spent his days buried in his cards and brandy, hiding from his family and leaving matters to his wife. That was how Evie ended up dumped at Penwich's at the age of twelve.

"Look at him," Evie pleaded. "He's your grandson."

His gaze dragged down.

"Henry," Georgianna warned in caustic tones. "Don't even consider it."

Evie watched, hope filling her chest as her father's expression changed, loosening, lightened.

"We can't do it!" Georgianna hissed. "It will ruin us! All of us, not just Linnie. An unwed mother is as good as a whore—"

"What if his mother were wed?" Evie quickly inserted before Papa could be swayed back to his wife's side.

"How is that possible?" Georgianna spit out. "Daft girl, everyone knows Linnie couldn't possibly have married—"

"Me," Evie blurted, pounding a hand to her chest. "What about me?"

"Yes!" Linnie struggled back up on her elbows. "Evie just returned from Barbados. No one knows she was forced to return home after that wretched man attacked her. She could say she met someone and married there, and returned to be with her family after his death—"

"Absurd. Who would believe such a tale?" Georgianna huffed and crossed her arms over her chest. "And why would we go to so much trouble when we could just dump the baby at—"

"Because he's our grandson," Papa broke in,

his voice solid, firm in a way that Evie had never heard before.

Georgianna blinked. "Henry, what are you saying?"

"It can work. Evelyn can raise the child. As a widow." Over her stepmother's sputtering, Papa handed Evie the squirming bundle, whispering near her ear, "Remember, you chose this."

Evie nodded, a lump forming in her throat as she gazed down at the child she had just claimed.

He stilled in her arms. It seemed that his liquid dark gaze found her, settling on her face with a curious intensity. Almost as though he recognized her.

"Well, this is idiotic! If the truth should ever come to light, we shall all fall from grace . . . especially you, Evelyn. You can never slip. No one can even suspect the truth!"

Evie touched the baby's cheek with the tip of her finger, wondering if she had ever felt anything so soft, so pure. "I know what I'm doing," she murmured. Or rather, she hoped.

For everyone's sake, she hoped.

Chapter 1

Crimea, 1854

Spencer Lockhart charged down the valley, leaving his regiment behind and hurtling toward the spot where he'd last glimpsed his cousin a moment before his line had disappeared in a volley of fire.

He vaulted from his mount, his throat thick in a way that had nothing to do with the cannon smoke filling his mouth and congesting the air.

The moment he hit the ground, a booming blast rent the air behind him. He ducked as chunks of earth, debris, and other matter he dared not consider showered over him. Artillery shells rained from the sky. His stallion screamed and dropped, shuddering on the ground. The creature's eyes rolled, wild with pain.

Spencer lifted the pistol and fired a round directly into his head. He forced back the tide of grief that threatened to cripple him. Later. There would be time enough later to grieve for the stallion that had carried him through the last years. Time enough if he survived.

Jaw clenched, he scanned the ground thick with bodies and horses until he found Ian. Jumping over soldiers, Spencer crouched near his cousin, using a fallen horse as a shield, all the while assuming he was no better than the rest of his decimated brigade—fodder for the Russian riflemen picking them off at every side.

"Ian!" He slid an arm beneath his cousin.

Ian fixed a glassy stare upon him. He opened his mouth to speak but instead coughed. Blood flew from his lips in a violent spray. Words finally came, a thick, desperate gurgle in the back of his throat. "Spencer! Find her . . . find my child. Make it right."

He spoke as though he were already gone from this world.

"Shut up," Spencer ground out, emotion clogging his throat. He ducked his head at a sudden whistling on the air. Another ball landed nearby, shaking the earth, spraying dirt and debris.

When he lifted his head, blood obscured one eye. His forehead stung. He wiped his face and hauled his cousin closer.

"We're getting out of here." His fingers clenched

Ian's shoulder. "You're going home." Then he added another lie—this one harder to spit past his lips. "Linnie's waiting for you. You're going home to marry her."

His throat thickened with emotion. He knew no such thing to be true, but he had to say it. It was the right thing to say . . . anything to give his cousin hope. To keep him clinging to life.

"You think so?"

"Absolutely. She loves you."

Ian jerked his head side to side. "I left her. I'm just like Cullen and Frederick. I don't deserve her. I should have married her . . . should have given my child my name."

"You couldn't—"

Ian seized Spencer's hand, brought it close to his chest in a grip of surprising strength.

Spencer squinted at him through the burn of smoke.

"Find her," Ian rasped. "And my child. See to them, Spencer. Protect them."

Spencer nodded.

Ian continued, his voice a hard bite on the air, "I'll have your word on it, Spencer."

"You have it." Over their clasped hands, Spencer glanced down at the blood spreading steadily over his cousin's chest. An ever-blossoming puddle, so deep a red it appeared black.

In this, the truth stared at him. It seemed wrong to pretend anymore. Ian was not long for this world.

He squeezed their clasped hands. "I will treat your child as my own. I pledge this to you."

Ian sagged back against the earth, seeming to find peace in Spencer's words. There was no point in reminding him that his Linnie had not responded to his many letters. That she had clearly given up on Ian long ago.

"That's good. Very good." Ian's gaze drifted up, as if he could see something through all the smoke and artillery fire. "Tell her I loved her. With my last breath, I thought of her."

Something soft brushed Spencer's hand. Glancing down, he saw that Ian had pushed a scrap of linen into his hand. The handkerchief initialed EC that he always carried with him.

Grasping it in his hand, Spencer studied it for a moment before looking back down. Into green eyes so like his own, only as lifeless as glass now.

"Ian!" he whispered, then again and again as pain rolled over him. Louder and louder, until the sound of his voice merged, lost with the roaring wind of battle.

Chapter 2

Yorkshire, England, 1855

Sudden wind stirred the icy-still air.

Evelyn sat back and lifted her face, pushing an errant gold-brown strand from her eyes with one dirtied glove. Angling her head, she waited. Listened. For what, she could not hazard a guess. Only something had changed. She knew it, felt it in the cold stroke of wind on her face. Almost like that night in Barbados when she awoke to the dark . . . no longer alone. For her, that night had changed everything. Brought her to this point now.

Shivering, she pushed the memory away and returned to her digging, determined to unearth the parsnips and turnips before the nip of snow she smelled in the air arrived.

Everyone in Little Billings concurred that this was the coldest winter in memory, but she had vowed against losing her vegetables to the late cling of winter. She had already unearthed the cabbage, small and pathetic as they were when she pulled them one by one from the ground.

And yet, as she toiled over her garden, she couldn't completely dismiss the unease sinking through her. Sitting back on her heels, she dropped her hands upon her stained apron and glanced around again, slowly turning her head left and right in exasperation.

Great-aunt Gertrude kneeled at one end of the garden, her rail-thin arms swinging wildly at the tenacious black birds diving for the cauliflowers. Desperation hung thick. Like Evie, her aunt was determined to bring in their meager crop before winter breathed death on them . . . and before the winged creatures devoured their only hope for survival.

"Blast you to perdition, you devils!"

Evie fought a smile. One wouldn't know from the look of her, but Aunt Gertie could eat more than the Queen's army. Ever since Linnie's death— and the subsequent halt to their allowance—food had become scant. Evie's father could offer no assistance. His son-in-law's generosity ended with Linnie's death. Evie couldn't fault her half sister's husband. Why should he support the few clinging relations of his dead wife?

On a nearby blanket, Marguerite played blocks with Nicholas. Evie watched her son as he carefully constructed a tall tower, biting his lip in concentration, sweetly unaware of the world that pushed and growled at every side. He paused to bask in Marguerite's murmurs of approval.

Sighing, Evie dug harder, pulling forth more parsnips, renewed with the resolve to feed her family—her child. *Linnie's child*, a small voice whispered across her mind.

Head bent, she stilled as a shadow fell over her.

"There's a gentleman waiting for you in the parlor."

Her stomach quivered. The words only confirmed her sense of foreboding, convinced her something *had* lurked in that cold kiss of breeze.

Her fingers loosened, dropping a parsnip. She watched it roll to a stop in the dirt before lifting her gaze to her housekeeper. Mrs. Murdoch leaned against the crumbling stone wall edging the garden, breathless, a hand pressed to her impressive bosom as though she had run the short distance from the house.

A gentleman. Harmless sounding, but Evie knew better, knew that the safe haven she had carved for herself stood on shaky ground.

Hopefully, this gentleman was not another bill

collector calling to demand recompense of an outstanding debt.

The Harbour, dubbed thusly when her aunt's fiancé jilted her the morning of their wedding some fifty years ago, belonged to Aunt Gertie. The majority of the once sizable property had been sold off in parts throughout the years. Only the house and a small parcel of acreage sat intact.

The Harbour and nearby village of Little Billings were a far cry from Evie's youthful dreams of adventure, but those dreams had belonged to another girl. She had sacrificed those dreams for Linnie's sake. And Nicholas's.

She wasn't a girl to believe in dreams and wish on stars any longer.

With a hand to her knee, she pushed to her feet. "Who is he?"

Mrs. Murdoch shook her salt and pepper head. "He ain't one of them collectors. Doesn't have the look. Said his name is Lockhart. Spencer Lockhart. Know him?"

Evie shook her head, frowning. "I've never heard the name."

"Yes, well, he looks a bit familiar."

"You have a caller?" Marguerite approached, her hand clasped around Nicholas's chubby one. She arched her dark elegant brows. "Dr. Sheffield, perhaps?"

Evie's cheeks warmed at the mention of the village doctor. "No."

Nicholas tugged Marguerite in the direction of the pond, very nearly pulling her down off her feet. "Maggie, c'mon."

"In a moment, darling. I'm talking to your mother."

"Go on." Evie slid off her gloves. "I'll see to our . . . guest."

Marguerite's dark eyes clung to hers. "You're certain?" Her friend knew her well enough to decipher when something bothered her. They'd spent too many years together at the Penwich School for Virtuous Girls, suffering through cold winters and meager rations—enduring the bullying of bigger girls, *enduring* Master Brocklehurst.

For some reason, the prospect of facing this unknown caller rattled Evie. She prayed Mrs. Murdoch was correct and he wasn't here to collect on a debt. But whoever he was, her stomach knotted at the idea of facing him.

"I'll see to this. You take Nicholas to the pond. It's your last day here. Enjoy yourself." Even as she said the words, a thickness rose in her throat to know that Marguerite would return to London tomorrow and she would not see her again for another year.

Shoving aside the grim thought, she pasted a reassuring smile on her face for the benefit of her housekeeper and Marguerite. Not for herself. That would be futile. Nothing could rid her of the uneasy fluttering in her belly.

She walked a steady line, entering the house through the kitchen. Mrs. Murdoch followed close behind, wringing her apron with one hand. Evie turned, nearly colliding with the overanxious housekeeper.

"No need to accompany me. I'll be fine."

Mrs. Murdoch's ruddy face scowled. "I'll fetch Mr. Murdoch. We might require—"

"I'm certain we don't need to bother Mr. Murdoch from his fishing. Besides, we need whatever he catches for supper."

Before Mrs. Murdoch could protest further, she spun around and departed the kitchen, taking the narrow steps two at a time to reach the main floor. Her feet moved silently down the worn runner leading to the front parlor.

Outside, the wind whistled, coming to life in earnest now. Belatedly, the thought crossed her mind that Nicholas might have needed his heavier coat for a trek to the pond.

That thought vanished, however, as she entered the parlor.

A lean figure stood with his back to her, staring out the window at the long-neglected front grounds. Mrs. Murdoch hadn't bothered to take his coat, and the elegance of the dark greatcoat only heightened the shabbiness of her parlor.

For a moment, she observed him in silence, staring at the back of him, tall and imposing. With his hands locked behind his back, he struck her as rigid as a rock. She struggled to swallow past the tightness in her throat and imagined that he was probably here to collect on a debt, after all.

She moved deeper into the room, preparing herself for the unpleasant task of pleading and bartering with the gentleman. Perhaps he had need of a good seamstress or laundress? Or possessed a fondness for skinny parsnips. A laugh strangled, died in her dry throat.

Her skirt whispered against the arm of a chair as she moved. The floor creaked beneath her feet.

He turned in a swift, fluid motion.

She opened her mouth to speak, but froze. Her gaze locked with his as her entire body seized, the breath freezing inside her lungs. Staring upon his handsome face, she knew. She understood. The premonition she had felt in the breath of that icy wind made perfect, horrid sense.

The blood rushed to her head. Suddenly dizzy, she reached out to grasp the back of a nearby chair to keep from falling to her knees. *Dear God.*

Staring into his face, she felt as though she looked through a window into the years ahead. That she stared at the future. At a face time had yet to mold.

The moment hung, words waiting to fill it. He did not speak, only further evidence, further proof. Her stomach rolled, rebelled.

It was he—her greatest nightmare come true. He could be no other.

The single fear that had lurked in the back of her head all these years, the remote possibility that she had convinced herself too remote, too impossible, had, in fact, become reality.

The father of her sister's child, Linnie's child—*her* child—stood before her in her parlor.

Chapter 3

Spencer gazed at the woman Ian had spoken of until the very end, and he couldn't help feeling . . . unsettled. This was Linnie?

He had known his cousin well, felt as though he had buried himself right alongside Ian those months ago in the Crimea.

Fighting for life beside Spencer, Ian had talked only of Linnie Cosgrove. With nary a letter from her, Ian had remained unflagging in his affections. Spencer never understood.

Hands clasped behind his back, Spencer surveyed this paragon of womanhood, the female who brought Ian to heel. Staring into her wide blue eyes, he searched his memory, recalling all the accounts he had heeded of Ian's paramour.

Was it possible Ian had never mentioned the color of her hair? Spencer had always imagined golden tresses. The marginally attractive female with sun-streaked brown hair spilling in untidy tendrils from a haphazard knot on her head did not coincide with the image he had constructed.

She was neither short nor tall. Her slender frame lacked any notable curves. As she stood before him, he was reminded of the many sturdy Turkish girls he had observed toiling the fields while abroad.

"Madam." He nodded his head in salute.

She said nothing. Her nose and cheeks glowed red. A smudge of dirt marred her jawline. She wore an old-fashioned pinafore over a dress so hideous that he couldn't help wondering why she took pains to protect it. The ugly brown wool that peeped out around the pinafore looked fit for the burn pile.

Her eyes stood as her one remarkable feature. Slightly slanted, the wide, crystalline blue pools surveyed him coolly, as if he were a bug to be scraped off the soles of her boots.

The untidy creature before him looked wholly woman—confident, mature, and bold as she raked him with her piercing blue eyes. Ian had praised her angelic smile and sweet shyness, but there was nothing celestial about her.

Perhaps motherhood had altered her. *Or marriage,* an inner voice reminded. Her father had revealed to him that she was a widow. A truth or fabrication to protect her from ruin? The latter, he suspected. All the same, he felt an instant response to her.

Because she belongs to Ian . . . belonged, he quickly amended. He finally faced her—the phantom woman to fill Ian's world, and, thereby, Spencer's. His response was purely that. Nothing more.

"May I help you?" She lifted her chin, staring down the slim line of her nose.

The sight of her, garbed so shabbily and yet facing him with temerity gleaming in her eyes, reminded him of the women that followed their armies. Haunted, haggard creatures, resigned but determined, prepared to toss their skirts for half a pence and a warm bed for the night. Camp followers ready to spread their thighs to guarantee a day's survival.

Despite his anger at her for failing to answer Ian's letters, the similarity to those pitiable women left a foul taste in his mouth. Clearly she'd suffered her own struggles.

"Sir?" Her eyes snapped blue fire. "Who are you?"

Not quite ready to answer, his gaze crawled over her, imagining her free of her drab attire, as Ian might have seen her—all lithe lines and smooth female flesh.

Clearing his throat, he struggled to swallow past the sudden tightness. Clearly, he needed a woman. He had not slaked his lusts in weeks, too focused on his grief for Ian and the business of selling off his commission and returning home.

He recalled the serving girl at the inn where he had spent the previous night—remembered the invitation in her eyes. He needn't leave immediately following this errand. A night's delay wouldn't hurt. He was in no hurry to reach his family's estate, after all. To face his duty. To enter Society.

"Miss Linnie Cosgrove?" he queried, bowing slightly and still struggling to reconcile the earthy, beddable creature before him to the paragon he had placed on a pedestal. A chore, that.

She nodded, face ashen, bloodless. "Cross," she murmured. "It's Mrs. Cross now."

That's right. She claimed widowhood. A ruse to protect herself from ruin, he felt certain.

Nodding, he drew his body taller. Focusing his gaze just above her head, he spoke the words he'd traveled here to say. "With heavy heart, I regret to inform you of the death of Lieutenant Ian Holcomb." A nerve ticked near his eye, his only surrender to emotion.

He continued, his words ripping fresh the pain he had lived with ever since burying his cousin. "I believe you were . . . acquainted."

Acquainted. A gentle euphemism to apply to

the girl who'd borne his cousin's bastard. If, in fact, she had. He'd yet to confirm that matter. Her father made no mention of a child, and he was not so bold or thoughtless to inquire.

"Y-yes," she stammered.

He dropped his gaze to her face again. Her unyielding exterior had vanished. She looked ready to crumble. Stepping forward, he clasped her elbow. A spark shot through him at the contact. He scowled at the unwanted sensation.

Clearly, she was not unaffected either. She gasped. Or perhaps his scowl distressed her. His glares had been fierce enough to inject his soldiers with a healthy dose of fear on more than one occasion.

With an inward curse, he released her and motioned to the settee. The last five years of his life had been in service to the crown. He'd forgotten how to conduct himself in Society. He possessed little in the way of social grace. None was needed on the battlefield. He could scarcely recall the last occasion he'd stood in a lady's parlor.

She sank down with a sigh. "When . . . how?"

"He died at Balaclava." Still standing, he fished the pouch from his pocket. "He wanted you to have this." He unraveled the bit of soiled lace handkerchief from the pouch.

She accepted it, her thumb brushing the EC embroidered in faint pink thread at the corner. "I remember this," she murmured, barely audible.

He grimaced at the blood on it. "I tried to clean it—" He shrugged. "He carried it with him always." Accusation laced his voice. "He never forgot you."

Clutching the scrap of fabric, her eyes snapped to his. "Is that so?"

He blinked at the bright fury there. It amazed him that Ian never mentioned her eyes when he extolled her many attributes. He had never seen such a clear blue before. Like sun glowing off the Baltic.

"If he cared enough to carry this, why did he not care to write me then?"

Incredulity tore through him, gnawing at the grieving wound in his heart. His fist knotted at his side. "Surely you jest! Ian wrote you. Tirelessly." He shook his head with a growl. "Clearly *you* moved on, forgot Ian." He nodded once. Hard. "Very well. The least you owed him was a letter of explanation. Every week, he wrote you. To his death." His voice sharpened to a razor's edge. "Even when he received no word from you, he still wrote."

Angry splotches of color filled her face. She closed her eyes and shook her head in weary motion. "Of course. They *would* . . . do that."

"They who?" he demanded.

"My parents."

"What did your parents—"

"Keep his letters from me, of course. They thought him the worst sort of reprobate and wished for me to break all ties with him."

His lips pressed into a grim line.

She continued, "He would have sent correspondence to my parents' residence." The statement brought a sudden frown to her face. "How did you find me?"

"I called on your parents in Surrey. They directed me here." His lips tightened. "Your father scarcely granted me a moment in his study before telling me where to find you. He seemed most eager for me to leave."

She tugged on her lower lip, twisting the tender flesh until it turned a deep, provocative pink. Sudden desire licked through him at the innocuous gesture, and he looked sharply away, inhaling a deep breath and barely registering her murmured, "Yes. He would be uncomfortable at your presence."

He glanced back at her, watching as she folded the handkerchief into a tiny square with trembling fingers.

"I must know. Did you bear Ian's child?"

Her shoulders pulled back and a militant gleam

came into her eyes. "It would seem Ian told you a great deal. How good of him to gossip with the soldiers of his regiment—"

"Ian," he broke in, his voice falling with the sharp clap of command he'd grown accustomed to using with his men, "was my cousin. Upon his death, he charged me with the welfare of his child."

The color bled from her cheeks. "Cousins?"

"On my mother's side. Ian purchased a commission in my regiment so we could serve together." He cocked his head. "Did he never mention me?"

She was back to tugging her lip again. "Um, that would seem to be the case."

His gaze narrowed on her pale face. Knowing Ian, he had been too busy trying to get beneath her skirts. Shaking the thought free, he focused on the only thing that mattered, the one thing that demanded his presence in her parlor.

"The child. Did you bear my cousin's child?"

"Yes." The word escaped her in a breathy rush. "Nicholas will be four in April."

"And I gather you're really not a widow."

Her chin lifted, blue eyes sparking in a way that made his gut tighten. "What else should I have done? The world is unkind to whores and bastards."

He flinched. "You're not a whore."

"But the world would view me as such."

He gave a single nod. "I don't fault your actions."

She clutched her hands around the small, folded handkerchief and smiled almost cruelly. "How kind of you to approve."

Impudent chit.

For a long moment they stared at one another. A curious tension washed through the air between them. He longed to wipe free the cruel edge of mockery curving her lips. The longer he stared, the stronger the impulse . . . and the warmer his blood heated.

Inhaling through his nose, he recalled himself and forced coldness inside him where the heat stirred. "I would like to see the boy. I'm certain you understand I have a stake—"

"No."

"I *will* see him."

She sucked in a deep breath. He watched the rise of her chest and decided she might not be lacking *all* curves. Her breasts appeared to be more than a handful beneath the straight fall of her ghastly pinafore. A fact of which he did *approve*.

She shook her head fiercely. "I thank you for coming here. You've honored me in journeying this far to deliver the news, but you must know your presence puts me in jeopardy. It puts Nicholas in jeopardy. You bear a striking resemblance to him. The last thing I need is speculation on—"

"Rest easy. I have no wish to expose you. But that said, I've a stake in the lad and I'm not leaving until I've seen him."

She moistened her lips. Her fingers tapped the arm of her chair as she weighed his words.

He arched a brow, waiting.

"Very well. Might I prevail on you to call later? I would like time to prepare him accordingly."

"Prepare him?"

"Introducing him to you will lead to questions. I must consider what to tell him—"

"Why not the truth? I am a relation to his father. That might also relieve outside speculation—"

"Or feed it."

He shrugged. "An unlikely risk."

"A risk nonetheless."

He shrugged again. "The boy is my kin. I'll take any risk to assure myself of his well-being."

She bristled, the color high in her face. "My son is well loved."

"There are considerations greater than love."

Her nostrils flared ever slightly. "Trust a man to believe that."

He felt the corner of his mouth lift in a sneer. Before he could stop himself, he shot back, "Trust a lady well and truly compromised to set store in notions of love rather than the practical matters of life that require attending."

A shocked breath crashed from her lips. The hand in her lap twitched as though she wished to strike him.

It certainly had not been his intention to provoke her, and yet he was doing just that. He said nothing more, merely held her brightly defiant gaze . . . and tried not to stare at the alluring way her dark lashes fringed those barely slanted eyes.

After some moments, she nodded stiffly. "Very well."

He gave a curt nod. "I will call on the morrow."

"Tomorrow," she returned.

Even as she agreed, he sensed more behind her acquiescence. Something lurked in the guileless blue of her eyes.

If he was not mistaken, he thought it might be fear.

Chapter 4

For one brief, panicked moment, Evie considered packing her family and belongings and fleeing. Then sanity returned and with it the cold reminder that she possessed no funds and had nowhere to go. Certainly, she could not rely on her father to save her. He could scarcely support himself since Linnie's death.

Hopping from the settee, she darted to the parlor window, watching as the devilishly handsome gentleman who had crowded her parlor and overwhelmed her senses rode away.

Spencer Lockhart. Ian's cousin. *Nicholas's cousin.* Her stomach knotted and she shivered as the ramifications of his arrival settled over her like a cold blanket of snow.

Should the truth come to light—that she was no widow, that she was not Nicholas's mother . . .

The prospect shook her. Her knees suddenly

felt weak and trembly. She reclaimed her seat, pressing a hand to her twisting stomach.

A pariah of Society *and* poor as a church mouse. A magistrate would well see fit to hand Nicholas over to Spencer Lockhart. The mere thought sent her pulse racing at her throat.

Ease yourself, Evie. You don't know that he even wants the boy. He just wants to see him. Meet him. Understandable.

She drew a deep breath into her lungs, letting it cool her panic.

"Evie?" Marguerite entered the room. "Did your guest leave?"

She nodded mutely as her friend sank down beside her.

"I saw him pass. A handsome man."

Handsome? Bitter laughter escaped her. "Indeed," she choked. A relation to Ian, was it any wonder? Her sister had often blamed her weak will on Ian Holcomb's face. Now a witness to such masculine beauty herself, she could almost understand why Linnie had succumbed. She frowned. It was more than Lockhart's handsome face and broad shoulders that unnerved her. He looked at her as no man had. As though he knew her intimately. Or would like to. His eyes mesmerized.

Marguerite's warm hands closed around one of her tightly fisted hands. "Who was he?"

She pressed her lips into a tight line, afraid to speak, afraid that if she opened her lips she would break, shatter into pieces.

"Evie, you're frightening me. Please say something." Marguerite's sherry-brown eyes searched her face, kind and encouraging. She always had that nurturing way about her.

"The gentleman who just left was cousin to the man who compromised Linnie." She inhaled before continuing. "He came to inform me that Ian died with the Light Brigade." Another deep breath. "And he wants to meet Nicholas."

"Does he know?" Marguerite quickly asked, her clever mind instantly grasping the situation, knowing where danger waited.

"No. He believes I'm Linnie. That I'm Nicholas's true mother. The name Linnie can just as well be a nickname for Evelyn."

Marguerite's hands chafed over hers. "Don't fret then. There's no reason he should suspect you're anyone else. Correct?"

"Correct," Evie echoed, but the word rattled around inside her head. There was nothing *correct* in this situation. Nothing *correct* with Spencer Lockhart's nosing about. A ragged breath shuddered past her lips.

Nothing *correct* about the tightness in her belly when he stood within five feet of her.

* * *

Spencer made short work of shedding his clothes. The serving girl waited for him on the bed, undressed, ready, her head cocked to the side and eyes gleaming with lusty approval as she watched him discard the last of his garments.

"You're a finely made fellow." Her hands stretched out to touch him as he came down on the bed.

Spencer was no saint, even if he wasn't quite the Lothario his pedigree demanded. His father, his half brothers, even Ian . . . scoundrels each, a score of peccadilloes to each their credit. In comparison, his sexual habits ran tame.

All the same, he'd taken his pleasure with women over the years. Faceless females. Usually camp followers or village women trying to earn money to survive the ravages of war.

They would come to the soldiers' tents in the dark of night and offer their services, so no one in their community would learn of their shame—or the means they took to support their families.

Such arrangements suited him best. No entanglements. No emotional involvements. Not since Adara, not since he'd borne witness to the horror of war, had he involved his heart with a woman. He doubted he ever could be that boy again. So trusting. A young fool who believed in the love poets spouted.

As he sank down beside the copper-haired maid, the wan, narrow face of Linnie Cosgrove—*Cross*, he supposed he should think of her—materialized in his head. Those impossibly blue eyes of hers watched him—*glared* at him. As though she stood witness to his cavorting.

Instantly, his ardor cooled. At least his ardor for the willing wench in his bed.

Thoughts of Linnie, however, consumed him.

He growled low in his throat. Why should thoughts of one colorless slip of a girl plague him when a well-rounded female kissed upon his neck? It was all Ian's fault. His cousin had imprinted her on his soul, it would seem. A tattoo etched for eternity in his head.

Squeezing his eyes tightly closed, he kissed the maid hard, deep. Desperate to rouse himself, his hands caressed her plump breasts. She moaned, her naked body arching beneath him.

Still, *she* remained firmly embedded there. In his head. *Miss Cosgrove . . . bloody hell, Cross. Linnie.*

The maid scored her nails down his back, pulling him closer, urging him to claim her. In a move that likely sent every Winters male turning in his grave, he tore free from her.

Collapsing on his side, he flung an arm across his forehead. The satisfaction he had hoped to achieve in a quick romp eluded him. His chest felt as hollow as ever, his body achingly unsatisfied.

The female beside him gasped for breath. "What's wrong? Did I do something—"

"No, I've simply had a change of . . . heart." He felt his lip curl in a grimace as an image of the disagreeable Mrs. Cross rose up in his mind.

"Oh." She lifted up on one elbow to trail a finger down his chest. "Pity. It happens."

His mouth twisted. She thought him incapable. He didn't feel compelled to correct the misapprehension. Easier than explaining that thoughts of another woman drove him to distraction.

"We can try again. Later perhaps?"

"Perhaps," he replied vaguely, wondering how to kindly request that she depart his room.

"You called on The Harbour today, I hear tell."

He grunted, idly wondering how he was to cope with Society when he could scarcely tolerate one maid's aimless chatter. How would he endure the dames of the *ton*?

The girl wiggled into a sitting position, brazen and comfortable in her nudity. "What business does a fine gentleman like you have with those there?"

"None of your affair." Didn't she have chores to attend to?

"You know the Cosgroves then? Widow Cross is an uppity prig. Not at all friendly."

A smile twitched his lips. The description was not amiss. "Indeed?" He imagined that she had built a certain distance between herself and the outside world. The better to protect her house of cards.

The girl continued, "Not that she has any right to such airs, given she's practically destitute. And she has no looks to speak of—"

"You may go," he broke in, beyond caring for her feelings.

Her cheeks reddened. She leaned forward, brushing a heavy, swaying breast against his arm. "Would you not like to try again—"

"Sadly, no." He did not smile, did not bother injecting kindness into his voice. His words rang out coldly.

"Very well." Snapping her mouth into a hard line, she hopped from the bed. "Is it what I said about the Widow Cross? Didn't mean no insult. You've no cause to feel protective over *her*. Everyone in these parts likes her well enough. Sour ways and all, she's made do." Her eyes snapped hotly. "Has a fine gentleman like Peter Sheffield faithfully trotting after her—"

"She has a suitor?"

"A lovesick puppy more like it," she sneered.

The notion shouldn't have bothered him, shouldn't have lodged like a rock in his chest. Ian himself had often wondered if Linnie had married another . . . if that explained the unanswered letters. A suitor shouldn't give him pause. On the contrary, Spencer should be relieved she'd found a gentleman to care for her.

So why did his hands curl at his sides at the thought of some faceless man daring to tread in his cousin's footsteps?

Or was that the true reason?

The servant girl left the room, coin in hand.

Spencer dressed quickly, his movements angry. After a few moments, he admitted his anger was directed at himself. Because he was lying. To himself. To his cousin's ghost.

He'd just fondled another woman . . . all the while thinking of Mrs. Cross. *Linnie!* The woman who had sat upon a gilded pedestal between him and Ian throughout the war, protected, revered. Today, he'd finally met her. And all he wanted to do was yank her down from that lofty pedestal and sample the woman's charms for himself.

He snorted, disgusted. He should possess more honor, more respect for Ian, than to think of her as he would any woman whose charms he itched to taste.

Striding from his room, his boots bit into the wood planks as he ventured downstairs into the taproom, ready to drown his guilt in drink. Tomorrow he would meet Ian's son, content himself with the knowledge that he was safe and in good hands, and then he would leave, forgetting this awful infatuation for Mrs. Cross.

And go where?

He pushed the unwelcome question aside. He'd sold his commission. He couldn't hide from the reality of his new situation forever. He must face his responsibilities. A sour taste coated his mouth. If he could only find some way to acquire the necessary bride and take up the reins as Viscount Winters without enduring Society and all its falseness. He would gladly suffer a battlefield and dine on cannon fire rather than walk the ballrooms of the *ton* where lily-handed aristocrats opined about a war they dared not fight in themselves.

The door to the inn flung open. A great gust of wind blew inside the establishment's toasty confines. A man stomped within, shaking his greatcoat about him as if that would rid him of the wintry cold. The innkeeper rushed to greet him, waving at one of the many empty tables. A night like this, the villagers were likely warming themselves before their own hearths.

The gentleman handed his greatcoat off to a serving girl and sank down at a table.

Hands cupped around his tankard of ale, Spencer assessed the newcomer, thinking him familiar. But what were the odds that he should know anyone in this small corner of Yorkshire?

At that moment, the man's gaze lifted and locked on him. "Lord Winters! Can it be I've actually found you?"

Spencer stiffened, recognizing him. Andrew Bagby, his late father's man of affairs. He'd changed, aged, but his lilting, Scottish brogue had not.

"Mr. Bagby," Spencer greeted as the older man settled his thin frame across the table from him.

Removing his gloves, Bagby chafed his hands together. "Frightful cold, is it not? Cannot tell you how relieved I am that I found you. This traipsing about the country is not for me. How you ever managed to do so the last few years—" Bagby paused to smile as a serving girl set a fresh tankard before him. "Do you have anything to recommend from the kitchens, my girl?"

"We've a tasty shepherd's pie."

"Brilliant." Bagby nodded happily. "My lord?"

The serving girl's eyes widened at the designation.

"I'm fine, thank you," Spencer bit out, displeased to have his title bandied about when he himself had not seen fit to adopt it. It had yet to sink in and feel a part of him. The girl left and Spencer focused his ire at the man before him. "What are you doing here, Bagby?"

At the edge in Spencer's voice, some of Bagby's cheerfulness evaporated. "Your stepmother sent me to find you."

"Of course." The very woman who made certain he felt unwanted and unwelcome in his own home, among his own family, now clamored for his return.

"You're the new viscount. She insists you return—"

"She's in no position to insist anything."

Bagby smiled almost pityingly. "Lady Winters is a formidable woman. She is not to be dissuaded."

"How did you find me?"

"Your sister."

"Ah," he nodded. He'd visited his stepsister first. Rose had always been sweet and loving despite her mother's influence. Rose gave a damn about him, unlike his father, half brothers, or the various Lady Winterses to pass through his life, all of whom had been happy to ignore him, a son no one deemed necessary, especially as he was a product of the viscount's most unacceptable wife—a nobody from Northumberland.

Bagby's gaze flicked about him with distaste. "Provincial little backwater, isn't it?"

"Better than the Crimea."

Bagby's food arrived and he dug in, murmuring his approval as he speared a greasy cube of potato into his mouth. "At least the food is palatable."

"Go home, Bagby," Spencer announced. "I'll put in an appearance soon enough."

Bagby shook his head. "Your stepmother won't accept that. She's determined you wed before the year is out and secure an heir. She sees it as her duty. In the last five years, she watched both your brothers die. One after the other." He tsked and shook his head at the tragedy of it.

Two young men struck down in the prime of their youth might seem astounding had they not been Winterses. The very nature of their existence had put them at risk. They'd expired as Society would have expected. Frederick shot dead in a duel, and Cullen when the brothel he'd frequented had caught fire.

"She counts herself fortunate that you did not die at Balaclava. When word reached us that you did not fall with your regiment in the charge, she wept with joy."

Spencer snorted. "Hard to imagine that."

"Not so much. She'd rather her fate rest with you than some distant cousin who would toss her and Lady Adara to the streets."

"And how are they so certain I won't?"

Bagby laughed. The sound grated. "You've a noble heart, ever since you were a lad. Always saving birds and stray mongrels. Remember the bag of kittens Cullen tossed into the river? We thought you dead when you jumped off the bridge after them."

Spencer grimaced. If a farmer hadn't pulled him to shore several miles downriver, he would likely be dead.

"Your stepmother knows you'll do right by her. Your honor would permit nothing less." Bagby dabbed at his mouth with a napkin. "She and Lady Adara are already working on the guest list and planning a grand gala for your return. The hope is for you to sign a betrothal contract that very night."

With a groan, Spencer dropped his head into his hand, picturing his return home with ugly clarity. His stepmother, with Adara at her side, would toss every eligible young lady of the season at him. He would be bombarded on every side with mealymouthed chits and their garrulous mamas. The harder he resisted, the harder they would push him into Society.

All he wanted was a little peace in his life, but he would have none of it until he married. Until he provided an heir. He straightened on the bench as a sudden thought seized him. He need only intercept his stepmother and Adara's aggravating plans and arrive home . . . *ineligible.*

But there was only one way to do that.

His blood began to pump as an idea grew, took hold.

Rising to his feet, the legs of the bench scraped the floor.

"Where are you going?"

"For a ride."

"This late, milord?" Bagby glanced to the door that rattled, buffeted from the wind outside. "In this weather?"

"I need to clear my head." In a firm and unflinching voice, he commanded, "Return home tomorrow, Bagby. Assure my stepmother all her wishes shall be satisfied. I will secure my title and perform my duty."

Bagby blinked, clearly startled by this happy turn. "Indeed. Very good, my lord. She will be most content to hear that. Most content."

With a curt nod, he swung on his heels and left the inn.

Chapter 5

Spencer Lockhart's name tossed through her head as violently as the winter winds blowing outside her window. Unable to sleep, she pushed down the counterpane and dropped to the floor, padding barefoot across the worn-thin rug.

Since his departure, she'd moved about in a daze, still seeing him in her mind. Imposing and handsome in her tiny parlor, his gaze blistering and intense, that deep voice of his rippling her skin in a way that both thrilled and scared her.

He was a handsome man, true. But she'd witnessed the devastation handsome men wrought over women. She would not be so weak.

At the first sight of him, at his striking resemblance to Nicholas, she thought she faced Ian himself. Linnie's lover.

She knew better now. Despite his resemblance to Nicholas, there was nothing soft or romantic about him, nothing that would have spoken to

Linnie's tender heart. Her sister would never have fallen in love with such a man—all hard edges and firm, unsmiling lips. The mere sight of him would have terrified her.

As he terrified me.

But for different reasons.

She crouched, opened the grate and stoked the coals, adding a few more from the nearby bucket, determined to keep the embers alive and burning. Not just for warmth. Even in summer, her grate burned, imbuing the room with a red-orange glow. Precious light. To stave off the dark. The always waiting dark, eager to pull her into its frightening maw.

Not since Barbados had she slept in the dark. Not since she'd learned that monsters lived and breathed, walked the earth in the guise of man. One couldn't see what was coming in the dark . . . or what was already there, lurking close, ready to pounce.

It was true. As helpless as a child, she feared the dark. None knew of her shaming secret, her embarrassing weakness. And none ever would.

Sighing, she strode to the window, her nightrail whispering at her ankles. The full moon sat high in the sky. Frost gleamed on the ground, glinting like diamonds on the grass. Soon it would snow. Relief ran through her to know they'd saved what they could from the garden. For a few months, at least, they would have enough food.

Shivering, she lifted her palm to the window, pressing her hand against the chilled glass. A few months. She swallowed against the rising thickness in her throat. After that, she had no choice. In the spring, she would approach her father. Beg, if need be.

The image of Spencer Lockhart flashed through her mind again. Another worry. At least until tomorrow. Tomorrow, he would leave. After he met Nicholas.

His presence rattled her . . . made her feel strange and alive in places she thought dead. He made her *feel,* made her remember, brought back, in a dizzying rush, her girlish dreams of adventure and excitement.

The moon gleamed full and bright overhead, casting the front lawn and drive with an iridescent sheen. She squinted into the distance, gazing at the horizon, and spotted a figure at the crest of the hill, just beyond the drive. A lone horseman etched perfectly in the moonlight. Spencer Lockhart. She knew it was he. It could be no one else.

Her heart seized in her chest. What was he doing here? Immediately, the impulse to run into the nursery and fold Nicholas into her arms overcame her. Foolish.

Dropping her hand from the glass, she took a hasty step back and drew a deep breath into her lungs. He wasn't the sort to steal a child. Even if her worst fear was true and he was here to claim Nicholas, he wasn't the sort to sneak into a house in the dead of night and do so. She didn't know how she knew this much of him, but she did. He would do so honestly, openly, using the law to his advantage. And she would fight him to her last breath.

"He can't. He can't. He can't." The words bled from her lips in a rushed mantra.

Why would he wish to saddle himself with a child? To take Nicholas from the only mother he knew? As long as he believed in her lie, believed her to be Linnie, he would not separate them. She tugged on her bottom lip, convinced of this. She need only to make certain he never learned the truth.

"Why are you here?" she whispered to the shadowy figure, so small in the distance, and yet he filled her whole world at the moment, larger even than the pulsing night.

Did he worry she would flee in the night with his cousin's son? Perhaps if she had some place to go, funds to support herself, a father that cared for her as much as he did for himself, she would.

But no. She needed to stay and convince him of what she had managed to convince the rest of the world. Then he could leave The Harbour, confident in the care being given to his kin.

Man and rider stood upon the rise for several more moments, the wind whipping his greatcoat, tossing it like a banner around him.

She held her breath, watching, bewildered.

The stallion pawed the earth impatiently. Fingers pulling at her lip, she shifted impatiently on the balls of her feet. What thoughts crossed his mind as he stared at her cottage?

Her voice cracked the silence of her bedchamber. "Go. Turn and go."

At last, he did.

She watched him disappear, praying that perhaps he had changed his mind and wouldn't return on the morrow.

Sliding beneath the crisp covers, she winced at the uselessness of that request. Of course he would. He considered himself some sort of protector, appointed by Nicholas's father. In his mind, that gave him the right to stay, to pass judgment on her. Anger simmered through her as she recalled his snapped words.

"Trust a lady well and truly compromised to set store in notions of love rather than the practical matters of life that require attending."

For years, she'd treaded a fine edge, guarding her deception, always counting pennies. She attended a great deal to the practical matters of life! Not a day passed when she did not.

Turning on her side, she rested a hand beneath her cheek. Her stomach twisted and flipped at the thought of seeing him again.

He frightened her. His size, his austerity, his very maleness. The intensity of his stare filled her with an uneasiness that had little to do with her closely guarded secrets and everything to do with how much he affected her and reminded her that she was a woman. A woman who had dismissed notions of intimacy and physical love long ago.

For the first time since she returned from Barbados, she questioned her determination to live life with no knowledge of the intimacies shared between a man and woman. Perhaps at five and twenty, she might, at last, hunger for the pleasures of the marriage bed.

With a man like Spencer Lockhart.

No, no, no. Not him, of course. Merely a man *like* him. Handsome. Strong. Broad-shouldered. Dark-haired. It needn't be him in particular.

Rolling on her side again, she almost believed herself.

* * *

"You're certain you don't wish for me to stay?" Marguerite squeezed Evie's hand with one of her own.

"No. Go. You'll miss your train." Smiling, Evie nodded to Mr. Murdoch waiting beside the carriage to take Marguerite into the village.

"Are you certain?"

"He only wants to see Nicholas." Evie shrugged, trying to project a level of nonchalance.

"But if he learns—"

"He won't. He doesn't even suspect."

Marguerite shook her head, her glossy, dark hair gleaming in the faint morning light. "Perhaps he was told something you don't know, something Ian shared about Linnie. What if you inadvertently say something . . ."

It wasn't anything Evie hadn't already considered, hadn't worried about late into the night. Especially given Spencer Lockhart's strange appearance outside her window last night. She couldn't shake the dark suspicion that he wanted more than to simply meet Nicholas.

"Come now, Marguerite. He would never consider that I am anyone other than Linnie. It's too incredible."

Marguerite's lips twisted. "Indeed," she mocked. "It's beyond fathomable."

Evie forced a smile. Marguerite had tried to talk her out of this charade years ago. Marguerite and her other old school friend, Fallon. Of course, recently sacked and returned from Barbados, Evie had not been in the proper frame of mind to heed their advice. A good thing. She didn't regret her decision. Even now. Who knew what sort of life Nicholas would have had without her?

Marguerite hugged her tightly, and there was surprising strength in the embrace for one so small, for one who had barely survived their years at Penwich. Pulling back, Maguerite's gold eyes drilled into Evie with stark intensity. "Take care. I'll fret every moment until I hear all is well. Write me as soon as he departs and let me know what happened." She wagged a gloved finger in Evie's face. "*Everything.*"

"Of course."

Moistening her lips, Marguerite suggested, and not for the first time, "You know, Fallon could be of help—"

"That's unnecessary." Wed to the Duke of Damon, Fallon possessed considerable influence, not to mention wealth. Evie had already prevailed upon her more than once when things had become too dire. She accepted Fallon's generous gifts—toys and clothes for Nicholas, oysters and chocolate-candied fruit every Christmas. Certainly, her friend would give more if asked, but Evie hated to ask.

"Don't be so stubborn," Marguerite chided.

"Of course, if I must prevail upon her, I will, but I'm still hoping my father will come through."

Marguerite snorted. "Don't wait too long. Any father that would dump you at Penwich can't be relied upon." Her gold eyes glinted, and Evie knew she was speaking from experience.

Linking arms, Evie walked Marguerite to the carriage door. "You'll visit again?"

"Same time next year," Marguerite promised, ascending the rickety carriage. "And I'll see you at Easter? At Fallon's?"

"Of course."

Evie stood back and watched the carriage clatter down the drive, crossing her arms and burrowing deeper in her cloak. She stiffened when the carriage rounded the bend, leaving the road clear for the approaching horse and rider. Spencer Lockhart.

Her fingers dug into her skirts. She forced herself to remain in place, fixing a tight, welcoming smile to her face.

As he neared, the paleness of his gaze came into view, settling on her with familiar intensity. Did he look at everyone that way? Or just her?

And did anyone else's stomach twist as hers did?

Chapter 6

"**M**rs. Cross," he greeted, doffing his head as he dismounted in one fluid motion.

"Mr. Lockhart," she returned. "Thank you for granting me time to speak with Nicholas. He's most eager to meet you."

The news of a cousin had incited all manner of questions in her son. Questions about the war, his father, and, of course, Spencer Lockhart, a kinsman who apparently cared enough to seek him out. It took so little to delight the boy. It twisted her heart. Because he deserved more. Everything. A mother *and* father. Siblings. A world rife with opportunity.

His deep voice rumbled across the air. "As am I."

Turning, she strode ahead, warning him, "I'm afraid he may pelt you with questions." He fell into step beside her. "Like most little boys, he has fanciful notions of soldiers and war."

A dark shutter fell over his eyes, and she suspected the war was a topic he avoided.

He said nothing, merely nodded, looking at her in that intensely unnerving way of his . . . as though he could see her, the real her. A most uncomfortable sensation for someone with her fair share of secrets.

"Must you do *that*?" she blurted before she could think better of it.

He stopped. Squared himself in front of her. Stared even harder. "What?" he replied, his tone exasperatingly even.

Fisting a hand in her skirts, she faced him and suffered his gaze. "Stare at me so, so . . ." Her voice faded on a growl. An itchy burn crept up her neck, suffusing her face. How could she explain that his stare made her feel exposed? As shaky and brittle as a leaf inside?

"And how do I stare at you?" He angled his head; waited for her answer.

She glanced away, then back again, shifting her weight on each foot. She dare not explain that when he looked at her he reminded her of a wolf about to devour its next meal.

"Linnie," he prompted, his gravelly voice lethal-soft. "How do I look at you?" He punctuated each word sharply.

Her gaze snapped back to him. Heat licked

her cheeks. She had not granted him leave to address her thus. And she didn't *like* it. Abhorred the sound of her sister's name on his lips. "You *stare*," she accused. "Ogle, sir. It's most rude."

His head jerked back ever so slightly. "Do I? I was not aware." For a fraction of a second, the corner of his lips twitched, and she was convinced that he *knew* the manner in which he stared at her. He knew and enjoyed every moment of it.

"Pardon me. I've heard much of you over the years. You are a curiosity."

She flinched. He had heard stories of her beautiful, charming and thoroughly tempting sister. Her sister. Not her. It must be difficult for him to reconcile such notions with the reality of her.

Her gaze narrowed on him. "I wish you would cease to look at me like I'm such a *curiosity* then."

"I shall endeavor to do that." From the bright glint in his eyes, she suspected he would do nothing of the sort. Indeed, she suspected he secretly laughed at her. Whatever Ian had told him of Linnie, it clearly made an impression. Why else would he look at her like a fine morsel to savor? Blast it. Not her, but Linnie. She must never forget that.

Lifting her chin, she turned away. "This way, please. Nicholas is at the pond with Amy."

"Amy?"

"His nurse, but we don't treat her like a servant. She's family."

He quirked a dark brow but said nothing. Amy had attended Penwich a couple years behind Evie's class. Evie remembered the girl with fondness and had written to her when she'd moved in with Aunt Gertie, hoping she would be interested in the post. Even now, when they could not afford to pay her wages, Amy remained. That made her family. Not a servant.

He fell into step beside her as they followed the small path around the cottage. Hands folded behind his back, the breadth of his shoulders stretched taut against the dark greatcoat he wore, she could well imagine him in full uniform.

"When do you . . . resume your duties?"

"I won't. I've sold my commission."

She cut him a sharp glance.

"It's time," he elaborated. "I'm needed here. My elder brother died last spring."

"I'm sorry."

As they strolled past the garden, she winced at the sight of her aunt, still at work driving the blackbirds away. Even with the winter vegetables harvested, she was determined to drive them off.

He eyed her aunt's efforts with speculation. "Is something amiss?"

"My aunt has appointed herself protector of our garden," she lamely explained.

"She is *armed*, you know."

Evie sighed. "Don't worry. She's a terrible shot. Harmless, really. Has never even hit a bird."

Almost to the pond now, Amy spotted them and set down the sketch pads upon which she and Nicholas drew. Rising to her feet, she pulled the lad up with her. Nicholas was all eagerness, dancing in place as they stopped before him.

"Nicholas," Evie murmured. "This is Spencer Lockhart. I told you about him."

Nicholas dropped his head back to stare up at the man, lips parting in a small circle of awe. With his usual directness, he reached up to stroke one of the shiny buttons on Lockhart's greatcoat.

"Hello, Nicholas. I'm your cousin."

"I've never had a cousin before. What will we do together?"

Mr. Lockhart blinked.

Evie fought down a smile.

"What *should* we do?" Mr. Lockhart wisely inquired.

"I like to fish. Mr. Murdoch lets me fish with him. Do you like to fish? We have a pole you can use."

"It's been some years, but yes, I've been known to fish." He crouched down before the boy, some of his stiffness evaporating. A dull ache began in Evie's chest at the sight of her little boy staring up at Mr. Lockhart with something akin to hero worship glowing in his eyes. "In fact, I fished with your father."

"Truly?"

Mr. Lockhart's face was all seriousness. "I wouldn't lie about that."

"Did you hear that, Mama?" Nicholas looked to her. "My father liked to fish, too. Just like me."

Tears burned her eyes. She lifted her face higher against the breeze to cool the sting. "Yes, Nicholas. Just like you."

Such a small thing to bring him pleasure, to connect him to a father he would never know. Mr. Lockhart turned, leveled her with his cool green gaze. She pulled back her shoulders, determined to present him with a show of indifference. Apathy. That she was unaffected by him, unmoved by his ease and charm with Nicholas. *That they did not need him here.*

"Amy," Evie broke in, "I believe it's time for Nicholas's nap."

"Mama," the child pouted with a small stomp of feet at her sudden announcement.

"Nicholas," she quietly reprimanded, "I'm certain Mr. Lockhart needs to be on his way if he wants to cover any ground today."

Nicholas's lip quivered, and although her heart ached to disappoint him, Evie knew it was for the best. They could not let this man into their lives. The risk was too great.

Lockhart reeked of disapproval, his green eyes cold.

She blinked and looked away, trying to rid the infernal burn from her eyes. He had only asked to meet Nicholas, not spend the day with him. The sooner Mr. Lockhart left, the better for all.

Gathering their sketch pads and supplies, Amy bundled Nicholas close and led him to the house.

"Good-bye, Nicholas," Mr. Lockhart called out, the deep sound of his voice stroking her somewhere hidden and deep. Shivering, she pulled her shawl close.

Without facing him, she held her ground and watched Amy and Nicholas tramp toward the house, letting the pair outdistance them even if it meant suffering his company alone for a few moments longer.

"You appear in a rush to get rid of me, Mrs. Cross." His words flew with well-aimed accuracy, striking at the truth, at her undeniable need to chase him from her life with all haste. She did not even possess the tact to disguise her eagerness. "Any reason why?"

Heat crept up her neck, spreading through her

face. "That's absurd." Shooting him the barest glance, she lifted her skirts and followed in her son's wake, stopping only when a hand fell on her arm, hard as a vise, forcing her back around. Lungs tights with an indrawn breath, she stared down at that hand, large and tanned on her sleeve, before meeting his gaze.

"I'll have the truth." A muscle rippled across the flesh of his jaw and her stomach clenched. "What is it about my presence that you find so offensive, Mrs. Cross?"

His hand burned her through her wool sleeve as she groped for the appropriate denial, only managing an evasive stammer. "N-nothing."

"Come, don't be vague. It hardly suits you."

She bristled. "And you know me so well, do you?"

A hint of smile curved his lips at her waspish retort. "That's more like it."

Wretch! He didn't *know* her. And she best be certain he never did.

"I merely thought to free you. You've already stayed the night. I would not keep you from the countless tasks waiting—"

"I have a duty to you and Ian's son."

Alarm tightened her chest. It was that sense of duty that worried her. Just how far did it extend? Did he intend to be a permanent fixture in their lives? *Dear God.* It couldn't happen. She couldn't risk him learning the truth. Her life was a charade. She was a fraud. He must never know.

She tugged on her arm. "Unhand me."

"Mrs. Cross," he ground out, his warm fingers flexing around her, sending sparks up her arm. "I had hoped that we might better acquaint ourselves. Become friends of a sort."

She strained away from him in horror. *Friends?*

His eyes darkened to a mossy green. "You needn't look so appalled."

"I—I—" When had she started stuttering? "You wish to be my . . . *friend?*"

His intense gaze roamed her face, dipped and traveled her person. Heavens help her if she didn't respond to that look, if her pulse didn't race just a small bit faster against her throat.

"Is that so wrong? I fear we've begun badly—"

Whatever he meant to say died abruptly, the words cut short on the air. His gaze flew wide, focused at some point beyond her shoulder.

Everything happened quickly then.

His hand on her arm tightened to a painful grip. A whimper rose in her throat. Before she could gain her voice and demand he unhand her a second time, he plucked her off her feet.

Her neck jerked with pain as he swung her around.

Colors blurred. Wind whistled.

She clutched his arms, hanging on for dear life, trying not to notice how strong and warm he felt against her.

What was he doing?

Air rushed from her lungs, blocking her scream, killing it in her throat. He pulled her to him, hugged her tightly against the hard length of his body. So tightly she feared he would crush her ribs. She had suffered broken ribs once before. She did not care to repeat the experience. She beat at his shoulder with tightly wound fists.

His body spasmed against her, his fierce clutch on her arms tightening, doubtlessly leaving bruises.

Buried in his arms, a violent shudder rippled through his body into her.

Then he stilled.

Chapter 7

Quite certain she was in the clutches of a madman, she loosened her lips and found her voice. The result was only a weak-muffled moan against his chest. "Mr. Lockhart! What are you doing?"

The arms around her dropped away. With a strange, ragged breath, he staggered back.

Gasping for breath, she glared at him, brushing a hand against her hair, thankfully still in place.

At the look on his oddly pale face, her hands froze. "Mr. Lockhart. Are you unwell?"

His lips looked gray as he spoke. "Not quite, Mrs. Cross." As if speech pained him, he paused and grimaced. "Appears your aunt finally hit something. Me, I'm afraid."

Her heart stopped. *No!*

Her gaze shot to Aunt Gertie. Her sticklike figure hunkered over her bow, as if attempting to hide the evidence of her misdeed.

"Aunt Gertie! Are you mad?"

Her aunt thrust out her chin and glared across the distance, her look mutinous. "It weren't my fault! A sudden wind blew me off course. I can't help it if he's such a large target. Did I kill him?" Aunt Gertie demanded, her voice petulant and resentful, as if his dying would be an affront to her.

Heat washed over Evie's face, a mix of shame and horror. Shaking, she stepped around Mr. Lockhart to inspect the damage. She swallowed a cry and bit her lip at the sight of the arrow embedded in the back of his shoulder.

In a tight voice, he demanded, "How bad is it?"

"It's—" *A bloody arrow in your back!* "Not too bad."

Striving for a calm she did not feel, she took him by the arm and led him toward the house, marveling at his composure, at his sure strides beside her own. "We'll settle you inside and send for the doctor."

He gave the barest nod, as though she did nothing more than suggest they adjourn inside for tea. Only the paleness of his face and the deep grooves on either side of his mouth indicated he felt any discomfort.

"I'm so sorry, Mr. Lockhart," she whispered fervently. "Aunt Gertie's never hurt a soul before."

As they passed the garden, Aunt Gertie called out again, "Did I kill him?"

"He's walking, isn't he?" Evie hissed, wishing her aunt would cease talking altogether.

"Years in the Crimea and scarcely a scratch," he bit out. "One fortnight home and I'm felled by an old woman's arrow." Then, astoundingly, the firm line of his mouth twitched. "I suppose that's irony."

She stared in astonishment at his profile, imagining most men would react with anything but humor in such a situation. Uncertain how to respond, she patted his arm awkwardly and assured him, "You'll be fine."

Slipping one arm around his waist, she reached for the latch to the balcony door, trying not to let the firm press of his body distract her. She'd never been so close to a man before—willingly, at any rate—and never such a virile male form. Her throat tightened.

He captured her gaze, holding himself still before the doors. "I'm glad it wasn't you. Glad you are safe."

Then she recalled that he had pulled her clear and taken that arrow. *For her, dear heavens!* She had been the one standing in the arrow's path. He had saved her life.

Her stomach heaved. She pressed a hand to her

belly and turned to stare at her reflection in the glass doors. "Why?" she whispered. "Why would you do that?"

In the glass, she could see he watched her; felt his stare on her face. "Why wouldn't I?"

She could think of a number of reasons— the most obvious being the arrow embedded in his shoulder. With a shake of her head, she said crisply, "I can think of no reason why you would risk yourself for me."

"Can you not?" Angling his head, he studied her as if *she* were the oddity. "You're Ian's Linnie. That alone is reason enough."

The words fell so matter-of-factly, so simply. She turned, stared at him bleakly. Sick at heart, only one thought raced through her head: *No, I'm not. I'm not Linnie. Not her.*

Only he could never know that.

Still fighting the churning in her stomach, she led him up the stairs to her bedchamber, the best room in the house. He would have it, of course. Anything to add to his comfort, to speed his recovery and hasten his departure.

Mrs. Murdoch soon arrived and took over, fussing over him as she eased him down on the bed, propping several pillows around him, careful not to jar the arrow until Peter arrived.

Evie stood back and watched, inhaling slowly

through her lips, vowing to see him restored to his proper self.

Later, she would ask herself whether he would have saved her if he'd known the truth. If he'd known she was a liar—an imposter and not his cousin's lover. Not Nicholas's true mother at all.

In effect, no one to him.

Resting on his stomach, Spencer felt a warm trickle of blood course its way down his back. He hissed as Mrs. Murdoch pressed another cloth around the arrow, catching the flow of blood. His shoulder burned like hellfire. He shook his head. *A bloody arrow.* That old woman was a menace. The shot headed for Mrs. Cross would likely have struck her. *Killed* her. He shivered. Clearly, his presence was needed here. What if Nicholas had been in that arrow's path?

"There you are, sir," Mrs. Murdoch clucked as she stuffed another pillow beneath his chest. "Mrs. Cross will be right up with Dr. Sheffield, and he'll remove that arrow for you. We'll have you comfortable yet."

Ah, Dr. Sheffield. The suitor. Even in his pain-muddled state, he tensed, anxious to meet Ian's replacement, if the maid from the inn was to be believed.

"Poor Miss Gertie," the housekeeper clucked. "I hope you don't blame the ol' dear too much."

Poor Miss Gertie?

Mrs. Murdoch continued, "Shame about your fine clothes. I'll launder and stitch them the best I can."

"Don't worry yourself," he murmured.

His clothing lay in tatters beside the bed. With the housekeeper's help, Mrs. Cross had cut away his garments, her cheeks flaming all throughout the task.

Footsteps sounded outside the door.

"Ah, here's Mrs. Cross with the doctor now."

Spencer didn't know what to expect of Linnie's suitor. Perhaps someone with a resemblance to his cousin?

I resemble Ian. He blinked hard, banishing the thought, not daring to consider that might make a difference to her . . . and make a difference to *him*.

The man who entered the room in no way resembled Ian. While tall, he was pale and fair-haired with muttonchop sideburns. "Mr. Lockhart, is it? Quite an injury we have here."

Stiffly proper, older-looking than his likely age, he smelled of musty books and rancid garlic.

The notion of her with this man filled him with distaste. "Doctor," he greeted as he discarded his coat and rolled up his sleeves.

Mrs. Cross paced beside the bed, her blue eyes brimming with regret. "I am so sorry—"

"You've already apologized, madam," he interrupted.

At his censure, she stopped pacing and dropped her luminous gaze, her long lashes casting alluring shadows on her cheeks.

He cursed himself for his snapped words. It wasn't her fault her choice of suitor struck him as uninspiring. For all he knew, the fellow breathed and bled honor.

He hissed as Sheffield's ice-cold hands prodded the tender flesh around the arrow; grasping the rod, the doctor jiggled with decided vigor. For a moment, spots filled Spencer's vision. A quick glance over his shoulder, and he knew such vigor was wholly intended. The good doctor's watery gaze revealed a decided amount of satisfaction.

"I hear you are quite the hero."

"Not at all," Spencer spat past clenched teeth, centering his attention on Mrs. Cross beside the bed. Her hands were on level with his gaze, the slender fingers entwined tightly, bloodless-white before her waist. Not the smooth, unblemished hands of a lady, but elegant nonetheless, sensual—hands that, he suspected, would know how to caress a man. At least in his imaginings they would.

"Fought with the Light Brigade, huh?" Sheffield paused long and looked at Mrs. Cross as he asked this, staring hard at her before returning his attention to Spencer. "That seems to mark you a hero. At least according to the papers." He prodded the arrow with jarring suddenness. Agony pulsed from the spot, vibrating throughout Spencer's back.

A cry strangled in Spencer's throat, and he heard Mrs. Cross whimper . . . as if she felt the pain herself. His gaze blurred gray at the edges. No question. For whatever reason, Sheffield was determined to cause him pain.

"Just widening the path so I can pull it out . . ."

Blood rushed warmly down his back.

Mrs. Cross gasped. "Please, be done with it," she pleaded over the roaring in his ears. Her hand grasped his on the bed.

Sheffield dropped a blood-sopped cloth on the bedside table with no thought to the lacy doily. "Very well."

Spencer lay gasping, his fingers clinging to hers, a random thought spiraling through his head: *Her hands are softer than they look.*

The doctor rummaged through his bag, muttering, "You're fortunate it didn't penetrate your shoulder blade. We would have to push it out through the front. That would have been most unpleasant."

Spencer winced, grateful for that. The doctor would likely have killed him with that maneuver.

"Just end it," he growled, bracing himself for the man's next move, locking his jaw and focusing on the soft, trembling hand joined with his.

Her gentle voice washed over him like a balm. "Can we give him something for the pain?"

Sheffield sighed as he brandished a knife. "I suppose. I have laudanum, but we can't wait for it to take effect. This arrow has been in long enough—"

"Never mind the laudanum," Spencer snapped. "Just get the damned thing out."

Sheffield tsked.

Mrs. Cross's hand shuddered in his.

With a curse, he tossed her hand from him. "And get her out of here."

"Mr. Lockhart! No—"

"Go," he ordered as the doctor sawed at the flesh around the arrow's shaft.

"Just need to widen this a bit more," Sheffield murmured. "He's right—you don't need to be here for this. Best leave."

As much as Spencer disliked the man, he was glad for his agreement.

"Come along," Mrs. Murdoch seconded, leading her away—but not before casting him a reproving look.

He snorted. He was the one with an arrow in his back.

The door clicked shut behind them, and he exhaled, relieved. True, he didn't want her to see him vulnerable like this—her beau carving him like a fish. But he also didn't want to distress her, and she appeared softhearted enough that the sight of him injured would distress her.

Thoughts of her vanished as the blade cut deeper into his ravaged skin. He held his breath until the torment ended and the arrow slid free. Blood gushed a warm stream down his side. Sheffield pressed something against the wound to staunch the flow. After some moments, he set to work cleaning the wound with deep swipes. Spencer clenched his teeth in a hiss.

"I thought of joining, you know."

Spencer blinked, his pain-muddled head slow to comprehend the comment.

"I simply concluded I was in better service here. Not fighting a senseless war on foreign soil. The next closest doctor is hours away."

Spencer's mouth twisted wryly. For some reason the good doctor sought his validation.

He droned on. "The Sheffields have lived in Little Billings since the reign of Elizabeth. My grandfather was the Squire Appleby."

"Remarkable." Spencer could not prevent the ring of mockery to his voice. Did the man think to impress him with a mediocre pedigree?

At that moment, a needle sank into his flesh. He held his breath as the tip wove in and out of his skin.

"And then there was Evelyn," Sheffield continued, his voice close as he bent over Spencer's back. *Evelyn.* Spencer had always wondered what Linnie was short for. Ian never mentioned it. "We've an understanding. Of sorts. I couldn't leave her on her own. In case you failed to note, she's in grave need of a man."

And Sheffield clearly considered himself that man. A strange tightness coiled through Spencer. "She appears to manage."

"Yes, well. She needn't *manage* at all." Sheffield's voice swelled with self-import. "Not with me about. I've invested a good deal of care and time into my relationship with Mrs. Cross. Naturally, a strange gentleman caller rouses my protective instincts."

"Naturally," Spencer ground out.

"You can understand how I would do anything to protect her."

Spencer detected the threat, heard what Sheffield wasn't saying; the doctor wanted him gone.

"I pose no—"

"You're a stranger, no matter your weak connection to her late husband." So, she'd apprised him of that much, had she? "A stranger. A man. Bleeding upon Evelyn's bed."

Spencer snorted. Did Sheffield think he'd manipulated himself into these circumstances?

The doctor tugged roughly on Spencer's torn skin, tying off the thread. Moving to his bag again, Sheffield rustled the contents within. "I trust you've finished your *business* here and will be on your way." He pronounced the word *business* with great skepticism.

An acerbic retort rose to Spencer's lips. Instead of replying that he would leave only when he was damn well ready, he shifted on the bed and inhaled, catching the faint scent of her on the pillow beneath his cheek. Lemons? Bergamot? Whatever the combination, it was a heady thing.

A smile touched his lips. The idea that he reclined in the bed where she spent her nights made his stomach tighten.

Sheffield finished bandaging his wound.

With a grunt, Spencer struggled to his side.

"Careful not to tear out my stitch work," Sheffield advised, slowly gathering his things. "So. You're the late Mr. Cross's cousin."

Spencer frowned. He already knew as much. "Yes," he replied, deliberately vague.

"And how did he die again? This . . . *cousin* of yours?"

Spencer's gaze narrowed. Was Sheffield nosing about for the truth? Did he suspect that Linnie fabricated a husband? *Had his arrival cast her into suspicion?* She had feared as much could happen, but he didn't let it dissuade him. He'd resolved to meet Nicholas. To know *her* better.

"Does Mrs. Cross never speak of him?" He tsked. "Given your relationship, I thought for certain she would have."

The doctor stiffened, acrimony writ on his pale countenance.

At that moment, the door opened and Mrs. Cross stuck her head inside. Her eyes locked with his, the blue bright with determination, daring him to try and banish her again. "Need anything, gentlemen?"

"I'm all done here." Sheffield stood, his movements stiff and jerky. "Your patient is on the mend. I don't see why he can't travel and be on his way—"

"Indeed not." She blinked, striding fully into the chamber. "How shall he ride?"

Sheffield's face colored. "He could take the post in the village—"

"And leave my mount?" Spencer shook his head.

"Of course not." Mrs. Cross looked at her beau as if he'd taken leave of his senses. "Travel is not possible in his condition. Not for days yet."

Sheffield exhaled heavily and leaned close to her, whispering indiscreetly, "You cannot mean for him to stay here, Evelyn. A veritable stranger in the house with you, a lone woman . . . what will people say?"

She pulled back her shoulders. "I'm not alone. I've the Murdochs and Amy and Aunt—"

"Hardly appropriate chaperones." He gestured to Spencer. "After this day's work, you should begin considering asylums for your aunt."

"Oh!" Hot color washed her cheeks.

Spencer frowned at the doctor, wondering why she tolerated his interference, much less his courtship. She should toss him out on his bloody ass.

The dim-witted man continued, either oblivious or indifferent to her outrage. "As to this . . . man, housing him in your home will only start tongues wagging."

Her eyes glinted. "I thank you for your concern on my behalf, but he stays."

"Very well. If you won't listen to reason and respect my infallible judgment, then think of Nicholas." Clearly the doctor was not yet willing to admit defeat.

Her head cocked at a dangerous angle. "I *am* thinking of Nicholas." Her next words astonished Spencer, considering her earlier eagerness for him to depart. "Mr. Lockhart is my late husband's cousin—he's Nicholas's remaining link to his father. He's welcome here as long as he likes."

"Indeed? Mr. Lockhart is your late husband's *cousin*?" Sheffield gathered up his bag, his spine poker-straight. "You are quite sure of that?"

Spencer's nape tingled in forewarning. Just like before the initial charge. The still before the first whistle of cannon across a battlefield.

Her blue eyes narrowed. "Whatever do you mean?"

"I only want to be certain on the matter. I have a right, after all."

With the color still high in her cheeks and her blue eyes sparking, she perched a fist on her hip and demanded, "Then by all means, be clear." She was a sight to admire, and suddenly he could see why Ian never shook free of her.

"I demand the truth, Evelyn! You owe me that much."

She tossed her head. "What in heavens are you talking about?"

Sheffield swung an accusing finger at Spencer. "Is this man Nicholas's father?"

Chapter 8

The stab of satisfaction Spencer felt was wholly inappropriate. He knew that—knew he should not relish Sheffield's accusation. But damn if he didn't relish the hot flash of jealousy in her suitor's eyes.

Yet as her wide blue eyes filled with horror, his satisfaction was quick to fade.

Why should she look so appalled? Did the notion of him—of *them*—repulse her so greatly?

She stared, gaping like a fish, looking back and forth between him and Sheffield.

"Nicholas is the very image of this man," Sheffield charged, still wagging a finger. "Any fool can see that!"

Her gaze flitted to Spencer, looking at him starkly, doubtlessly seeing him through Sheffield's eyes.

He lifted his one good shoulder in a shrug. Valid point. Spencer and Ian had often been mistaken for brothers, strikingly similar with their dark hair and green eyes.

"Do you deny it? Deny this is Nicholas's father?" Sheffield shook his head, his eyes crinkling at the corners as though the sight of her hurt. "You're no widow, at all! Are you?"

"Tread carefully, Sheffield," Spencer warned, his voice thick in his mouth.

A flush of outrage crept up the other man's neck, the only sign he heard Spencer. "Your silence speaks for itself, Evelyn. Have I been naught a fool? Wasting these last years in my hopes for a future with you—"

She shook her head wildly, gold-brown tendrils falling free, loosely framing her face in charming disarray. "I made you no promises." Her voice rang hotly, all outraged tones. He liked the sound of it. Too much. Even with his back throbbing, the passionate sound stirred him.

Astonishment washed over Sheffield's face. He seized her arm and thrust his face close to hers. "Are you daft? What did you think I was playing at all this time?"

With no regard for his injury, Spencer shot up in bed. "Unhand her," he growled.

He had meant to merely observe, to let her maneuver this interesting turn of events on her own, but that was before Sheffield touched her. Before

Spencer saw her wince. Before that hand on her arm fueled him to a cold rage.

With no regard for his injury, he swung his legs over the bed and pushed to his feet. Legs braced wide, he squared off in front of Sheffield, struggling to ignore his dizziness.

"Mr. Lockhart!" She scowled at him. *Him.* Didn't she realize he only sought to defend her? "You musn't stand," she cried. "Get back in bed."

His gaze narrowed on Sheffield. "Release her."

Uncertainty flickered in the other man's eyes, the fingers of his hand flexing upon her arm, as though considering Spencer's command. "You've no stake here," he challenged, although his voice gave the slightest tremor. "Whomever you *may* be."

A dark and angry beast twisted inside Spencer, and before he could stop himself, he spit out, "I have every claim here. Whomever I *might* be, I'm family."

Let Sheffield infer what he wished from that. At that particular moment—with a primitive burn sizzling through his veins—Spencer was only too glad to foster Sheffield's misapprehension. *Let him think I'm Nicholas's father. Her lover. That she belongs to me.* Recklessly, he tossed out, "Unlike you, I belong here."

Black fury passed over the man's face. He

dropped his hand from Mrs. Cross's arm and stiffly stepped away.

She glared at Spencer with wide eyes of glittering ice. Frozen. Astonished. Her mouth a perfect little O of horrified wonder.

"Evelyn," the doctor bit out, smoothing a hand over each muttonchop sideburn. "We'll speak again. When I've regained my composure . . . and your *guest* has left." He turned for the door.

Sparked to action, she took a step after him. "Wait! Don't go. You misunderstand the situation—"

Shaking his head, the doctor stormed through the door, slamming it after him.

She spun around, her flashing eyes settling on Spencer in a way that made his blood pump faster. "What have you done?" She tossed her arms in the air. "You permitted him to leave thinking— wondering . . ." She closed her eyes in one long blink, pressing a hand to her forehead as if it were too awful to contemplate.

He shrugged, then winced at the pull on his sore shoulder. "I did not care for the way he addressed you."

"How he addresses me is none of your affair. You are not my protector. I can look after myself. I've done as much all my life." She dropped her hand from her forehead and advanced on him. "However will I convince him you are not Nicholas's father now?" Her cheeks deepened a becoming pink. "That you and I are not . . . were not—"

"Lovers," he readily supplied, the word practically a growl.

She blinked, startled at his bluntness. Her gaze slid over him then, seeming to realize his state of undress. The pink in her cheeks burned brighter. For a lady of experience, she affected modesty most convincingly. A man could almost believe she was untouched. But then he knew all about the duplicitous nature of females. Long ago, the one girl he had thought to marry had only treated him to lies and deceit.

Heaving a deep breath, she demanded quietly, "What are you doing here? Truly?"

He wondered that himself. He'd intended this to be a simple errand. A quick matter to attend to—the fulfilling of his promise to Ian and a welcome delay to his entry into Society as the new, bride-seeking Viscount Winters. Wretched prospect, the latter.

"You know why I'm here. Ian wanted—"

"Wanted you to cast me into scandal? Place the taint of illegitimacy on his son?"

Her words jarred him. She was correct, of course. What in bloody hell was he doing letting that jackass leave thinking he was Nicholas's father? That Linnie might not be a widow at all but a fallen woman?

Her blue eyes shimmered with entreaty. "I've walked a fine line since Nicholas's birth, adding one lie to another until I can scarcely remember what I've said . . . or who I am anymore . . ." She glanced away, blinking fiercely. A hoarse laugh escaped her. The sound shuddered through him. "Believe it or not, it's not *my* shame I fear so much . . . but Nicholas?" She shook her head. "Illegitimacy is a cruel stamp to bear."

No worse than Society judging her a whore.

He really was a selfish bastard, thinking only of himself. Injury aside, he was in no hurry to depart, no hurry to take leave of the female he found a fascinating study of contradictions. Vulnerable yet strong. Innocent yet experienced. Indeed, the idea that had seized him last night pressed upon him with even greater fervor.

The more time he spent in her company, the greater she affected him. Staring at the sensual fullness of her mouth, he imagined himself tasting her, savoring her at his leisure.

He sighed. Only one thing remained to do in this situation.

Fortunately, he was in the market for a bride.

Perhaps it had been his intent from the start,

the moment he had been crawling toward ever since setting sail for home. Since Ian first whispered stories of her to him across the fire.

"An easy matter to rectify." He stared hard at her bewildered face, testing the idea in his head before he spoke the words that would seal his fate, and hers.

Words that would satisfy his vow to Ian.

Words that would fulfill his obligation to his title and family.

Words that would satisfy his inconvenient longing for her.

"Marry me."

For several moments, silence held, hung on the thick air. Shock flashed across her face, lasting only a moment before the outrage arrived. Outrage and something else. Something fleeting and wistful. It passed over her lovely eyes and then vanished before she slapped him full across the face.

The crack of her hand on his cheek reverberated on the air. She tucked her arm close to her body, folding a hand over her stinging palm.

Marry me.

Flexing her hand, she instantly regretted her loss of control. So uncustomary for her. Bold demonstrations of emotion were more Fallon's forte.

Evie had always rebuked her for that. Yet here she was. Striking the man her aunt shot with an arrow. Because he possessed the temerity to offer her marriage?

Heat stung her face. She pressed her offending hand close to her side, as if the hand acted of its own will and could not be trusted.

He fingered his cheek, cocking a dark brow at her.

Her chest lifted and fell, as if she'd run a great distance.

Her gaze scanned his taut, sinewy forearm, moving on to his broad chest and flat, muscle-ridged belly. Her mouth dried and watered alternately at the firm, warm-looking flesh.

She did not know gentlemen like him existed. He was bred for the fields, not a drawing room. He could easily crush her. *And she had slapped him?* She'd been on the receiving end of a man's fists before and it was not an experience she intended to repeat.

Although the way he stared at her, his eyes gleaming an unholy ice-green, she did not think he wished to return her slap for one of his own. Indeed, the way he stared at her brought to mind all manner of illicit thoughts involving the two of them, their bodies locked together, her hands exploring his delicious masculine form.

He spoke in a slow, deep voice that made her belly tremble. "Not the reaction I was expecting."

Lifting her chin, she fought to reclaim her composure. Dignity. "What did you expect? You're cruel to mock me—"

"I do not mock," he bit out. "I can assure you, marriage is not a topic a man makes light of."

She pressed her lips shut, supposing that to be true.

Studying him warily, she took several steps away from his imposing figure—large and masculine and potent. Anything to distance herself from him. To lessen his overwhelming impact on her senses. "You best get back in bed. I wouldn't want you to collapse."

His lips twitched. After a moment, he obliged, lowering himself down. "I offer marriage in all sincerity."

She stared. "You are serious."

"If we wed, you shall have my name, my protection. Anyone who suspects you've lied about your past shall keep the opinion to themselves." His jaw tightened. "Or court my displeasure."

Tugging her bottom lip, she moved to the window and stared out at the lawn where she had spotted him the night before. Had he been contemplating this even then?

His voice curled toward her. "Think of the boy."

Evie swung her gaze back to where he lounged on the bed. The sight of his bare chest made her stomach flip. "And he is the reason you offer marriage?"

She had to know. Needed to know what drove him. Certainly there were ladies far more eligible than she.

That unnerving intensity was back in his eyes. "He's Ian's son—my own kinsman."

She nodded. "I see." And she did. Spencer Lockhart was Nicholas's kin. She was mired in lies regarding all else except this single truth.

"He deserves a future beyond what you can give him. I can give him that. The finest homes. Travel. Horses, hunting. The best tutors, and when the time comes, he shall attend the university of his choice."

She pressed her fingertips to her forehead, suddenly dizzy. It was more than she had ever dreamed for Nicholas. More than her own father had ever given her. But it would require her marrying this man, a stranger with eyes so piercing a green she could scarcely think when he stared at her.

A shaky breath escaped her. "And what of me?" She had to know, had to ask.

"Ian loved you. For that, I can offer you the protection of my name. I am not without means. You shall never want for anything. Forgive me for saying so, but I believe that to be a marked improvement from your present circumstances."

But they would be wed. Bound before God, together in this life and the next. A high price to pay for security. "That's a great sacrifice on your part."

His gaze raked her then, a slow-blistering perusal thorough enough to weaken her knees. "The arrangement won't be without benefit." His rich voice suffused her with a warmth she had no right to feel. He wasn't offering to wed her because he fancied her in the way a man regarded a woman he wished to wed. *To bed.* Honor compelled him. Duty. No matter the manner he looked at her right now, she would do well to remember that.

He continued, "Since my half brother's death, the family relies upon me to marry and provide an heir. I want that heir." She shivered. The way his eyes glittered at her, she could almost imagine he said, *I want you.* "The sooner the better. Clearly, you are capable."

Heirs? He wanted children. *With her.*

Her throat tightened. Fear hissed through her, urging her to refuse him. For her sake. But she couldn't summon forth a refusal. What kind of mother would she be? It would not be fair to Nicholas. "If I am to consider this, we must have certain matters between us understood."

He cocked his head. "The matter of marriage should be fairly straightforward."

"Marriage, yes, but—what I mean to say is . . ." With a deep breath, she plunged ahead, "I can't countenance intimacy with a stranger."

His eyes narrowed to menacing slits. "I'll be your husband—"

"A stranger still."

A dangerous light entered his gaze. "It's what married couples do, *even*"—he angled his head sharply—"*unmarried* ones."

She stiffened at the express reference to her. A direct cut. Hot embarrassment swept over her.

He continued, "Is it the thought of sharing my bed you find so offensive?"

Her gaze skimmed his masculine form. He was a well-made man, and she had not reached the age of five and twenty without some curiosity about the pleasures to be had between a man and woman. Despite her past. The memory of waking in the dark to savage hands had never left her. If Stirling's wife, the very girl Evie had been charged with accompanying to Barbados, had not burst in upon them, he would have completed his vile business with her.

And yet she knew the rough, drunken groping of Hiram Stirling couldn't be all there was to the whole matter. She was confident that Mr. Lockhart would never take his fists to a woman for rejecting his advances. Indeed not.

The notion of sharing Spencer Lockhart's bed was far, far from offensive. Since she'd met him, the idea had been there, a sensual nibble at the edge of her awareness. The very thought of *having* him—of him having *her*—sent heat shooting to most intimate places.

The man before her radiated adventure, reminding her that once upon a time she had been a girl who'd longed for that very thing. She had once been someone who wanted to explore the world. Her stomach dipped and fluttered. Spencer was that—the adventure she'd always wanted, but from which she might never recover. If the warmth he stirred in her belly was any hint, she would easily welcome his touch, allow him to do to her the sort of things a husband did to his wife.

Except then he would know.

A woman did not give birth to a son without knowing a thing or two about the happenings within the marriage bed. How could she explain her inexperience . . . her *virginity*?

She pressed a hand to her belly, hoping to quell the flutterings, and lifted her chin. "I can't even entertain the notion of sharing such intimacies. I scarcely know you." The lie tripped from her tongue with surprising ease.

His green eyes glowed. With a wicked twist of his lips, in a mocking tone that implied he knew she lied, knew that she *did* entertain such notions, he assured her, "No worries. You'll get to know me."

The words, their very suggestion, sent a lick of heat twisting inside her belly.

She shook her head. "If I'm to seriously consider your proposal, I'll have your word that you shall not . . ." She paused, moistening her lips. Her stomach clenched tighter at the sight of his eyes following the movement of her tongue. Clearing the thickness from her throat, she finished, "I'll have your word that you will not require that of me."

"*'Require'*?"

She gave a jerky nod.

His green eyes frosted over. "I've no use for a female who is less than willing. There are plenty of women who would welcome me in their beds."

Heat scored her cheeks. His words shouldn't have stung, but they did.

He continued, his voice as chilly as the cut of his gaze. "I've never taken an unwilling woman to my bed. I'll not begin with my wife."

Wife. The word jarred her. *Was she actually doing this?*

His hand moved over the taut flesh of his stomach in a lazy circle. Her gaze followed the movement, mesmerized.

"That is not to say I won't persuade you into changing your mind. As I've said, I need an heir."

Her pulse jumped in alarm. She snapped her gaze back to his face, fearful that he was correct—that with one look, he could persuade her into doing just about anything. "I-I need time." Perhaps forever.

His green eyes swept over her appraisingly. "I need a wife in the truest sense. At least until you've conceived an heir. Then we can assume a more relaxed arrangement."

"A more relaxed arrangement?"

"Of course. I've never subscribed to the notion of a love match. That's for novels and starry-eyed virgins. Marriage is a practical matter. It should be treated thus. You can live the life you wish. Wherever you wish. In Town. In the country. Travel, if you like." He shrugged, as if it were of little account.

"And you?"

"Will do the same, of course."

She considered him carefully, weighing the prospect of living with him, sharing his bed, if only for a short time. It would certainly lessen the risk of his learning the truth, assuming she managed to keep it from him through their initial intimacies. One could survive anything with the end looming in sight.

She clasped her hands tightly together. "How long do you think until we can live . . . separately?"

For a moment, he looked annoyed. Then his face turned to cool marble. "I imagine that depends on how vigorously and frequently we put ourselves to the task of begetting an heir."

Her cheeks burned. "Of course."

"Of course," he echoed, his tone clipped and officious.

She sucked in a breath. *Are you mad? How can you consider marrying this man? Sharing his bed?* Pushing the hissing whispers aside, she asked herself how she could not. For Nicholas's sake, how could she refuse? He offered her son a future. Not to mention an end to their dire straits. No more worrying over their dwindling pantry stores. She would make a pact with the devil himself for such security.

Folding her arms across her chest, she lifted her chin. "Very well. I accept."

He stared at her a long moment, assessing her before nodding. "We'll leave tomorrow."

Her arms dropped. "Tomorrow?" She gestured to his figure lying upon her bed. "You are in no condition to travel—"

"On horseback, no. We'll be comfortable enough in a carriage."

"I can't possibly be ready tomorrow." It would take more than a day to explain matters to everyone in her household and set their concerns to rest.

He frowned. "Then the day after tomorrow we shall leave for Scotland."

"Scotland?" She shook her head. Everything was happening too soon, becoming too real much too quickly. She squeezed her hands even tighter.

"Know you of any quicker way to wed without special license?" He grinned suddenly, his teeth white and gleaming.

She blinked. "Why do you look so . . . pleased?"

"In the matter of one afternoon, I've righted an issue of honor on behalf of my cousin and managed to settle the bothersome matter of finding a bride."

"Oh." Deflated, Evie moved toward the door.

Certainly he wouldn't be smiling because he was marrying *her*. That would be absurd. How many men would feel *pleased* about entering into marriage with a veritable stranger? He didn't know her, and what he did know of her wasn't her. It was Linnie.

Their marriage was merely a point of honor for him. A cold calculation. Nothing more. She would do well to remember that. In a few months, they would put the farce behind them and continue their separate lives.

Chapter 9

The smile faded from Spencer's lips as the door clicked shut behind Mrs. Cross—soon to be Lady Winters. He winced, recalling that he had neglected to mention that fact. It wasn't deliberate. He could scarcely remember it himself. The formal address felt strange and alien on him. Unwanted. A loathsome title that had belonged to his father and brothers before him. It was never intended for him. A fact of which they had made certain to keep him apprised. Daily. Still, he ought to have mentioned it. Not that he imagined she would mind. What woman wouldn't want a title before her name?

He shook his head. Had he actually proposed marriage to Ian's precious Linnie? What's more, had he actually placed a stipulation on her for an heir? To be conceived in all haste?

He laughed hoarsely. He might claim duty as his motive, but make no mistake, he longed to strip Mrs. Cross of her dowdy garments and explore her at leisure . . . to discover for himself all her hidden charms. The urge to bury himself in her softness had nothing to do with his need for an heir and everything to do with his desire to possess her.

He carefully resettled his weight on the bed, mindful of his throbbing shoulder. Lusting after Ian's woman was no way to honor his memory. And yet, he couldn't seem to cease the lascivious bent to his thoughts.

His guilt was alleviated somewhat at the thought of all he could provide Ian's boy. Reason enough to marry her. And presenting Linnie to his stepmother and putting an end to all her matchmaking schemes held decided appeal. No doubt Adara had a hand in her schemes, too. She would be particular about who took her place as Lady Winters.

Five years ago, he had been crushed when Cullen announced his engagement to Adara at the family's annual Christmas ball. Especially considering the fact that the day before, the chit had promised to run away with him. When Spencer left England, he never thought to return. Never thought to see his degenerate brothers, his heartless stepmother, or the faithless Adara again.

With no warning, the door flung wide.

Mrs. Cross's aunt strode inside, splotches of color staining the parchment-thin skin of her face.

"What are you about?" she demanded.

"At the moment?" He arched a brow and replied drolly, "Recuperating from an arrow you shot into my back."

She snorted. "You're alive, aren't you? Now." She stabbed the air with one wrinkled, crooked finger. "Evie says you're planning to marry her."

"I am."

Her rheumy-blue eyes narrowed. "Why would you want to do that? She's ruined, you know." She slapped a hand through the air. "She told me that you know everything. And let me tell you what else I know. *I* know that no man wants another man's leavings."

Charming. "Apparently, I do."

With a disdainful sniff, she crossed her bony arms over her thin chest. "I don't trust you."

"The boy's father was my kin."

She rocked back on her heels. "Ah, 'tis honor that drives you, then?"

"Your niece has agreed to marry me. She trusts me. Nothing else matters. Not even your approval." He inclined his head. "Although desired, it is not necessary."

Her thin gray brows winged high, reaching

toward her hairline. "Indeed. Aren't you the arrogant one?" She curled a finger toward him. "Now heed this, I'll be watching you." Her gaze scanned his face. "A handsome face and fine eyes won't fool me. Hurt her and next time my arrow might find its way to your heart."

Before he could respond to that dire threat, she drove a hard line from the room, nearly knocking over the sturdy Mrs. Murdoch as she entered.

"I believe," he said drolly to the wide-eyed housekeeper, "had she been on the front line, the war would have ended a great deal sooner."

Mrs. Murdoch chuckled. "No mistaking that, sir." She set a tray on the bedside table. Tendrils of steam floated above a bowl of creamy soup. Standing back, she cleared her throat. "She's worried for our girl. We all are. None of us want her to make a mistake. And this is the sort of mistake a woman can spend a lifetime paying for."

He nodded grimly. "True. And by that token, a man can suffer, too."

"No denying that, but with all due respect, when a marriage suffers, the woman's left with fewer choices." She shrugged one plump shoulder. "The world belongs to men. I've seen many a woman crushed beneath a husband's"—she paused, eyeing the length of him stretched out in her mistress's bed—"displeasure."

"I won't hurt her," he vowed. "I have too much regard for my cousin's memory to do such a thing."

"And what if that regard were lost?" she broke in, her brow wrinkled, clearly troubled. "What if you learned she was not . . ." Her voice faded, her gaze dropping away.

"Not what?" he prompted.

Her gaze lifted, her eyes bright and resolved. "What if it turns out she's not the woman you thought you were marrying?"

How could he be disappointed? Could he even claim to know her? He merely knew she was Ian's Linnie. The mother of Ian's child. Beyond that, nothing. He needn't know anything else. That was enough.

Ah, but you know something else. Something more. You know you want her. You want to know her intimately. As Ian knew her.

Shaking the thought off, he gave the housekeeper a reassuring smile. "Truly, I don't know her well enough to punish her later if she doesn't live up to my expectations. I have no expectations."

With an unconvinced nod, she moved for the door. "Enjoy your dinner."

"Thank you," he murmured.

Hand on the latch, she paused. "Contrary to what you say, you have expectations. Whether you admit it or not. Whether you even realize it. We always do."

The door clicked shut behind her. Spencer stared at the dark paneled wood. As the housekeeper's words rolled through his mind, doubt crept in.

What did he truly know of the woman he planned to wed?

What do you need to know? a small voice whispered. He had thought he knew Adara. Knew her heart and mind. Lucky for him he'd escaped that noose.

Shaking his head, he picked up his spoon. He supposed Mrs. Murdoch was right. He did know something about his bride-to-be . . . he did in fact possess one expectation.

He would have her in his bed.

Millie Anderson, the village laundress, rented rooms above the blacksmith's. Rumor purported that the blacksmith accepted payment upstairs in her private rooms every Sunday after church. Payment was not rendered in the typical fashion.

Shunned by gentlefolk, her situation was one for which Evie felt great empathy. Linnie would have faced the same ostracism had the world known of her fall from grace. Evie could yet suffer such a fate if her lack of a husband ever came to light. The threat of that scandal forever nipped at her heels.

Convinced Millie could help her, Evie knocked lightly on the door. Light seeped from the wide crack beneath until a shadow fell there, blocking the glow. The pungent odor of manure floated from the stalls below.

"Yes?" a voice called from within.

"Miss Anderson? It's Evelyn Cross."

After a moment, the door opened. Evie stared at the hard-eyed woman. She was handsome. Perhaps once beautiful. The flesh edging her eyes sagged; her face was gray where it was not chafed red and raw. Ice-gray strands streaked the dark plait hanging over her shoulder.

Exhaling a great breath, Evie proclaimed, "I need your help."

Millie arched a brow, hesitating only a moment before holding the door wide and motioning Evie within.

A sparse room greeted her. A single bed, unmade. Table, chairs, a large chipped basin on a stand. A tattered sofa sat near a smoldering grate. Millie plopped down inelegantly upon its worn cushions, curling one leg beneath her.

She jerked her chin at Evie. "What brings a fine

woman such as yourself here? I'm not accustomed to entertaining ladies."

Evie cleared her throat and settled beside the woman on one end of the sofa. "You know who I am?"

"Aye, I know you. You're the one that lives with that old bat, Miss Gertrude." Millie sniffed and brushed at her soiled hem.

Evie reached for her reticule, ready with coin for the favor she would ask. She didn't possess much, but she considered this a necessary expense. If she was to wed Lockhart, she needed expert counsel.

"I need information."

"From me?" Millie grunted, the sound deep and skeptical.

"Of an intimate nature."

"Ah." The woman smiled then. "I suppose I know a thing or two about matters of an *intimate* nature."

Heat crawled into Evie's cheeks, her mind moving ahead, trying to form her first inquiry. "I had heard you might."

"I was a rich man's mistress," Millie shared. "My life wasn't always this." Her tired eyes flicked around her room in distaste. "If you would believe it, I served a fine lord. Loved him even, faithfully, for nearly fifteen years." Her eyes gleamed wetly.

Evie flexed her fingers over her reticule. "What happened?"

"He took everything from me. My youth. My beauty." Her mouth whitened at the corners. "He used me up, he did, and then tossed me aside when he was finished." She fluttered her hand. "Never thought a wedding ring was all that important. I always scoffed at the priggish matrons marching along Bond Street. I had other jewelry. Emerald necklaces. Ruby brooches." She snorted. "But I'm not telling you anything new. You know what it's like to be abandoned by a man. Even in death. It's not much different, is it?" Her gaze searched Evie's face, clearly seeking confirmation of this.

"No," Evie whispered. "Alone is alone."

Millie nodded.

Evie didn't know that precisely, but she did know, staring at the pitiable Millie Anderson, that she saw Linnie in her. She saw what could have been. If she were not careful, what still could be.

Her sister never would have survived such a life. Not even a fortnight. Evie thanked God that she had been there to help. So Linnie could live her last years in peace and comfort as a rich man's wife. So Evie had the privilege of being Nicholas's mother, even if she lived in a perpetual state of fear that she would end up like Millie Anderson, a pariah shunned by Society should the truth ever come out.

With a grunt, Millie pulled her tattered shawl tighter. "Now. What's your business with me?"

Evie swallowed past the thickness in her throat and plunged ahead. "The fates have been kind enough to give me a second chance at marriage."

Millie's brows winged high. "Indeed. What's that got to do with me?"

"I'll be leaving for Scotland." She swallowed again, the lump back. "Shall be married before the week is out."

"Congratulations." Millie rose and opened the grate to add more coals from her dwindling supply.

"Yes, but I find myself nervous about . . . er, the wedding night . . ."

Millie turned, a frown marring the tired lines of her face. "You've been with a man before. What's to be nervous about?"

Heat licked Evie's cheeks. "Yes, that was some time ago. I was scarcely a woman."

"That bad, huh?"

Her cheeks burned hotter. "No," she hastened to say. "I was merely young. Inexperienced. Really, it's all a . . . blur—"

"Isn't the first time usually?"

"I would like for it to be better . . . er, more

memorable." She choked on the words. "I want to appear—"*not a virgin*"—natural with the entire process."

"I see." Millie stared at her intently, and Evie fought not to fidget.

To fill the sagging silence, she asked, "Do you have any tips on how I might come across as more proficient?" She wet her lips. "How I might please him?"

So that he doesn't notice how woefully inept I am and reach the obvious conclusion?

Evie bit her lip and waited.

Millie's lips twitched. "Aye, I've a tip or two that always worked for me." She dropped back on the sofa, flinging her arms along the back. "They might offend your fine sensibilities, though."

Evie shook her head. "Please speak plainly. I'm ready."

"Are you now?"

Evie's thoughts flew to the man sleeping in her bed. Was she ready?

For marriage?

For *him*?

She fidgeted on the sofa, suddenly restless. "Yes." She inhaled deeply through her nose. "Please proceed."

* * *

Well over an hour later, Evie departed Millie Anderson's room with her cheeks afire and a low throb pulsing in her belly.

She had a difficult time accepting everything the woman imparted as fact. Unfortunately—or fortunately, depending on the way she viewed it—Millie's information included detailed descriptions, which resulted in vivid images permanently etched in her mind. Scandalous images of Evie and Lockhart acting out every one of the ribald scenarios described.

Now that she was informed, could she behave so boldly? Could she perform the intimacies Millie had described? To convince Lockhart of her experience, did she have any choice?

On the bottom floor, stalls that smelled like they hadn't been cleaned in over a year lined the walls. Pressing a hand to her nose, she hurried forward, jerking to a halt when the burly blacksmith stepped in her path.

Wiping his hands on his stained leather apron, he pressed close. "Have a nice talk with Millie, Missus?" His dark eyes skimmed her figure insolently.

"Quite so." She lifted her chin, scanning him distastefully and thinking of poor Millie crushed beneath his sweaty hulking form. At that thought, she fished the coin from her reticule that Millie had refused to accept. "See that Miss Anderson has fresh coal supplied to her room every day."

With narrowed eyes, he snatched the coin.

"And you'll deliver just coal . . . not your"—she wrinkled her nose—"unwelcome person on her."

His fleshy lip curled over stained teeth. "What do you care happens to some tart?"

Staring at the blacksmith's red, bulbous face, she simply couldn't stomach the thought of Millie suffering his attentions another day. "If she cannot pay your rent, see me," she ground out. She'd worry about explaining that expense to her husband later.

"The arrangement I have with Millie suits me well enough."

Pig. "If you refuse my money, I'm sure we can find Miss Anderson quarters elsewhere. Perhaps your wife might recommend somewhere else?"

"Very well," he bit out, his ruddy face burning red.

Evie smiled brightly, suddenly feeling lighter inside. "Thank you. Good day." She pulled her shawl tight and started toward home. For the first time, the future did not loom quite so grimly. She could manage this—manage her husband.

Wrong or not, she permitted herself to feel hope. What were a few months if she and her loved ones gained lifelong security?

Chapter 10

Lockhart joined Evie for à private dinner that evening. It was Mrs. Murdoch's idea. Dinner was usually a noisy, boisterous affair with her son leading the charge. They all dined at one table— Aunt Gertie, the Murdochs, Amy, and Nicholas.

She'd been unable to pay the Murdochs or Amy a proper wage for nearly a year. They remained only out of love and goodwill. Considering that, Evie refused to be waited upon. And yet tonight, Mrs. Murdoch insisted on serving, claiming the evening required more dignity. She even arranged for Amy to take Nicholas to bed early . . . leaving Evie to dine alone with her future husband.

He sat across from her, stiff with military bearing. His firm lips fell hard and unsmiling as he sat rigidly in his chair. An eternal soldier . . . or did he simply regret his proposal? She didn't know—didn't know him enough to hazard a guess.

With her dinner tasteless in her mouth, she chewed and tried not to fret over the future. The entire matter was decided. They would leave the day after tomorrow. Lockhart wanted to be off sooner, but he didn't stand a chance against the intractable Mrs. Murdoch. According to the housekeeper, he would be fit for travel only then. No one suggested calling Sheffield back for his expert opinion on the matter.

It was settled. She would be a married woman before the week was out. Evie reached for her small glass of sherry and downed it in a swift gulp. Mrs. Murdoch's eyes widened from where she stood sentinel along the paneled wall.

Her future husband lifted an arrogant brow at her.

"How is the sole?" The sound of her voice breaking the silence almost startled her.

He looked up. "Fine. Delicious."

She nodded, glad for that at least. Mrs. Murdoch had worked a small miracle, trading some of her special drawing salve for fresh fish in the village. Otherwise the night's fare would likely have been stew. Mrs. Murdoch knew how to stretch out a broth.

He studied her in that intense, almost frightening way. Her stare fell to his mouth. Full, well-carved lips for a man. A man that seemed incapable of smiling. He was handsome, true, but so very stoic. Her mind wandered to her conversation with Millie.

Would he even *want* her to put her lips . . .

She shook free of the scandalous thought.

He wanted her in his bed. He had admitted as much. She shivered, pressing a hand to an overly warm cheek. No, *needed*. He needed her in his bed. He needed an heir. He'd said nothing of wanting her. There was a distinction, and she would do well to remember that. Even if he entranced her and made her feel warm in places she never knew *could* feel, she must keep their marriage in proper perspective.

At that moment Nicholas broke into the room in his nightshirt, bare feet flying, an apologetic Amy fast on his heels. Clambering onto her lap, indifferent to the dishes he sent rattling with his flailing elbows, he demanded his good night kiss.

With Lockhart watching in brooding silence, Evie rained kisses on his sweet little face, feathering his shock of dark hair off his brow. "Now off to bed with you."

Nicholas paused before returning to Amy, eyes landing on Lockhart with a curious intensity. "Are you going to marry my mother?"

Evie sucked in a breath and shot a questioning look to Amy. Her friend shrugged.

She should have been prepared for this. Nicholas was a precocious child, and earlier today she had explained to him that she would be leaving for a short time and that when she returned, she would be married. Still, Evie had not thought he'd fully understood. Coward that she was, she judged it best to leave him with only a vague sense of the changes to come. She did not wish to rip away all that was comfortable and familiar. At least not too suddenly.

Her husband-to-be stared solemnly at her son. "Yes, Nicholas. I am."

"Will you be my father then?"

She blinked. Such an innocent question. Yet to hear it from her child's lips, she felt as if she had been struck a blow. Had he wanted a father so very much then?

"Yes," Lockhart said again, his voice solid and firm.

She closed her eyes, grateful for the answer, for the unflinching promise that gleamed in his gaze.

"Would you like that?" he added.

Nicholas cocked his head, clearly considering. "I don't know. Will you take me fishing?"

"If you like."

Nicholas nodded fiercely. "Very much. Mr.

Murdoch takes me fishing, but I've never fished with a father before."

A breath shuddered from her.

Satisfied, Nicholas moved toward Amy, stopping at the last moment to rush back toward Lockhart. Without invitation, he climbed up into his lap and pressed his little mouth to his cheek. "Good night."

"Good night," Lockhart returned, his lips a little softer now, almost bending into a smile. His eyes had changed as well, glowing softly as he watched Nicholas hop down and depart the dining room.

Alone with him again save for Mrs. Murdoch, Evie stared down at the buttery peas on her plate. She chased a glistening pearl onion slowly with her fork, focusing on suppressing the hot sob that rose in her throat.

Had she been a fool all this time, convincing herself that Nicholas didn't need a father? That he didn't want one? That he would never feel the lack?

She gave her head a small, violent shake. Not even five years old, but he already understood that a father had been missing from his life.

Any lingering doubts fled. She settled her gaze on Spencer Lockhart. Nicholas needed this man. It was enough. Enough that her son needed him.

Even if she did not. Even if she could not permit herself to feel anything more than gratitude toward him. The loyalty a wife felt toward her husband.

She could not afford to need him, and could not risk more than she already had. She could not risk her heart.

After dinner, Evie walked the garden alone, her thoughts on the man occupying her bedchamber for the night. He had tried to give her back her room, but she'd refused and taken the smaller guest room, along with its drafts, for herself. He was already healing from an arrow wound; she would not have him catch ague.

She inhaled the chill night air and stared out at the neat rows of her barren vegetable garden. No crows in sight. Her lips twitched. Aunt Gertie would be pleased.

She would miss this place. She had felt safe here during the last years. After Barbados, she had so badly needed to feel safe. And purposeful. The thought of leaving, even for a short while, made her feel like a child preparing to give up a favored blanket. Lengthening her strides, she chafed her arms against the brisk air.

Soon. Soon, she would be back. Married, yes, but

otherwise unchanged. Well, perhaps with child if Lockhart achieved his goal. Her heart tightened, not liking the notion of becoming some man's broodmare. Shaking off the vile comparison, she reminded herself that she was being more than compensated. Lifelong security for Nicholas and herself—for *all* her dependents—was no small matter.

But where was the love? Desire and affection between two people?

An image of Lockhart's hands filled her mind. She saw them so clearly—broad–palmed and masculine, a light sprinkling of hair at the wiry wrists. They had fixated her at dinner. Her belly fluttered at the memory . . . at the prospect of those hands moving languidly over her body.

Very well. Desire mightn't be lacking. At least on her part.

She would take what months they had together, share his bed until he either tired of her or she conceived. She would seize what pleasure she could from their arrangement and accept when it ended.

She couldn't blame him for using her. Not when she was using him, too.

Not when she was less than honest with him.

She shivered and buried herself deeper inside

her shawl, recognizing that she might be shivering for reasons other than the chill night.

Sighing, she walked on, wishing she were brave. Like Fallon. Composed like Marguerite. Her friends would not feel this stark terror that was shooting down her spine and settling in her stomach like a ton of bricks.

She wished she was a bit like her old self. The girl who had hopped on a ship bound for Barbados ready to conquer the world. That girl would embrace the notion of marriage to an exciting, enigmatic man . . . a man who made her toes curl inside her slippers.

Her gaze drifted to her bedroom window. A low light glowed there. She thought back to this evening's dinner, to that indefinable tension on the air. To Lockhart . . . *Spencer*. A man who said little but spoke volumes with his watchful green eyes.

And she knew. Felt it in her core.

He had something—*everything*—to do with her desire to go back. To turn back the clock and return to her old self. A girl ready to embrace life and adventure. *Him*.

The chill in her bones faded, replaced with a simmering warmth as she contemplated that in mere days she would be sleeping in the same bed with Spencer Lockhart. Well. Perhaps not sleeping.

"Is it true?"

Evie spun around, feeling very much like Romeo caught in the act of gazing at Juliet's window.

Dr. Sheffield stood before her, his thin chest rising and falling as though he had run a great distance. Noticing his lack of hat and his wild, windblown hair, she suspected he had in fact executed a mad dash from his home.

"Sheffield," she murmured, slipping her hands beneath her shawl and chafing her arms briskly. "What are you doing here?" An inane question, voiced only to grant her time, a reprieve, however brief.

She knew why he was here.

Word had reached him that she was marrying Lockhart. Mrs. Murdoch had likely mentioned something in the village today. Gossip like that would spread with the speed of wildfire.

"Sheffield?" His head snapped back a fraction. "I thought we had dispensed with formality long ago, Evelyn."

Her cheeks warmed. "Of course. Peter."

"Is it true?" He punctuated each word, his voice a deep bite.

"I don't know what you mean," she lied. She blinked once, slowly, painfully, understanding perfectly what he was getting at, but still hoping to avoid the impending confrontation.

He moved swiftly, grasping her by the arm. "Don't play daft," he hissed in her face. "You owe me an answer. I'm the laughingstock of the entire village!"

She gasped at his cruel voice, his rough grasp. She had never seen him this way before. The sight of his red-mottled face shot alarm through her and brought back the bitter fear she had felt only one other time. But with that fear followed another emotion. Anger.

She would not be a victim again.

"Unhand me." Her voice rang with authority, all politeness gone.

"Not until I have the explanation I deserve."

His voice, his face . . . she did not know. All these years, she had thought Peter kind. A true friend. Yes, he deserved an explanation, but he had no right to treat her in this fashion.

She twisted her arm, trying to break free of his unrelenting grip. "You're hurting me."

Something akin to pain flashed in his eyes. "Not, I assure you, how you have hurt me."

Hurt him? Surely he jested? Despite his attentions, she had never imagined he truly *loved* her. In three years, he had never pressed her for a declaration.

"I made you no promises, Peter. On the contrary, I urged you to find someone worthy—"

"Indeed. Perhaps you should have told me a bit more of *him*." He motioned wildly toward the house. "Had you mentioned you were waiting for his return—"

"I was not waiting for him!" The truth, at least. How could she have known her sister's past would come calling? She had not considered the possibility. As far as she knew, Ian Holcomb had abandoned Linnie. "Peter, please—"

"I've waited all these years for you—"

"No one asked you to," she bit out, her temper flaring hotly.

"I thought you grieved! I did not wish to push you."

She shook her head, helplessly frustrated. "What do you want from me, Peter?"

He loosened his grip on her arm, no longer hurting her. Emotion burned in his eyes, making her feel the veriest wretch. "The moment I saw you, I knew, Evelyn—" His voice stopped, strangled in his throat.

Good heavens. He truly cared for her? Had she been so blind? Or merely indifferent?

Shame ran prickly-hot inside her chest. "Peter," she whispered, "I am sorry. I never intended to hurt you."

His woeful gaze crawled over her face. "A little late for that, though, isn't it?"

Her lips worked, searching for a suitable response. She brought her hand up between them, covering his where he grasped her. "I'm sorry. I wish I could give you back the time you've wasted on me, but I've no doubt a young lady of sterling quality waits you. You really are a most splendid catch."

He nodded slowly, scratching one muttonchop sideburn and opening his mouth to reply, when another voice intruded, a dark growl that shattered the brief accord she had reached with Peter.

"Take your hands off her."

Evie tore her gaze off Peter to gawk at her soon-to-be husband. With almost guilty haste, she slipped her hand off Peter's. Unfortunately, he did not copy the gesture. If anything, his grasp on her arm tightened.

And that was the only place Lockhart seemed to stare.

Chapter 11

Spencer's fists curled and uncurled at his sides as he gazed at his future wife in another man's arms. With a grim press of his lips, he wondered if he had not made a colossal mistake.

It was one thing to contend with a ghost, a cousin he loved and for whom he himself still grieved, but it was quite another thing to contend with a flesh-and-blood man who appeared to have a firm footing in his future wife's affections.

Affections, hell. Since when did he require that? He'd thought loyalty and the necessary heir were his only requirements in a wife.

A feeling that he had never experienced before burned down his throat, settling in his gut in an angry, roiling froth. The longer he stared at her—at *them, together*—the feeling only intensified.

There had been no mistaking the tender look on her face, or the gentle tenor of her voice when she'd spoken to Sheffield. Just as there was no mistaking the scalding anger in his veins.

Did she love him? A foul taste filled his mouth. The good physician who had attended her so faithfully these last years? Whilst his cousin had dodged bullets and choked on cannon smoke and thought only of her, *talked* only of her and filled Spencer's ears with stories of *her, her, her*?

If she cared for him, why did she not wed him? Did his pockets not run deep enough?

He locked gazes with Sheffield, his stare unblinking, hard and intent, hopefully conveying what he would do to the man if he did not take his hand off her. Understanding flickered in Sheffield's eyes. Defeat.

At last, Sheffield looked away, his hand slipping from her arm. "I'll go now, Evelyn." He nodded with tight courtesy, his face drawn, eyes flat. Lifeless. "Happy wishes on your nuptials."

"Thank you," she murmured, her voice scarcely audible. And why was that? Shame? Or sorrow? Grief for this man she released from her life?

Alone now, she studied him, her gaze cautious.

"Impressive," he bit out.

She shook her head. "What is?"

"To have won the utter devotion of two men. And still so young. At this rate, you'll have quite a collection of men before you reach thirty."

She pulled her shawl tightly about her shoulders. "You speak of Ian and Peter."

His lips twisted. "Are there others yet I don't know of?"

Her chin jerked. "Of course not." She motioned in the direction Sheffield had taken. "I did nothing to encourage Peter. I gave him no promises—"

"That did not stop him from falling in love with you, did it? Tell me, what is it about you that so thoroughly beguiles men?"

He cocked his head and ran his gaze over her. Even in the twilight, he made out the bloom of color in her cheeks and the wild pulse thrumming at her throat. The insane urge to press his mouth there and suck seized him. He closed his eyes in a long blink and looked away. He really was mad to want his future wife this much. Especially as he only intended to keep her around for the time it took to conceive an heir.

The last thing he needed was to form an attachment to her. Wives meant domesticity and seasons in Town. Balls and routs and shopping excursions to Bond Street. He had no intention of being dragged into Society, where nosey busybodies would clap him on the back and pronounce him a hero and ask him to speak to their garden club. He only wanted solitude—to manage his properties and retire to Northumberland, where he could find a measure of peace. Where dreams of dying men and exploding artillery did not fill his nights.

"I haven't beguiled Peter. We are good friends. Nothing more."

Nothing more. There was everything more. There was the fact that she drew men like bees to the honey pot.

And in that moment, he vowed he wouldn't be another man on her list—another fool to fall at her feet.

He might marry her, but he would stand strong. He would not love her. Would not let those blue eyes ensnare him.

"You're so certain of that?" he demanded.

She angled her head, the gold-brown strands drowned black in the shadows. "Can one truly love someone who can't love them back? I would not call that love. I would call that infatuation."

She was clever. He wondered why Ian had never mentioned that. He had extolled her beauty, her grace, her sweetness and delicacy. Never her wit. Had she changed so much? Or did Ian never really know her?

"What of Ian then?" he demanded, his words carrying an unintended bite. "He loved you. I can attest to that. Did you return the sentiment, or was it a mere fancy of youth?"

A stillness came over her, and he held his breath, marveling at why he would ask when he knew the answer. Of course she loved Ian. Why else had she remained unwed these many years?

"I—" Her mouth parted, worked for speech. "Yes," she finally answered. "That was love. Real and true. Once in a lifetime."

Brilliant. Her heart was irrevocably bound to the past. To Ian. It rooted their marriage even more in cold practicality. She would not pine for his love and affection. It wouldn't disappoint her that he could do no more than offer fleeting passion. He could not offer himself. He was but a dead shell of a man, his heart, his spirit lost somewhere on a battlefield in the Crimea.

Even so, his hollow chest ached as he stood there in the gloom of the garden, gazing down at the woman that should have been his cousin's wife but was to be his. Even as he determined to let her go in a few months' time, he wanted to leave his mark on her. Brand her as his.

He felt like a thief. A wretch for plotting how quickly he could seduce her into his bed and make her forget Ian. Ian and any other man—Sheffield included.

"I trust you'll behave yourself in the future with your overly solicitous doctor."

"*Behave* myself?" Her blue gaze snapped fire in the night. "What are you accusing me of?"

"It was quite the loving scene that I interrupted. For all that you claim not to love him, you clearly have tender feelings for the man." He moved, circling her. "Once we decide to part ways, you may wish to return here, no?"

"Perhaps," she admitted.

He stopped directly before her. "If that's the case, I won't have you cavorting with him in the manner I just witnessed."

She crossed her arms across her chest angrily. "Why should it matter so much to you? Our marriage will scarcely be *real*."

His gaze dropped to her mouth. "It will be real enough."

"For a time." She gave the barest nod of agreement.

He lifted a hand and ran a finger over the plump line of her mouth. So soft. "It will be enough. You'll have no doubt that you've been wedded . . . and *bedded* by me."

She slapped his hand away and stepped back. "Is that your definition of a real marriage? Marriage involves more than the act of consummation."

"View it however you like. After we part ways, when you return here . . . or anywhere, you'll still be mine, and I'll not be made a cuckold." He flexed one hand into a fist at his side and wondered at the stark surge of possession burning through him.

Standing this close, he saw her lips quiver. She lifted her chin, staring down—if possible—the slim column of her nose at him. "I'll not shame you. You need not fear that. I will behave with utmost decorum. I wouldn't dream of behaving in a less than circumspect fashion."

"Well." He cocked his head. A dangerous churning started in his gut. "It wouldn't be the first time if you did."

She gasped.

He blinked hard, angry with himself. What had possessed him to fling out that unkind remark? So she'd fallen from grace. He was no saint himself. Unlike the rest of Society, he was not one to hold ladies to impossible moral standards.

Was he so jealous of her indiscretion with Ian? If it hadn't happened, he wouldn't even have been standing here with her now. He wouldn't even have known her.

She edged back a step, clearly on the verge of flight, and he didn't blame her.

Her gaze swept over him like he was something foul she found beneath her slipper. "Let us be clear now. At every encounter, must I account for my past? Is it something for which you will forever condemn me?"

Bloody hell. "Linnie," he started.

"No. *No.*" She held up a hand, her slim fingers splayed wide in the air. "Please. You are correct, after all. I can make no claims to decorum. None that you should believe, at any rate. I'm merely the silly, stupid girl your cousin ruined before he left for the war. And you"—she looked him up and down—"are the honorable kinsman sacrificing himself on the altar of matrimony." Her blue eyes glowed brightly. "How very proud you must be."

"I did not say that—"

"No, but you meant it." Her voice shook, rippling through him like a cold wind. "It's only the truth." Clenching her shawl tightly around her shoulders, she swung a wide circle around him, striding past with fiery dignity.

He stopped her with a hand on her arm.

He couldn't help it; he couldn't let her go. This stranger he would wed.

He felt he should know her, understand her for all that Ian had shared about her. And yet he did not. He didn't know the first thing about this creature with wit and courage and fire in her eyes and an expressive face that carried its own unique history. He didn't know her. Yet. But he intended to.

She glared at his hand on her arm and back to his face, her firm, narrow little chin jutting at an obstinate angle. He burned to grasp it in his hand, pull her to him and sample her mouth, see if her lips tasted as soft as they felt.

"You have more to add?" she fairly hissed. "I think we've said entirely enough for one night. Perhaps we can begin again on the morrow with fresh insults."

His lips twisted. God, she was a spitfire.

Even beneath the wool sleeve of her gown he felt the humming pulse of her warm flesh. She affected him. He thought back to the eager servant girl at the inn. Perhaps he should have taken her up on her offer. Because at this moment, this close, with his hand on Linnie, he wanted her with a blood-pumping intensity. The kind of intensity that forced him to act. Seize and claim her now.

He tugged her closer. She came, tumbling against his chest. He hardened instantly at the soft press of her breasts through her hideous gown. Her head tilted back to watch him, her brilliant gaze softly questioning. He studied the length of her long lashes, inky cobwebs framing the vivid blue of her eyes. He would see them even in the deep of dark. In his bed. He would see her eyes even as their bodies rocked together, locked in passion.

Aroused, shaken, he dropped his hand from her arm as if burned.

Wide-eyed, she stared at him.

"Go," he snarled. "Just go, Linnie—"

"Stop!" Her chest lifted with a giant breath. "Don't call me *that*. I'm Evie." Her tongue darted out to moisten her lips. "No one calls me Linnie." She looked away from his eyes abruptly, adding in a softer voice, "Not anymore."

He nodded jerkily. He'd heard the others call her Evie and thought it just another nickname for Evelyn. He hadn't realized she now preferred it exclusively.

"Evie," he said, tasting it on his tongue, savoring it.

It suited her. *Linnie* belonged to a little girl. He scanned her slender length, the breasts she hid beneath the rag she called a dress. Evie was a woman. All tempting woman.

"Evie," he repeated, brushing a stray strand off her cheek and tucking it behind her ear.

Her eyes gleamed in the night, uncertain as they moved from his eyes to his mouth. Tension still hummed on the air, volatile and crackling. A cinder waiting to catch fire. Her gaze flickered with some emotion before dropping half-mast.

He dipped his head, holding his mouth above hers, sighing her name against her lips. "Evie." He liked that he could call her something Ian never had. Linnie was Ian's. Evie would be his.

"Yes."

He breathed in her gaspy reply, his gaze devouring her face, every curve and hollowed line. "Call me Spencer."

"Spencer," she whispered, her stare back on his mouth.

He nodded, liking the soft roll of his name on her lips.

"Evie," he tasted her name again. "I'm going to kiss you now." He let his meaning hang, hover, sink deep.

Her eyes flared wide, but she didn't move as he lowered his head. He brushed his lips to hers, tasted gently the hint of warm sherry on her lips. Her lips moved tentatively, almost like a beginner. Or at least someone very rusty.

Blood pounded in his veins. He shuddered, hard-pressed to keep his desire under control.

She leaned into him, gave herself up, and he snapped. Slipping a hand around the back of her neck and an arm around her waist, he hauled her off her feet.

With a firm grip on the back of her neck, he angled her for his mouth, groaning against her soft lips, forcing them apart for his invading tongue.

Soft skin filled his palm. Silky tendrils brushed the back of his hand as he held her close, deepening the kiss, hungry, starving for more. He dragged his mouth down her throat, licking and gently biting at the wildly thrumming pulse in her neck.

Her moan swung into a gasp.

As if the sound frightened her, she lurched her face away. Too soon, it ended.

Reluctantly, he released her, let her slide down the length of him.

Like a woman drunk, she staggered back from the circle of his arms, pressing one shaking hand against her lips. Lips he still tasted on his own.

His hands opened and curled at his sides, aching to haul her back, to clutch her close, to feel the slim, giving length of her against him again.

Her wide eyes looked strangely wounded as she gazed upon him. "This is too soon. I'm still adjusting to the notion of marrying you . . . of, of—"

"Sharing my bed," he finished with a snap. Would she prefer he be someone else? He inhaled, his chest lifting. "I told you my expectations. This should come as no surprise."

She shook her head. Sun-kissed tendrils escaped the confines of her simple coiffure, framing her face and making her look young and fresh. Utterly desirable. "We're not even married yet."

He couldn't help himself. He tossed his head back and laughed. The harsh sound filled the garden, echoing all around. A kiss before marriage scandalized her? When she had done so much more before? With Ian?

Her eyes flashed with outrage, understanding the meaning behind his laughter.

Even in the gloom, he detected the burning rise of color in her narrow face. She made a sound, a low, animal-like noise in the back of her throat. This time he saw her hand coming—but unlike the last time, he caught it in his grasp. He flexed his hand over her slim fingers. So fine that the slightest pressure would crush them.

She whimpered and tried to pull free.

"You struck me once," he bit out. "Don't make it a habit."

She tugged harder, color unevenly staining her cheeks. She possessed mettle, he'd give her that.

"Then don't make it a habit of treating me like a whore."

"Very well." He inclined his head ever so slightly, unable to deny that charge.

For whatever reason, she provoked him into flinging her past at her time and time again. Bewildering, that. He didn't condemn her; he was certainly no paragon of morality. On the contrary, he came from a long line of scoundrels. To be fair, he had to count himself among their ranks a time or two. Before the war, he'd almost been as wild and unrepentant as the rest of the men in his family, all in the hope to fit in among them.

And yet her past with Ian plagued him. Drove him to fling angry words. He sighed, not particularly liking himself just then.

He dropped her hand. "Go," he commanded.

She didn't move.

"Go," he barked.

Like a startled hare, she bolted, leaving him in the garden. He stood alone for several moments, dragging a hand through his hair. Tomorrow he would depart for Northumberland, to the one place that always felt like home. They would stay the night there before moving on to Scotland.

The prospect should have settled peacefully in his chest. During the war, he had dreamed of returning to Ashton Grange. When his mother took him there as a boy . . . those had been good days. He hoped to reclaim a measure of that again.

Only now he would possess a wife. *Evie.*

He rubbed a palm against his thigh. He heard a door shut in the distance and knew she was gone. For now. Soon she would have nowhere to run. Soon she would be his.

Chapter 12

E vie looked up and stared through the parted curtains as if waking from a dream. "What is this place?"

"Ashton Grange. The estate came to me through my mother." Spencer swayed slightly on the squabs as the carriage turned onto the drive. "It's the only thing I've left of her aside from a few rusty memories." He shook his head. The barest scowl crossed his handsome face.

She found herself staring at his well-formed mouth. Felt her own mouth part, her lips tingle and loosen on an inaudible sigh with the memory of their kiss.

She'd thought of little else throughout their journey north. She couldn't have imagined how much it would stir her. How much she would ache to feel his lips on hers again.

She closed her eyes in a long-suffering blink.

Millie's voice filled her ears, her explicit descriptions dancing through her head. Heat swamped her, creeping up from her too-tight chest, to her neck, her face . . .

She saw herself naked with Spencer, their bare limbs tangled, their hot mouths kissing, dragging . . . everywhere. To all the intimate places she now knew—courtesy of Millie—could be touched, kissed, loved.

Cheeks burning, her breath fell faster. Embarrassed that Spencer might detect his mortifying effect on her, she quickly turned her attention back out the window just as they stopped before the sprawling country house.

His voice slid across the closed confines of the carriage, brushing her skin like a feather's stroke. "We'll stay the night here."

Although he'd declared himself well-heeled, she certainly had not expected him to possess anything of this level. With its great mullioned windows and the flawlessly maintained front hedges circling the house, Ashton Grange looked like something that might belong to a duchess like Fallon.

A sick little feeling stirred in her belly. With wealth and property came rank and position. Neither of which she wanted. The privileged were always scrutinized. The last thing she needed was scrutiny . . . where someone could pry loose a few truths best left buried.

Mr. Murdoch hopped down from his perch to open the carriage door, looking so weary that Evie felt a stab of regret. The man needed to be resting beside his fire, his feet propped on a footstool, not haring off across the north of England atop a carriage in the cling of winter.

Spencer must have read her mind. Or maybe he saw the tired lines around Mr. Murdoch's eyes himself. "You can return to Little Billings on the morrow, Murdoch. I've a carriage here. One of my footmen shall take us the rest of the way."

Murdoch snapped to attention. "I'll not be leaving Missus Evie alone—"

"She won't be alone. She'll be under my protection. From here on, she'll be my concern."

Apparently that wasn't good enough. Murdoch cut his gaze to her, arching a bushy, caterpillar brow in question.

Spencer tensed, looked at her, waiting to see how she would respond. Whether or not she would give herself over to him as a wife ought.

Evie nodded. "It will be all right." She glanced at Spencer. "I'll be safe."

The wicked way his mouth quirked, she wondered if she perhaps misspoke.

The front door swung open at that moment. A tall, ruddy-faced woman emerged. "Spencer?" She rushed down the steps. "Is that you, my boy?"

Before Spencer could answer, she flung her arms around him in an unseemly display of affection. "Sweet boy! My sweet, sweet boy. I never thought these old eyes would see you again. Oh, dear, you're here and we're only with half staff. It shall take me a week to outfit the place properly—"

Spencer patted her back, sending Evie a glance. "It's good to be here, Mrs. Brooks. And no worries. I should have sent word of my visit."

"Indeed, you should have," she chided. The woman pulled back and clasped his face with both hands. "Ah, look at you. You've the look of your mother. A fine, handsome man you turned out." Her gaze drifted to Evie. "And who's this you've brought with you?"

"This is Evelyn Cross. We'll be journeying to Scotland in the morning. To wed."

Mrs. Brooks clapped her hands together. Before Evie could offer a proper greeting, the larger woman enveloped her in her arms. "Ah, lass! I always knew the right one would come along for our lad."

"Easy there, Mrs. Brooks. I'd like to keep her in one piece."

Mrs. Brooks pulled back, releasing Evie with quick hands. "Forgive me. I'm quite overcome."

"We've been traveling hard, Mrs. Brooks."

"Of course." She waved Murdoch away from their luggage. "Good man, leave that for one of the footmen and move on to the kitchens with you for a meal." Beaming, she lifted her skirts and led Evie and Spencer inside. "I'll have you both settled in no time."

Evie snuck a glance at Spencer as he walked beside her, his face impassive, one hand on her elbow. Strange, but that hand on her elbow felt natural. *Good*.

"Cook made shepherd's pie—"

"Ah. I remember it well. The best I ever ate."

Mrs. Brooks nodded gravely. "It's the red wine. She uses a liberal hand."

In the foyer, Evie tried not to gape at the crystal chandelier. The spectacular monstrosity would not fit inside any room of her house. She blinked against its sudden light, welcoming the intrusion, letting it jar her awake, reminding her that this wasn't natural. None of this was. Not his hand on her elbow, not him, not her . . . together in this mausoleum, soon to be married.

And how could it be natural? Right? He didn't know her, and he never could. Not with subterfuge sitting between them. Not with a union that would only *resemble* a marriage, and even then last only a few months.

His hand moved from her elbow to the small of her back as they ascended the stairs. She shivered, that single touch undoing her. For the barest instant, a mere breath, she longed for this to be real and not a sham. For a moment, she considered confessing the truth. Telling him who she was. *Who she wasn't*.

A breath swelled up from her chest as she followed Mrs. Brooks down the corridor, her husband-to-be an imposing presence at her side. She exhaled, the air shuddering from her lips as she imagined herself saying the words. *I'm not Linnie.*

No. She couldn't risk it, couldn't risk losing Nicholas. Her gaze scanned the lavish surroundings they passed. Clearly, Spencer possessed the means to wrest her son from her. No magistrate would deny him. Especially in favor of a woman that wasn't even Nicholas's birth mother.

She would keep her secret—and she would keep Nicholas. As for her marriage, she would do her best to be a good wife. For however long they were together. According to him, it wouldn't be very long.

For now, she would simply concentrate on making it through tonight.

* * *

Later that evening, Evie brought her brush down vigorously and caught a snarl. Her reflection in the vanity mirror winced back at her. Still, she continued to brush the cloud of golden brown until her scalp tingled and the strands crackled.

Tomorrow they would cross the border into Scotland. Tomorrow they would marry. Tomorrow she would add a new lie to the ever-growing pile.

She'd always justified her decision to take Linnie's place. Nicholas had needed a mother, and Linnie hadn't been able to manage it—not without the support of Papa and Georgianna. Evie, however, had been expendable in their eyes.

Somehow she did not think Spencer Lockhart would be pleased to know he was marrying Evangeline Cosgrove's older half sister. No matter the altruism of her motives.

Unable to stare at herself any longer, she set her brush down and pushed up from the stool. Rubbing her arms, not yet ready for sleep, she turned from the large tester bed.

Muttering to herself, she snatched up her nightrail, convinced there was a library about. Swinging it around her shoulders, she stepped out into the corridor, intent on finding a good book to occupy her thoughts.

* * *

With his solitude stolen, Spencer hungrily watched Evie from where he sat ensconced in a wing-backed chair, careful not to alert her of his presence in the library as he drank deeply from his brandy.

He ceased to breathe altogether when she stretched up on her tiptoes for a thin volume on a shelf just beyond her reach. He'd never seen her hair loose and he drank in the sight, following the trail of waves brushing the rounded curve of her bottom. In the low glow of light, her hair gleamed like sun-kissed honey. His palms tingled, itching to bury themselves in the thick locks.

The light from the fire's dying embers sketched her silhouette perfectly. He stared hungrily at the upturned breasts outlined through her nightrail. Even more tantalizing was the beautiful view of her tear-shaped bottom. His palms itched, tingled to cup and feel the shape for himself.

He shifted, adjusting himself through his robe. No good. He was hard as a rock. It didn't help that he was nearly naked. That one pull of his belt would free him. That one stride would bring him directly behind her, only the thin cotton of her nightrail separating them. A lift of her hem and he could press himself against the length of her, rub himself between her sweetly rounded cheeks.

Book in hand, she lowered herself back down, examining the pages and tugging her bottom lip in that achingly erotic way. With a decisive nod, she turned to leave.

And he couldn't have that. Not yet.

"Couldn't sleep?"

She gave a small start and dropped the book at her feet. "Spencer. I didn't see you there." Firelight moved over her face. With her hair loose, she looked different. Younger. Fresher. The narrow lines of her face less angular, soft.

"You should be asleep," he murmured. "We've a long day tomorrow."

"I could say the same to you."

He lifted his glass to his lips, drank deeply, welcomed the warm burn down his throat.

She observed him warily, her gaze traveling over the long stretch of his legs before him.

"I'll be to bed shortly." He motioned to the small rosewood table beside him. "Care for a drink?" He leaned over and filled a waiting glass sitting on the tray. "Might help you sleep."

She opened her mouth—to decline, he would guess—then stopped. Surprising him, she simply shrugged and stepped forward to accept the glass. Her fingers brushed his, igniting a spark.

Sucking in a breath, she sank into the chair across from him, clutching the glass with both hands. She sipped delicately. "When do you expect we'll arrive?"

"Gretna Green is just a skip over the border."

Nodding, her gaze drifted, roaming the room, the shelves of books lining the walls, stretching toward the mahogany domed ceiling. "Fortunate your mother left you this house. More comfortable than a posting inn."

"According to my father, she was one of his greatest mistakes." His lips twisted. "And he had many."

"Why was she his greatest?"

"A poor match, he claimed. She was somewhat of an embarrassment to him. Her family possessed a bit of money—owned a factory in Morpeth, but her provincial ways, her inability to accept his many affairs . . ." He shrugged.

She paused to sip again. "Your father must have loved her very much once. In the beginning," she murmured.

He laughed, the sound low and rough, void of humor. "Yes, he did. She and every other wife. He loved them all in the beginning. In the beginning, he only saw their lovely faces."

Her eyes widened. "How many wives did your father—"

"Four. My current stepmother, Camila, was the fourth and final. She lasted the longest. She was the most understanding of his . . . habits, his many lies."

"Lies," she echoed, her voice strangely quiet.

"Yes, he was a proficient liar, excelling at convincing any woman that he loved her alone." He felt his lip curl involuntarily over his teeth. "He could make anyone believe anything. Even me. Sometimes I even imagined I meant something to him."

"He sounds an unpleasant sort."

Spencer paused to clear his thickening throat. "When I was six, I caught my father with the midwife's assistant soon after my mother delivered a stillborn son."

She drew a sharp breath.

"She didn't live long after that. A fortnight. Then came Camila. Fortunate for her, he beat her to the grave."

Eyes wide, she gulped from her glass and winced. "You're not saying your father—"

"Was a murderer?"

She nodded mutely, no doubt horrified at the prospect of marrying a man whose father murdered his wives. A man who spewed forth nothing but lies and venom.

"No. Simply unlucky. His first wife died in a fever. The second in a carriage accident, the third—" His throat thickened here. "And my mother never recovered from giving birth to my brother." While his father shagged another woman in the next room.

"I'm sorry."

He grunted. "My father wasn't. It freed him to marry Camila."

Evie cleared her throat and sipped again. He wondered if she had considered any of this. That marrying him was entering into his world—a world she knew nothing about. A world she had seen fit to ask little about.

"You look frightened."

Her gaze snapped back up to his.

"Reconsidering?"

"Of course not. Everyone in Little Billings has seen you and is likely jumping to the same conclusion Peter reached. There is nothing to consider."

"Perhaps I should have reassured Sheffield that I am not Nicholas's father—merely a relation who bears a strong resemblance."

Her eyes widened. "Are you reconsidering?"

"Me? No."

She moistened her lips. "It's as you said. This is the best thing for Nicholas. And it's not as though our lives shall change that greatly." She smiled, her lips wobbly.

"You think not?"

She blinked, her smile slipping. She set her glass down on the table beside her with a clink. "It isn't as though it will be a true marriage. It's more like a partnership. A business relationship."

"Ah, that is how you see it, then?"

She nodded. "Indeed. Should I look at it differently?"

"Hmm," he murmured, his mind immediately drifting to that kiss in the garden, brief, but intense. He certainly didn't think their relationship could be characterized as businesslike.

"Things will change." He felt the need to point out the obvious.

She twisted her fingers in her lap. "How so?"

"For one." He motioned around him. "You'll share my bed. Sex changes everything."

Her head snapped up at this announcement. Her cheeks burned an attractive pink at his bluntness. "Not for any length of time."

He angled his head. "Long enough." And perhaps if she proved as passionate as he suspected, they could arrange the occasional visit . . .

She cleared her throat. "About that . . ."

"Yes?"

"I think it ill-advised for us to immediately engage in conjugal relations—"

"Ill-advised?" He leaned forward in his seat.

"You wish us to wait?" He couldn't wait. He could hardly sleep at night without thoughts of her tantalizing him.

"Until we became better acquainted."

"I know you well enough."

"Do you?" Her voice rang almost angrily.

"Well enough to know a few weeks won't change anything. I need an heir." He set his glass down with a dangerous clink, gazed at her with a hunger he didn't care to disguise. "And I'll have you in my bed."

She blinked. "You said you never would force a woman—"

He chuckled. "Think you that I would need to resort to force?" He slowly appraised her. "With you?" A small shiver rippled over her. "You'll be willing."

"Arrogant—"

"Have you never been seduced before? You were just an inexperienced girl when you met Ian . . . I'm sure there was some gentle persuasion involved."

Her hands strangled fistfuls of her nightrail. Her blue eyes looked almost haunted, pained. "That was a long time ago."

"I'll be more than happy to reintroduce you to the joys of seduction."

She moistened her lips and forged ahead as

if she hadn't heard his offer. Only the bright spots of color on her cheeks told a different tale. "Truly, must we rush into it? Give it some thought—"

He leaned forward in his chair, hands dangling loosely from his knees. "I was clear on what kind of relationship we would have."

Her nostrils flared. "Not everything goes according to design."

He shook his head, glaring at the obstinate thrust of her chin. "You don't grasp the concept of marriage, do you? It's not that tricky."

Grimness filled him as he studied her tight expression. Her absolute distaste over becoming his wife was clear to read. It galled him. She should be thrilled at any distance from the scandal hanging over her head, an avalanche ready to bury her should the fact that she'd invented a husband come to light.

Instead she looked as though she faced a hangman's noose.

"We had an understanding. Unless you've changed your mind. In that case, we will need to discuss what's to be done about Nicholas."

She frowned. "Nicholas?"

"I intend to be a part of his life, with or without you as my wife. We've already discussed all the advantages I can provide him. He can live with me some—"

"You're not taking my son from me!" Sparks glinted in her eyes. Her body quivered where she sat, vibrating with anger. His blood warmed at the sight, and he imagined that this was how she would look lost to passion, naked and writhing beneath him in his bed.

"I wasn't suggesting that. Precisely."

She glared at him hotly, her blue eyes fevered and bright. "You make it sound like my son has suffered a lack with me as—"

"You love him. You're his mother. He needs you. There's no discounting that. But what happens when he's older? When his needs change? When he wants to go to university? I can provide that. Guidance and the kind of opportunities a boy needs to become an estimable man. Even your home—"

"What about my home?"

He waved a hand about him. "A finer home shouldn't signify, but to the rest of the world it does. What the rest of the world thinks does matter . . . determines what doors will open for him—"

She surged to her feet. "You arrogant . . . *ass*!"

Spencer stared, his mouth twitching. "Did you just call me an ass?"

She nodded fiercely, her hair tossing wildly over her shoulders.

He couldn't help himself. He smiled, certain that no woman had ever spoken to him thusly. A short bark of laughter escaped him. He could not even recall a female losing her temper with him before. It was . . . *refreshing*.

She glared at him as though he'd taken leave of his senses.

He rose to his feet as well. "*I'm* an ass?"

"Yes. You are."

"Because I want the best for Nicholas?" He stepped nearer, arching a brow in challenge.

She stomped her foot, color burning her cheeks in the most fetching manner. "I'm his mother. I've raised him since—"

"You're ruined," he stated baldly. "How you've managed to keep it under wraps this long is a miracle unto itself."

She stopped and scowled, crossing her arms tightly. "Not that surprising. A humble country widow doesn't attract much attention."

"Scandal," he continued, stalking her, "nips at your heels, waiting to cast its taint on Nicholas. Marrying me doesn't mean your little subterfuge will forever stay hidden, but it does mean people will care less if it should come to light."

Her chest heaved with angry breath, but she

said nothing. What could she say? He spoke the truth.

"Which leaves me wondering . . . are you merely senseless or . . ."

"Or?" she prompted, her eyes snapping blue flame.

"Or the thought of being married to me—sharing my bed—repels you so much that you clearly won't do what's best for yourself and Nicholas."

Some of the angry color ebbed from her cheeks. She looked nervous, her gaze darting over him. "I didn't say I changed my mind. Only that I wanted some time before we engaged in intimacies." She moistened her lips.

His mind turned again to that kiss in the garden. Sweet, but too brief. Her response before she'd pulled free had promised great passion. He dropped his gaze to her lips, hungry for another taste.

She fumbled a hand over the loose fall of her hair, continuing, "I couldn't have come this far with a man I found repellent. I simply don't know you."

Don't want to know you.

She didn't say it, but she might as well have. He heard it. Saw it in her stiff, angry posture. Felt her unspoken words dig deep in his gut. For whatever reason, she was attempting to construct a wall between them.

And he didn't like it.

"You're right."

Her eyes brightened. "I am?"

"Some things don't go according to design."

She smiled uncertainly. "Yes. Precisely."

"Precisely. Sometimes"—he cocked his head—"one doesn't even wait until the wedding night to begin carnal relations."

Chapter 13

He closed the brief distance separating them, his eyes glittering as he stalked her, the green lit from a fire within. Her back collided with the bookcase at her back. *Trapped.*

She clung to her composure. He'd rattled her enough during their conversation. She wasn't accustomed to losing her temper, but with him it was alarmingly easy. "What are you—"

Whatever she'd meant to say fled, vanished from her head as his body surrounded her, pushed against her, large and masculine, overwhelming. His chest mashed her breasts. His leg slipped between her thighs, the muscled thigh wedging against the core of her with shocking intimacy.

She gasped, swallowing down the urge to cry out. Certainly a virgin would not appear so skittish.

Inhaling deeply through her nose, she hissed. "What are you doing?"

He pushed his thigh higher, raising her until her toes brushed the carpet. The act pulled her nightrail high, lifted the worn fabric to her knees, bringing her eyes nearly level with his. This close, his eyes gleamed brightly, the green so pale, so light.

"What does it look like?" He lowered his hands, dropped them to her hips, slid them around and cupped her bottom. Squeezed her flesh in his large hands.

She gasped. Heat shot directly from his hands to her core.

His gaze traveled her face, dipped to her throat and lower. She swallowed. Or tried. She seemed to have trouble with that. And breathing.

He smiled, the white flash of his teeth wicked and wolflike.

"I suppose," she managed to choke out past her constricting throat, "this is your attempt at seduction."

He slowed his hands, massaging her cheeks deeply and thoroughly until a moan welled from deep in her chest. "How am I faring?"

She shrugged one shoulder. "Not too affecting," she lied, desperate to conceal that what he was doing left her utterly shattered.

His dark brows winged high. "Really?" His eyes glinted with such determined light that she immediately knew she'd taken the wrong approach.

Before she knew what was happening, he tugged her nightrail up and over her head. His large, bare hands clutched her naked bottom. A strangled, guttural cry burst from somewhere deep inside her, tearing past her lips.

Mortified, she quickly attempted to extricate herself, squeezing out between him and the bookcase at her back. No use. He was too big. Too strong. Panicked at the naked press of her body against him, she struggled, thrashed, her hair a wild tangle around them.

"Sssh," he soothed, dragging his hand down the bare line of her side, over the flare of her hip, grasping her thigh and pulling it high, wrapping her leg around his waist. The bulge of his erection prodded directly at her heat.

She stilled, air sawing from her lips. Her gaze locked with his. Longing ripped through her. *Need*. Her body trembled, ached, wakened after years of dormancy. A lifetime.

Her gaze shifted. Dropped. The air rushed from her lips, drying her mouth. His robe was parted, revealing all the gleaming hardness of his chest. The chest she remembered in her dreams. In a burning instant, everything became horrifyingly clear.

He could do anything he wanted to her. She didn't have the will to stop him.

Her request for him to wait, to give her more time was absurd. She couldn't resist him.

Was this what Linnie had been up against? Why she'd succumbed? In the back of her mind, Evie had always rather arrogantly thought her sister naïve. Sweet, but weak-willed.

If that had been true, the same could now be said of her.

"Please, just a little time." She stopped, gulped a breath.

His eyes changed, the pale green deepening to a dark green, a forest after heavy rain. He thrust against her. A throbbing ache began low in her belly. "Back to that again, are you? Never took you for such a coward. What are you afraid of?"

You, she thought, but held her tongue.

After a tense moment in which neither spoke a word, he dropped her leg and stood away from her. She quickly snatched her nightrail from the floor and wrestled it over her head. With her face burning at the eyeful he viewed, she smoothed the fabric down her body, grateful to feel the worn cambric covering her again.

Tying his belt back in place, he turned, granting

her only a glimpse of his profile, the strong line of his jaw a bristly shadow.

He dragged both hands through his dark hair, declaring, "I'll give you until we're married. Then, my patience runs out." He looked at her then, his eyes hard as polished malachite.

She inhaled sharply, nostrils flaring at the forbidding sight of him.

He hated liars. She'd gathered that much when he'd talked about his father. And she was one colossal lie. She shivered to think how he would react to the fact.

For a moment, she considered demanding that he leave her alone, that he renounce all demands on her—on her body. But then she recalled how he'd reacted when she'd tossed down the gauntlet a few moments before.

Her nightrail had ended up on the floor.

Simply eager to escape, she snatched up her book. "I think I should be able to sleep now." Her voice rang tight and clipped, as proper as a schoolmistress's despite her thundering heart. "Good night."

"Good night, Linnie." The moment the name slipped out, he knew his mistake.

Halfway to the library's door, she froze. "Don't," she bit out, slowly turning.

He hadn't meant to call her by the name. It was simply habit. Years of thinking of her as Linnie, Ian's Linnie. Imagining what she would look like, be like . . . and finding she was none of that.

She was more.

He cocked his head, watching her, slightly puzzled over her extreme reaction at his slip.

"I'm not that girl." An emotion he couldn't name washed over her face. "Not anymore."

He nodded, studying her . . . wondering if he would ever understand her. If she would always be this mystery. A woman who tightly clung to her barriers even as she responded to his touch. "It was a slip."

She looked away, blinking, almost as though battling tears.

"*Evie,*" he drawled, saying her name firmly, wanting to give her that, to appease her. Because, for whatever reason, it mattered to her. "Good night."

"Good night." As she stepped from the room, he couldn't be certain, but he thought he heard her whisper his name.

Evie blinked back stinging tears as she fled the library, rubbing her knuckles in each burning eye. Foolish, stupid tears.

She didn't cry.

Ever.

She had not cried since Barbados.

Nor during those wretched years when Papa had abandoned her at Penwich to suffer hunger, fend off bully girls, and, on occasion, endure Master Brocklehurst's strap on her back.

She had not even wept when word had reached her of Linnie's death. Her sister had never fully regained her strength after Nicholas's birth, and she'd fallen even weaker within the misery of her marriage.

Linnie's death had devastated Evie. It was Linnie who'd written her at Penwich after all. Only ever Linnie. And still, Evie had not wept; she had stoically borne it all.

Why now must she feel the need to shatter into sobs?

The answer skittered across her mind, plain as day. *Because after tomorrow, your safe world will be ripped from your fingers.*

The Harbour had never seemed so far away as it did now. Even when she'd spent time in London and the country with Fallon and Marguerite, home had felt close. Always within reach.

Nicholas, Amy, Aunt Gertie, the Murdochs— she missed them. Missed them all. Already she felt adrift without them.

Spencer would take her from all that, keeping her with him until he finished with her and then return her as if nothing had happened.

Ascending the winding stairs, she slid her fingers over the railing, polish-smooth and warm beneath her palm. Once in her room, she stopped and flexed her chilled toes on the plush rug beneath her feet.

A knot formed in the pit of her belly. *Ian's son*. That's what mattered to him. And a future heir. Not her. She was only a peripheral concern. Any courtesy given to her merely extended from his obligation to Nicholas.

It wasn't as though he wanted her. Cared for her.

He would bed her simply because he was her husband—a *man*. She'd long understood the nature of men. She would do well to remember all the hard lessons of her life and not lose her head with fanciful thoughts.

Spencer stared at the open doorway where Evie had vanished as though a pack of hounds chased her. He did that to her. Sent her running. His stomach twisted at the unwelcome notion. His wife-to-be couldn't escape him fast enough. *Brilliant*. Precisely what every groom hoped for in his bride.

The whisper of his name still trembled on the air. As did his last glimpse of her, bare feet peeping beneath the flash of her white hem.

He'd struggled not to stare at those bare feet as she'd sat across from him, hugging her glass of brandy as though she'd clutched the Holy Grail. He had struggled and failed. Those slim feet, so feminine, so bare, had made it hard for him to remember that he should wait until they were properly wed. The flash of her lithe, naked body had made it impossible. If she had not stopped him, he would have taken her on the library floor.

She was to be *his* wife. His. Not Ian's. Whether or not Ian had her first, in the eyes of God and law, she would only ever belong to him. The fact gave him a dark, primitive satisfaction, chased by another feeling. A niggle of guilt. What would Ian think?

Shaking his head, he reminded himself that his cousin was gone. If it wasn't him, some other man, likely Sheffield, would eventually claim her. His gut twisted at the thought.

And there was the matter of doing right by Nicholas. He rubbed his fingertips together, imagining he still felt the silkiness of her skin. She was no monument to a dead man. He realized that. Perhaps that's what she needed to realize, too.

A slow smile curved his lips. Tomorrow, he

would resume his seduction. He would use every method he possessed in his arsenal to bring her to his bed. Like it or not, he was a Winters. He knew a thing or two about talking reluctant ladies out of their gowns. It was his birthright.

Although she didn't realize it, Evelyn Cross's life was about to change.

Tomorrow they would marry.

And she would be his.

Chapter 14

Sitting in the small parlor at the back of The Black Boar, Evie nibbled her way through her dinner. The savory lamb and parsnips would have more than satisfied her appetite on any other occasion, but given the circumstances, she could scarcely choke down a mouthful.

Chasing a pea with her fork, she stared at the frosted panes of the window, where snow fell in a hazy blur of white. As good a place to look as any, certainly better than staring across from her, where Spencer sat. The journey north had been bad enough. She'd endured his close proximity for hours, feeling his intense stare as she'd constantly struggled to keep her feet from tangling with his boots.

Giving up on her pea, she reached for her glass and took a healthy swig of sherry.

Would she ever be comfortable in his presence?

His nearness, his utter maleness, swirled around her like a heady fog of perfume. The quick little fluttering in her belly whenever she broke down and feasted her gaze on him mortified her. Considering the lie that stood between them—that he would forever believe her to be her sister—the situation was nothing short of misery; all in all, untenable considering they were about to be married.

"How much longer, do you think?" she inquired, mostly from a need to fill the uneasy silence.

When the innkeeper's wife had offered them the parlor, she had informed them that a good many couples were marrying today, no doubt choosing wintertime to elope in the hopes that the abysmal weather would slow down irate papas in their pursuit. She would fetch them the first available reverend.

He shrugged one broad shoulder. "Can't say."

A clock ticked on the mantel, a lonely sound in the silence. Her gaze fell on his large, masculine hand resting casually on top of the small table. He sat at an angle, his knee peeking out the side. A very muscled knee. She hadn't known a man's knee could be so well shaped. Heat crawled up her face, and she hastily moved her gaze back to the window. The wind howled a desperate song, shaking snow-spotted branches outside.

"Nasty bit of weather," he murmured. "Fortunate we arrived when we did. Looks as though it's worsening."

Her gaze snapped back to his. "Will this delay us from returning home?"

He shrugged. "Depends if the roads are passable."

Nodding, she tugged on her bottom lip, her legs shaking beneath the table at the prospect of being stuck at this inn with him. For how long? She'd braced herself to endure one night. But two? Three?

"It wouldn't be so terrible. Since we're not having a proper honeymoon, this might at least give us the time you wanted."

She shook her head, confused, unable to recall wishing for time alone with him, time for him to rattle her senses and rob her of her composure. She would hardly wish for that.

He cocked a brow, smiling harshly. "You expressed a desire to become better acquainted."

"I never—"

"You did. In fact, you cited that as the reason we should wait before consummating our marriage. Now we shall have that time." His smile deepened. He waved a hand airily. "In idyllic solitude."

"Oh." She pulled at her sleeve, suddenly feeling

like she couldn't draw air deep enough into her lungs.

"Are you well?" He frowned. "You look pale."

"I don't know if I can do this." Her gaze darted to the door. She rose to her feet in a swift motion, jostling the table. Dishes rattled a protest. She hated this. Hated the compulsion to run. Nonetheless, she heard herself say, "Perhaps I have not thought this through enough. It is all happening too quickly. Marriage is so very . . . permanent."

She loathed the tremor in her voice. Loathed feeling fear. Since that long-ago night in Barbados, she had worked so very hard to rid her life of fear. Perhaps impossible to completely prevent, but she had managed thus far.

Then this man had arrived and shaken everything up. She stared down at him. Suddenly something else warred with the fear clawing her throat.

"I can't do this," she repeated, her voice stronger as she moved for the door.

He was on his feet. Grabbing her arm, he swung her around. "Linnie—"

"No!" She blinked hard and hissed, "I told you not to call me that!"

Every time he said her sister's name it was a knife in her heart. A reminder of the lie she lived . . . the lie she must always live with him.

A lifetime of never dropping her guard, never relaxing her breath—it would send her to an early grave.

She tried to twist her arm free, but it did no good. He grabbed her other arm, pulled her close, shook her a little. His hands on her arms felt like manacles.

"Stop! Let me go!"

"What are you so afraid of?" he hissed, his glittering gaze darting sharply over her face, achingly close. The strong, square jaw, the well-cut lips, the deep grooves on either side of his mouth—all combined to overwhelm her senses.

This. You.

His voice gentled. "I'll not hurt you, Evie."

"You keep calling me Linnie," she accused, the connection so easy, so clear to her. Calling her Linnie hurt, wounded her in a way that would only strike him as irrational. As it should. Ignorant of the truth, it should.

"It *is* your name," he reminded. "In a manner. Short for Evelyn. It's all Ian ever called you. How I first came to know you." His stare drilled into her, stripping everything bare. She quivered deep in her belly, wishing he stared at *her* in such a hungry, visceral way but knowing that he was not. He was staring at Linnie . . . at whatever extraordinary pillar of womanhood he believed her to be, courtesy of Ian. "Forgive the slip. Evie will take getting accustomed to."

His words made her throat ache. Would he ever become accustomed to her? She shook her head, felt the pins of her coiffure loosen, her unruly hair fighting for release. She froze.

"Listen," he continued. "The whole of Little Billings knows you left with me. They expect you to return as my wife. To not do so will sink you into ruin, mire you so deep you shall never recover. The effects of which would spill over onto Nicholas. You can't very well run like a frightened rabbit now, can you?"

He was right, of course. She could not walk away now. She could not be so selfish. She'd never been weak or cowardly before. By damn if she would begin now.

She nodded once. "You are right, of course."

"This is settled then." He arched one brow. "At last?"

"Yes." She swallowed hard. "At last."

"I'll hazard to guess that marriage is scary under the best of circumstances." His lips twisted. "But I vow to never hurt you." His hands gentled on her arms, flexing. "You needn't fear me, do you understand?"

She gazed into his eyes, drowning in the woodland green, soaking up his words, letting them fortify her. "I'm not afraid."

"But you were." Something sparked in his eyes then. "Is it him? Is it Ian?"

Ian? She shook her head, frowned. Ian? The dead man hadn't crossed her mind. An irrational laugh bubbled in the back of her hot throat, but she fought against it, bit it back.

She *should* be thinking of him. He was Nicholas's father, after all. But only Spencer filled her head. Spencer's nearness, his overwhelming maleness, the memory of his bare chest, ridged with muscles that resembled a Greek sculpture. The thought that he would be her husband, that he would finish what they started in the library, made her heart pound faster.

And it dawned on her. She didn't fear Spencer at all—she feared herself. That's what she was running from.

She melted in his arms and watched him like a starving woman. Even now, the night ahead tormented her. Enticed and tormented her—*equally*.

She *wanted* to consummate their marriage. She could finally learn all that transpired in the marriage bed with a man who brought her body to life. But that would mean he would likely uncover all she sought to hide. The secret she had guarded so closely these years. What a mess.

His fingers slid up her arms, singeing her through the fabric of her dress. "Answer me. Do I have a ghost to contend with?"

She held his gaze, read the stark need in the brilliant green depths. The demand for truth.

She licked her lips, considered her answer, and blurted, "Yes."

He jerked.

As much as she loathed adding another lie to the web, if it stayed his impulse to seduce her, it was worth it.

"I feel as though I'm betraying Ian." A logical enough reason to keep Spencer at arm's length, however much it pained her to spit the lie past her lips.

Something passed over his features then. "Betraying Ian," he murmured. His hands fell from her. "Legitimizing his son? Giving Nicholas a future he could never hope to have as a bastard? Hardly rings of betrayal."

She nodded. "Of course not, but feelings of the heart are not always logical. Just because we marry today doesn't mean we have to consummate tonight—"

"You've made your wishes clear on that matter."

His eyes stared at her. Hard. Intractable. "Tirelessly so."

A knock sounded on the parlor door then, followed by Mrs. Macgregor, the innkeeper's wife. A tall gentleman with wind-chapped cheeks fell close on her heels.

Cold washed over Evie, dulling everything else—even the usual heat she felt in Spencer's presence. Fortunate, she supposed. She needed to be dulled. Numb to this farcical undertaking.

Mrs. Macgregor introduced Mr. Hart.

Somehow, a proper greeting passed her lips.

"Sorry to keep you waiting," Mr. Hart said. "If you'll stand here, we can proceed."

Spencer took her elbow and guided her before the window. Cold drifted from the glass, penetrating the wool of her dress. She shivered and folded her arms in front of her. Spencer must have felt her shudder. He stepped close, the length of his arm lining with her body, which only made her tremble more.

The reverend began.

She watched his lips move, tried to absorb his words. It was as though she drifted underwater, in a great vacuum, void of time and noise.

Turning, she studied the strong profile of the man at her side. Stoic. His mouth didn't give the slightest bend. His features looked carved from marble.

He would be a part of her life now. Forever. Unto death. She struggled to wrap her head around that. To appreciate the significance of the moment. The enormity of marrying a stranger. Even as she tried to absorb all that, to see through the blur, to hear past the dull roar in her head, nothing the reverend said penetrated. Not her name. Not his.

Nothing until Mr. Hart uttered the words *man and wife*.

Man and wife. *Man and wife.*

She was married.

As a girl at Penwich, she had dreamed of adventure, of leaving the ordinary behind and flying away from the familiar. Even in those days, marriage had not played into her notions of adventure. And afterwards, after Nicholas was born and she'd given up on the notion of adventure, marriage had loomed ever further, the most distant and remote of possibilities.

And yet now, here she stood. A wife.

"You may now kiss your bride."

The pronouncement launched her heart into her throat. She turned.

Those pale green eyes stared down at her, inching closer as his head lowered. She felt the others watching her, cheerful, interested, blind to the fact that they watched a set of strangers wed . . . prepare to kiss.

His hands took hold of her shoulders, firm but gentle.

Her gaze fixed on his descending lips.

At the last moment, she turned her face away. His lips landed on her cheek, stilled there for a moment, a warm press to her chilled cheek. She fixed her eyes on the frosted windowpane until his mouth lifted. Until his hands fell away.

Slowly, she settled her gaze on his face.

A breath shivered from her lips. Something dark and angry glittered in the green of his eyes, and she understood at once. He did not like being denied. Especially this. Their first kiss as man and wife. Not an auspicious beginning, but she could not help herself.

Mrs. Macgregor clapped heartily, unaware of the tension. For a few moments, they preoccupied themselves with signing a leather-bound register. Well, the others did. She could narrowly function. With a shaking hand, she signed her name, an indistinct scrawl. And it was done.

Now she had the rest of her life to become acquainted with her husband.

And pray he never became too acquainted with her.

Chapter 15

"**W**e're sleeping here?"

Spencer watched as Evie stood in the center of the inn's finest room and tried to grasp that she was his wife.

"Yes." Leaning against the armoire, he broodingly watched as her gaze flicked to the bed, then away, then back again. His lips twitched. "Is there something wrong with the room?"

Alarm filled her brilliant blue eyes even as she managed a calmly murmured, "No."

His gaze dropped to the fingers that she was twisting blue. To hide his smile, he sank into the armchair beside the window and began tugging off his boots, certain he would hear more on the matter of their shared room. If he knew one thing about his wife, it was that he made her uneasy. His smile slipped. Being in love with another man, even a dead one, would do that to a woman.

True to form, she inquired, "Were there no other rooms available?"

"Inn's full." His first boot hit the floor. "Didn't seem logical to move to another inn across the village simply for a second room. Not as we're married."

She nodded, clearly suppressing her thoughts. Not that he needed her to speak her feelings to know her thoughts. The fine skin of her jaw feathered where she clenched her teeth. He knew. He knew she was staring at that bed and thinking of them in it together. Thinking of Ian . . . . and that the moment she climbed in bed with him, she betrayed Ian. A deep growl swelled inside his chest.

Why, he wondered, did he not suffer the same sentiment? How is it she felt a greater loyalty to Ian than he did? He dragged a hand over his jaw. He had loved his cousin, mourned his loss. Shouldn't there be a token of shame twisting his gut for wanting to part her thighs and claim her? Mark her as his own?

With a vicious yank, he dropped another boot to the floor. "I suggest we get some sleep. Weather withstanding, we'll depart early in the morn."

She moved to her valise, pulling out her nightrail. With a guarded glance over her shoulder at him, she stepped behind the screen.

He stripped off his shirt, then paused, hands on the front of his trousers. Deciding to respect her sensibilities, he left his trousers on.

She emerged from the screen clad in the same white nightrail as the night before. Even so, he was stirred. He watched her as she moved to the mirror and unpinned her hair. It tumbled over her shoulders like dark honey in the candlelight. Her eyes flickered to him and away. She looked very young.

The thought came to him, unbidden: had Ian ever seen her with her hair unbound? More than likely their secret trysts had not afforded them time to fully unclothe. Jealous, stupid hope unfurled in his clenched chest. Perhaps his cousin had not even seen her entirely naked.

Dragging a hand through his hair, he silently cursed. He couldn't change the fact that she had been with Ian. It was the reason he even knew her. The reason he'd married her. Perhaps, to some degree, the reason he wanted her so badly.

He was a fool to feel jealous over the past . . . or to seek a *first* with her.

You married her. You're her first in that regard.

"Bloody hell."

She shot him a quick glance, blinking at his harshly muttered expletive.

"Did you say something—"

He pulled down the bed with a rough yank. "No," he bit out, angered beyond reason. "Nothing at all. It's been a long day. Let us just go to bed."

She slid beneath the coverlet, pulling it up and folding it neatly at her chest.

For a moment he paused, staring at her on her far side of the bed. She clenched trembling hands together over her stomach. Bloody hell. He terrified her. Did she think he would pounce on her?

He turned away and quickly doused the lamp. Climbing into bed beside her, he was careful not to touch her. More for himself than her. He didn't trust himself. Didn't trust his control.

Lying in bed, the low-burning fire from the hearth cast the room in a lazy glow. Outside, a flurry of white fell.

He thought of their vows. She had turned her cheek to him at the end. His hand curled into a fist at his side in memory of that rebuff. Could she not bear even the smallest kiss to seal their union? Did Ian's ghost prevent her from even so small a gesture? And why the hell should any of it matter so much to him? He had his wife. Soon he would have his heir. It wasn't as though he wanted her affections.

In that moment, he couldn't abide himself. He couldn't stomach the jealousy he felt for his cousin.

And he couldn't understand this overriding need to claim the woman he had wed, to prove to her that she wanted him, that *he* could make her burn with desire. More than any ghost she loved ever could.

Evie feigned sleep.

That's not to say she didn't attempt to sleep. She tried. Valiantly, she tried.

She told herself the night would fly past if she could only surrender to dreams. She wouldn't even know a man slept beside her—a man as virile and handsome as the one she had wed. The bed yawned large enough between them. They would likely never even brush against each other.

In the morning they would wake and return to Ashton Grange. To the separate beds that awaited them there. One night in a bed together was nothing about which to feel alarm.

It was not Barbados. She would not wake in the dark, confused and terrified at the rough hands on her. He was a gentleman, a man of honor. Clearly, or why would he have bothered to marry her in the first place?

Lying there, watching shadows chase across the walls with the wind howling outside, she listened to his breathing slow and deepen, his body so close to hers but not touching.

Exhaling, she closed her eyes and told herself to relax. He had vowed not to hurt her, and she believed him. This was not Barbados and he was no Stirling. He would not force intimacy on her. Would not pound her with his fists. She need only withstand their unfortunate attraction.

He began to snore gently beside her. Unable to resist a peek, she turned her face in his direction, unreasonably miffed at how easily he drifted to sleep. Clearly, she need not fear seduction from him.

She mustn't be that desirable. She was nothing more than the mother of Ian's child. A convenient bride for a man in need of a wife. She frowned, disappointed. Absurd, she knew. She should feel nothing save relief over that fact.

Squashing her hurt over his lack of interest, she sighed and rolled onto her side, sliding a hand beneath her cheek. The fire popped and a log crumbled. She shivered and buried deeper into the bed.

She would learn to ignore the feelings he roused in her.

She *would* learn to overcome this bothersome attraction to Spencer, to rise above it and never, ever act on it no matter what methods of seduction he might employ on her susceptible body.

* * *

Spencer feigned sleep.

That's not to say he didn't attempt to sleep. He tried. Valiantly, he tried. He told himself the night would fly past if he could only surrender to dreams.

He was aware the moment Evie fell asleep beside him, and he couldn't help wondering if she and Ian had ever shared a bed. He didn't think it possible. Another first for him, then. His lips twisted. The thought perversely pleased him— gave him something to consider as the minutes rolled past and she slept peaceably beside him.

He doubted he would sleep at all tonight. Not with his cock hard and the slim female body lying next to him. Linnie—*Evie*, he quickly amended. His wife. She was his for the taking, yet he did not make a move toward her. Not with her recent words ringing in his ear. She loved Ian still. She didn't want him. She wasn't ready for him. Perhaps she never would be.

Suddenly, she woke, surging upright beside him with a ragged breath. He glanced sharply at her but could make out little in the gloom. The fire had died. The room was as quietly shrouded as a battlefield at dusk after the fighting had finished and the last sound of artillery ripped the air.

"Evie?" He sat up beside her, lightly touching her arm. "Did you have a nightmare—"

She released a small shriek at the touch, and he drew back his hand.

He pronounced her name again hard, determined to reach her. "Evie!"

She was quiet for a moment, still beside him before she at last spoke, the shadow of her face turning toward him. "Spencer?"

"Yes. It's me."

With a deep breath, she lowered herself back down, trembling beside him on the bed. "Sorry. The darkness . . . surprised me. There was light when I fell asleep."

He paused, thinking. "Does the dark frighten you?"

"Of course not," she replied. Too quickly.

He lay beside her, not touching, still feeling the tremors of her body. Something frightened her. If not the dark . . .

"I'm not a child," she added, her voice ringing defiantly.

He smiled grimly. He knew that. Every time she walked into the room his body came alive. "I know."

Several moments passed and she still shook. He was on the verge of demanding an explanation when her voice stroked the air, small and anxious. "I wouldn't mind if you wanted to stoke the fire. It *is* a strange room. A little light wouldn't be . . . unwelcome."

Without a word he stood and moved to the hearth, locating the poker. In moments, a soft glow filled the room. When he climbed back in bed, he noticed she had stopped shaking. He settled beside her.

"Thank you," she murmured, rolling on her side, presenting him her back.

He grunted a response, staring at the waterfall of gold-brown hair. His palms tingled, itching to gather the mass and feel the silken texture.

His wife was afraid of the dark. And she didn't want him to know it.

Interesting. What else would he learn about her?

Curled on her side, Evie shivered as cold air stroked her neck. Foggy with sleep, she whimpered and tugged her coverlet higher, snuggling closer to the pulsing warmth that felt like satin beneath her seeking palms. She rubbed her chilled nose against the silky smooth pillow.

Burrowing deeper, she sighed contentedly, dimly aware of the snapping cold outside her bed, and grateful for the heat cocooning her. There was nothing like a cozy warm bed when winter closed its teeth on the land.

The slightest pressure at the small of her back urged her deeper into her pillow. She obliged, moving closer to the source of heat, welcoming, seeking, pressing her lips against . . . *skin*.

Her eyes flew wide but found nothing but darkness. *Awful darkness*.

Gasping, she jerked—lifted her face off her warm wall, desperate for some light, for saving light.

Relief flowed through her at the low glow of firelight suffusing the room, staving off complete darkness.

The relief lasted only a moment before she remembered, before she grasped the terrible truth.

She was *not* snuggling against a pillow. She was not alone. She shared a bed with Spencer. Her husband. The pressure at her back was his hand. A large, warm, masculine hand pulling, urging her closer. The warm wall at her front was his body.

She pulled back and studied his face in the murky room. He was asleep. Eyes shut, lips loose and relaxed, he looked like a dark angel. Relief swept through her.

He doesn't know you're awake. Close your eyes and go back to sleep.

Jamming her eyes tight, she fought to relax, to reclaim the sleep of moments ago. The peace. Sweet oblivion.

The hand at her back shifted, fingers fanning out, spreading wide, branding her like fire.

With nowhere else to place her hands, she laid them lightly against his chest, praying she did not wake him. Air hissed between her teeth at the contact—a bare chest like hot satin.

How could she have thought him a pillow? There was nothing soft about him. She chalked it up to his warmth, to the incredible smoothness of his skin. Skin that seemed everywhere. All around her. His broad chest spread out like a wall before her. Afraid to move, to alert him that she was awake and clinging like a vine to him, she waited.

She waited, growing achingly aware of how truly mortifying the situation had become.

Her nightrail was bunched around her thighs, her left leg wedged intimately between his. Thank heavens he had left his trousers on.

His hand moved again and she sucked in a silent breath as it slid down, cupped her bottom in a grip that felt achingly familiar. A twist of heat licked through her belly. He brought her closer, adjusted her against him as though searching for the right fit.

She bit back a groan and forced herself to remain perfectly still. Stone against him. With her face buried against his chest, her lips tasted his skin.

Her body hummed, alert, alive, a wire strummed. Her heart hammered wildly within her chest and she could not imagine he did not hear its wild fluttering.

Dear God, she had to move, had to extricate herself from this shocking situation. She could not remain as she was, his hand clutching her derriere and pushing her up against the impossibly hard length of him.

Still feigning sleep, she sighed and twisted, breaking free in what she hoped to be an artless maneuver. Turning on her side, she was mindful to put a few inches between them.

Her body now gratefully separate from his, she dug her fingers into her pillow in a bloodless grip and waited. Listened to a log pop and crumble in the hearth. Watched the flurry of flakes against the deep blue of night outside the room's window.

Moments crawled past. Gradually, relief glided through her. And something else. Regret perhaps? That she had moved. That he slept while her body ached with need. That he had not woken and made the choice for both of them.

Then she forgot about regret, sucking in a sharp

breath as an arm circled her waist and dragged her back. A shudder racked her at the hot press of his body. He spooned her, her back perfectly aligned to his chest, her legs bent with his, her derriere cradled in his hips.

She should never have moved. This position was much worse. Her skin prickled, flushed with heat. *So much worse. So much better.*

For several moments, neither moved, and she thought that was the end of it. He slept, unaware that he had pulled her to him. She would simply resign herself to sleeping this way in torment. All night long.

Then, he moved again.

A broad palm closed over her breast. The air seized in her lungs. Her heart jumped, its fierce beat drumming against his hand, shuddering in her rib cage like a wild bird.

She waited, held herself motionless, her eyes so wide that they ached.

He held himself still—didn't move. Not his body. Not his hand on her swelling breast. Evidently he was *still* unaware of his actions.

Brilliant. She could *not* sleep like this. She would go mad.

She prepared to pull free, but she froze when she felt his hand flex. Her nipple hardened, beaded against his palm, betraying her.

That hand began a slow, steady knead on her breast.

She bit her lip, stifling her pleasured cry.

Would he do that in his sleep? Was it an unconscious act?

To her horror, she arched, pushing her hardening nipple deeper into his palm.

There was no fear in this moment. Nor in the deep throbbing ache between her thighs.

Without thought, she began to move, wriggling, pressing herself back into him, grinding into his groin, nudging at the hard erection prodding her backside. His fingers found her nipple and her world grayed.

A low moan built deep in her throat as his fingers started to softly roll her nipple, teasing, plucking lightly until she was panting. His touch grew harder, more insistent on her breast. The ache between her legs almost hurt now, pulsing and clenching, desperate for satisfaction. She bit her lip against a moan.

His breath fogged at the crook of her neck. He sounded like her, his breathing fast and heavy.

Her nightrail became an unwelcome barrier between them, a nuisance that prevented her from feeling his skin flush against hers. She whimpered, writhing against him.

His other arm came around, slipped beneath

her. This time there was no suppressing her moan as both his hands cupped her breasts, playing with the nipples until she thought she would scream.

Her thighs worked, feverishly opening and closing, seeking, desperate to find relief for the throbbing squeeze there. One of his hands left her, sliding unerringly down the front of her rumpled nightrail. That hand delved between her thighs before she could protest.

Not that she would have. Not that she could.

Her entire body quivered, burned for him. Her mouth parted on a cry at the first brush of his hand—at the smooth slide of his fingers against her slick folds. She closed her eyes, lost in sensation. She lurched, shuddered, swallowing the tiny sounds at the back of her throat.

"God, Evie," he groaned. Alert. Awake. *Awake*. She stilled.

"You feel so good."

Chapter 16

It was the sound of his voice. The confirmation that he was awake and aware of his actions that turned her to stone in his arms.

If she had taken a moment to consider the matter, she would have realized he no longer slept. Only lost to his touch, to the hunger clutching her body, she had permitted herself to ignore what should have been patently evident.

His breath warmed her neck. "Do you taste as sweet as you feel?"

At the rumble of his voice, she could no longer delude herself. Those words, so deep and throaty, so full of sexual intent, made her feel the fool. Duped and ill-used.

He'd known this would happen. Had planned for it—the very seduction he had threatened.

Anger churned inside her, washed through her in embarrassing heat even as her body responded, arched into his fingers playing in her moist heat, unerringly finding *that* place—the spot Millie had told her about. Where a woman would forget herself, forget the world around her and dissolve into a puddle of quaking, screaming nerves.

The part of herself she'd never even known existed before Millie told her. Before he found it. Touched her there. His fingertips slid against her, wringing desire from her.

He knew. Of course he knew.

And he used the knowledge to torment her, enslave her. He dragged that tiny nub in small, tight circles until a strangled cry ripped from her throat. Hating him—hating *herself*—she flew off the bed, lurching upright, coming apart.

He pulled her back down to the bed, working his hand faster between her legs, his face close now, the planes and hollows harsh and relentless in the low glow of firelight.

Moaning, she strained, arched, fisting the bed linens.

"That's it." His eyes gleamed down at her with a primal satisfaction as he continued his sensual assault, his fingers stroking her in deep drags.

Her thighs spread of their own volition, parting wider for him.

"Please," she begged, mindless to what she asked for.

However, he knew—answered her plea by thrusting his finger inside her, filling her in agonizing slowness. In and out he penetrated, pausing to caress and tease the little nub before diving back inside her with a deep surge.

At last she surrendered to the building pressure, exploding, crying out as white-hot waves of sensation rushed through her.

Panting, quivering, she collapsed back on the bed, loosening her fists, convinced she would never be the same, never be right. Never want anything but this—*him*. Every moment of her life.

He shifted, looming over her, his shoulders a vast shadow above her, darker than the murky air surrounding them.

Cool air rolled over her thighs, brushing the exposed flesh he had just ravaged. She squeezed her legs together, shaming heat crawling over her face at the feel of her own wetness, at how totally she surrendered herself—his bride who had demanded distance and time, who had pledged her love and loyalty to a dead man. What a weak fool she must appear.

She squeezed her eyes shut. "I didn't want this to happen."

His voice rumbled through the near darkness. "Indeed? It seems you did."

Heat licked her cheeks. She opened her eyes, stared at his shape, wishing she could see his face more clearly and read what thoughts she could in the ice-green of his eyes.

"You tricked me. I was asleep—"

"You knew what was happening. You wanted it."

"*Stop* saying that!"

"Then stop denying it . . . and be relieved I don't finish what we both so clearly want. Despite your maidenly protestations."

"Finish . . ." She frowned, shaking her head in defiance.

He snatched her hand. Before she realized what he was about, he forced it down between their bodies, pressed her palm over the hard evidence of his desire. She shook, her hand trembling over the hard outline of him against her palm. She quivered at that treacherous, curious part of herself that yearned to move her fingers, to feel him, test the shape and length of him.

"This," he bit out. He was large and pulsing, straining against his breeches. "Be grateful. You achieved your satisfaction while I'm left wanting." His voice was harsh, tight, a growl that shivered across her skin. "Unless you care to rectify that?"

She snatched her hand free, rubbing her palm against her bare thigh as though burned. Then, realizing how much flesh she still left exposed, she tugged her nightrail down.

"Of course not," she hissed. "Perhaps my body responded to you, but I didn't ask for you to ravish me!"

"No? What do you think happens when you tease a man until his cock grows hard?"

She jerked as though slapped. "I did no such thing!"

He moved suddenly. She tensed, half afraid, half hoping he would touch her again.

The bed lifted as he dropped to the floor in one lithe motion. "Rubbing your sweet little body against me the way you did definitely qualifies as cock-teasing."

She flinched from his crude language. Bolting to her knees on the bed, she stabbed him in the chest with a finger. "Anything I did was unintentional . . . while I slept," she snapped. "It didn't help that we were forced to share the same bed. In the future, we can avoid that. When we return to—"

"Evie, you're my wife now," he growled, his voice thick with warning. "And no shrinking virgin." He held up a hand. "Don't mistake me. It's all very affecting. A brilliant act. The coy-maiden-just-wakening-to-desire act certainly arouses me."

She gasped, the blood rushing to her face. What

could she say to *that*? She could scarcely inform him that it wasn't an act!

He jerked himself into his clothing, his voice a low snarl as he added, "Perhaps you should simply admit that you've an itch that needs appeasing and put an end to these games."

"Games! I never—"

"Yes," he snapped. "Pleading for time in one breath because you're still attached to Ian, then teasing me like any hungry tart in the next." He drew a ragged breath. "Well, it doesn't work like that, love. If Ian's watching, he knows."

"Knows *what*?"

"Whether you can face it or not, you want another man—you want *me*." His voice took on an edge, sent a shivery twist through her belly. "You crave me deep inside you."

Outraged, the air painfully tight in her chest, she watched his large shadow move around the room, gathering his boots and jacket. Still on her knees, she hobbled to the end of the bed, closer to where he stood. "Y-you're a monster!"

"Indeed?" He jabbed a finger through the air at her. "Then next time don't expect this *monster* to stop what you started."

His shadow moved then, coming at her, a fast blur in the room's dull glow.

He wrapped a hand around her neck and

hauled her against him. His lips slammed over hers in a brutal kiss.

With their bodies mashed together, she pounded her fists on his hard shoulders, sputtering hotly against his lips. He took advantage of her open mouth and swept his tongue inside.

With his grip on the back of her neck and his other hand cupping her face, she was a prisoner.

Like a cinder catching fire, the ache between her legs renewed with a vengeance. His mouth singed her lips. The stroke of his tongue against hers robbed the last of her will.

She sagged against him, dead weight, fingers digging into his shoulders, loathing the fine lawn of his shirt, wishing to feel the smooth ripple of his flesh again. Moaning into his mouth, she kissed him back, loving his devouring lips, his hungry tongue.

As quickly as it began, his hands dropped free.

He wrenched away. Panting, she fell back on the bed, fingers flying to her lips, bruised and stinging.

Her eyes burned with furious tears, hating him in that moment. But hating herself even more. Because everything he said was true.

She wanted him. Burned for him.

Spencer's eyes glittered down at her. "That's the

kiss you denied me earlier. *Now* we're man and wife."

Then he was gone, slamming from the room. The wood door vibrated from the force.

Alone, bereft, she sank down on the bed. Snatching up the pillow, she wrapped both arms around it and clutched it close, wondering if she had not made the biggest mistake of her life.

Lifting her hand, she lightly fingered her mouth and turned her face to gaze blindly out the window, at the snow flurrying past. And she knew.

With heart-stopping intensity, she knew.

If he wanted her in his bed, she lacked the willpower to resist. And then all would be revealed to him. Her inexperience. Her lies. Her growing fascination for him that bordered on obsession.

Her skin shivered. It was only a matter of time.

Spencer stormed into the dark predawn, welcoming the bite of icy wind and the wet fall of snow on his face, hoping it might cool his ardor.

Naked branches creaked and groaned in the wind. He walked, his hard strides crunching over the slushy ground and carrying him from the inn into the empty, shadowed streets of the village. He walked to the edge of the sleeping hamlet, stopping deep within a well of tall trees. Jerking to a stop, he leaned against a moss-frozen trunk.

How many men were forced to walk off unspent ardor the morning following their nuptials?

He cursed. Angry at Evie . . . but even angrier with himself.

Why must he plague her? Why could he not leave her be as she wished him to? Where was his pride?

He never begged. Had never worked to seduce a woman before—had never had to. To what point? There were plenty of women willing to satisfy his needs. Was he simply obsessing over claiming the piece of heaven Ian had found in her arms? Or was it something more?

Was it *her*?

Shaking his head, he pushed off the tree and continued his walk, not yet ready to return and face her.

Despite her body's response to him, her head—*her heart*—still said no. He was beginning to suspect it always would. As much as he wanted her, she would always hold a part of herself distant from him, forever locked away. *The part she held for Ian*. The belief burned through his veins, fed bile to the back of his throat.

He was not his father or brothers, brutes that acted out every base instinct with no thought to the female in question. She was his wife, Linnie, no matter what he called her now. He owed it to Ian to be more considerate of her than that.

Unfortunately, when it came to Evie, logic and thought did not arise.

Chapter 17

Ashton Grange was ablaze with lights when they arrived. She was grateful for that. Always grateful when light broke the unrelenting dark. It was not until the carriage door opened that she thought to wonder why.

Even as Spencer assisted her down, he trained his eyes on the house. The perplexed expression on his face gave her an uneasy feeling. She glanced from him to the house and back again. "Is something amiss?"

His gaze scanned the house. "It appears we have guests—"

The front door flung open. Mrs. Brooks descended the steps. "Ah, praise the heavens! You've returned. I haven't known what to do! I've been beside myself trying to make"—she dropped her voice to a hiss—"that *female* happy. Nothing pleases her. She arrived shortly after you departed. She and her friends."

Breathless, she pressed a single hand to her side as if she suffered a stitch. With a quick, furtive glance behind her, she continued at a low whisper, "She pestered me something fierce on your whereabouts." The housekeeper motioned over her lips as if she were locking her mouth with a key. "Not a word . . . not a word I said on where you be"—she slid her gaze meaningfully to Evie— "or with whom. I informed her that your business is your own and it's of no—"

Spencer held up a hand and shook his head, as though dizzy. "Mrs. Brooks. Please. I haven't made sense of a word you've uttered. Who is here?"

The housekeeper blinked, as if that much were obvious. "Did I not say? Oh, me! The viscountess." She flicked Evie an apologetic glance. "The dowager viscountess, that is . . . I'm guessing. Why, your sister-in-law, the Lady Adara."

Lady Adara? Evie swallowed. He was related to a *peer*? A viscountess? Her head whirled.

She shot Spencer a quick glance. Why had he not mentioned this before? Thoughts spun through her head. Pieces of a puzzle slowly clicked together, fitting neatly into place.

Lady Adara was his sister-in-law—his late brother's wife then. The elder brother who left him with everything.

Including a title.

Fury radiated through her. Spencer's gaze locked with hers. How could he have neglected to tell her this? He was titled. *She* was titled now. A viscountess. She belonged to a world she had never aspired to enter.

As a Penwich girl, she had never even thought it possible. And later, after Barbados, she never would have wanted entry, would have loathed the scrutiny on her. She would still loathe it.

Betrayal burned hot in her chest. How could he have failed to tell her? It certainly bore mention.

A glance down at her rumpled and horribly unfashionable traveling frock heightened her sense of distress. A fine lady she was not. This Lady Adara would see that in an instant.

Suddenly she wanted to crawl behind one of the large hedges lining the front of the house. How would his family react to their marriage? A woman with no prospects. With only loose ties to a family of questionable means. A woman with claim to a vague first husband of mysterious origins.

A lord could be counted upon to marry an heiress. Or a lady. Or both.

"Adara is here," Spencer announced grimly, sounding decidedly unsurprised. "Just as well. She can carry the news to Camila and appease her on the matter of my marriage."

Really, if he'd thought his relations might descend upon them, he ought to have explained who he was to her.

The housekeeper's lips curled back from her teeth. "She and her friends have been having a high time of it in the drawing room this evening."

Spencer clasped Evie's arm and guided her toward the housekeeper. "Take Evie. I'll see to our . . . guests."

Relief swelled through Evie. She wouldn't have to stand witness as he explained his *wife* to his blue-blooded relation. Cowardly, she supposed, but she was glad to absent herself from the encounter.

They started up the steps, halting as a sudden feminine squeal pealed across the air.

"Spencer!" In the threshold emerged a creature so beautiful that Evie felt like a gorgon, all her flaws magnified—her lack of curves, a narrow face that could only be described as marginally attractive.

Lady Adara was a goddess in a gown of blue silk, her hair gathered in golden ringlets at each side of her head. The dark choker at her neck only drew the eye to her creamy expanse of cleavage.

Others arrived, crowding the threshold. All

brightly plumed peacocks. Lady Adara lifted her skirts and hurried forward in a dainty rush of tiny-slippered feet. She tossed herself against Spencer, her arms wrapping around him in warm embrace.

Evie's face grew tight and itchy as she watched the female hug her husband.

Feeling very much the outsider, she edged closer to the housekeeper. She might be Spencer's wife, but she clearly didn't know him. Not as Lady Adara did. She doubted the day would ever arrive when she would fling her arms around her husband in such abandon. A dull ache throbbed beneath her breastbone at this realization.

"Adara," he greeted, disentangling her from his body. "What are you doing here?"

She slapped lightly at his chest, blinking her thickly lashed eyes. Big, melting brown eyes. "I should ask you that. Why have you not yet come home? Your stepmother and I have been waiting with bated breath. Especially me."

Evie stiffened. *Especially me.*

Was it her imagination, or was his sister-in-law a little too affectionate?

Spencer's voice rumbled, "I assured Bagby—"

"Bagby, pfft! You expected me to take a servant's accounting that you truly mean to acquire a bride? Spencer, darling, would you even know where to look for an eligible lady? You've been at war, for heaven's sake. Never fear, I've a list of only the most exceptional girls from this season's crop."

She flattened both palms over Spencer's chest as though it were the most natural thing to do. "At least you've returned with all your parts intact. Young brides can be particular about that sort of thing." Fingers splayed wide, she skimmed the broad expanse of his chest and giggled. "At least you *feel* intact, but I might require a closer inspection in private."

The little witch! Evie had never witnessed a more sordid display. Heat scalded her cheeks. Her fingers curled at her sides in barely checked violence. Incredibly, the urge to seize the woman by her blonde ringlets and toss her to the ground consumed her.

Would it begin then? So soon? Before they even set about making that heir he so desired? Must their marriage already appear the sham it truly was?

She swallowed against the tightening of her throat, horrified at the unwelcome burn in the backs of her eyes. Would he seek out other women with her watching? She blinked fiercely, wondering why she should care so greatly. Could she fault him when she had not obliged him in the marital bed on the very eve of their wedding? Marriage was lifelong. Men did not engage in life-long abstinence.

Unable to trust herself to not assault the exquisite Lady Adara, she nudged closer to Mrs. Brooks, ready to flee, eager to leave the company of Spencer's sister-in-law.

"Adara, there is someone I would like you to meet."

Evie froze. Slowly, she turned.

Spencer stretched a hand toward her.

Adara's gaze followed, skimming the length of his outstretched arm before lifting up to Evie. Her face registered surprise. Apparently, she had not noticed Evie until now.

"Spencer," she murmured, her voice chiding. "Who is this?"

"Adara, this is my wife. Evelyn—"

"Your wife!" Her eyes grew enormous in her face, rendering her almost unattractive. Evie suppressed a smile, secretly wishing she would maintain the expression.

"How can that be?" Adara continued. "Bagby made no mention of a wife when he returned from seeing you, only that you were agreeable to *acquiring* a bride." Splotches of red broke out over her face. "Is this some kind of jest, Spencer?" She propped delicate fists on her waist.

"Because I assure you, I am not amused. This, this . . . person cannot be your wife. Camila and I had plans, far more suitable candidates than this—"

"No jest, Adara," he replied, his voice cutting. "You and Camila must suffer your disappointments. I decided to choose my own bride." His broad palm splayed against the small of Evie's back. "Won't you properly greet my bride? She is your successor."

Evie slid a glance to his stone-carved face, certain he was receiving some sort of twisted pleasure from the entire episode, and sure of the fact that it failed to register with him that he did so at her expense.

After a moment's hesitation, Adara skirted a curtsey, her brown eyes no longer melting brown but hard chips of obsidian. "Lady Winters, welcome." *Lady Winters*? Was that her name then? "We have much to . . ."

Her words faded to a droning buzz in Evie's head. *Lady Winters.* She glared at Spencer. At her questioning stare, he gave a single hard shake of the head. A warning. The message in his eyes was clear. *Not now.*

She bit her lip to keep from demanding an explanation then and there. Only pride kept her in check. She would not have his sister-in-law learn that she did not even know her own name. She would not have her learn she knew close to nothing about the man she'd married. If possible, she would keep that shame to herself.

"Adara, if you will excuse us. It's been a long journey, and Evie and I would like to rest."

Adara's face grew splotchier. "Of course. You're newlyweds, after all." Her head cocked, dark eyes snapping malice. "I well remember what that was like." Her lips curved into a brittle smile. "Your brother and I didn't surface for days." Stepping aside, she waved them within.

Spencer urged Evie ahead. Evie snuck another glance at his face. He showed no sign of even hearing Adara. His gaze remained fixed on her, his green eyes glittery and hard, probing. With a lift of her chin, she snapped her gaze straight ahead and fled up the stairs, letting him trail in her wake. She could not stroll side by side and muster the pretense of happy newlyweds. Inexplicably, emotion clogged her throat.

Hoping to leave him far behind, she hastened down the corridor toward the room in which she'd previously slept.

Only Spencer had other ideas. He caught her arm and whirled her around, ushering her inside another room. *His* bedchamber, if the sheer size and dark masculine furnishings were any indication.

She tried leaving, but he blocked her path to the door, his expression cross.

"Let me pass."

"Not yet. We need to clear up a few matters."

She propped her fists on her hips. In that moment, the sight of his handsome face irritated her to no end. "I'm not one of your soldiers to be commanded—"

"No," he bit out. "You're my wife."

She angled her chin. "Not quite."

"No?" He advanced on her. She couldn't help it; she backed away, moving deeper into his vast bedroom. "And how is that? I seem to recall taking vows."

"The union can still be dissolved," she tossed out, reckless in her anger. "It's not too late, Lord *Winters*," she snapped with heavy emphasis, fuming over his omission . . . fuming at the way his sister-in-law fawned over him. It failed to signify to her that he had not appeared to return her interest. The woman wanted him. Evie read it in her face, heard it in her voice.

She charged ahead, "How could you not mention such a thing to me?"

"I did include my full name and title when I signed the register—"

"Oh! I failed to notice. Not so shocking when I scarcely remember signing my own name!"

"I confess it hasn't been something I've quite learned to accept yet. I planned to tell you."

"Pay it no mind! I'm certain the Church will grant a fine lord such as yourself an annulment once they learn you married a little nobody like me."

"I never said—"

"A fallen woman, no less." She emulated a shudder. "Imagine if the truth ever came out? A man of your position, what could you have been thinking?"

"Enough," he thundered.

"You can't order me about. Let's not forget, we're not man and wife in the truest sense."

He cocked a dark brow. "Oh, I haven't forgot, my dear."

"Good," she snapped, nodding fiercely, her heart pounding loudly in her ears.

"That I haven't bedded you is a fact I'm acutely conscious of." His expression grew menacing, and he advanced a step.

She blinked, not liking the militant light entering his green eyes. She edged back a step.

He followed, his lips curving in a cruel, humorless smile.

"You are right, of course," he growled, his hand moving toward his cravat, tugging it free.

"I am?" She bumped the bed.

"We aren't wed. In the truest sense." His cravat flew through the air. "Perhaps I'd best rectify that."

She rounded the bed, placing it between them. Alarm and excitement pumped through her blood. She mentally cursed the latter. She had no business feeling excitement. "An annulment can't be too complicated to arrange. You're a lord, after all. Doesn't the world bow to your whims?"

"On this matter, I don't intend to find out." He rounded the bed. "Cease being so dramatic. You're stuck with me. For a few months, at any rate. Can you not endure me that long? If you want to trim some time off that sentence, then I suggest you make yourself more amenable. Now come here."

Panic fluttered in her chest. She darted past him. He caught a handful of her cloak, and she cursed herself for not yet removing the garment when she entered the house.

Her fingers clawed the ties at her throat loose so that it dropped to the floor and she burst free. Triumph zinged through her.

His curse flew behind her, stinging her ears.

She flew to the door, her hand closing around the latch.

Then he was on her, crushing her against the door with the hard slam of his body. Air rushed from her lips. Still, she scrabbled for the latch near her hip, trying to open the blasted door. A hard hand clamped on her shoulder, spinning her around.

"Oh!" The back of her head bounced against the door.

He glowered at her, the grooves on each side of his cheek stark and deep. She'd never seen him in such a temper.

Never felt so alive in all her years.

"Is this how you want it to be?"

"To be manhandled?" she hissed, thrusting her face close to his. "Oh, indeed. It's the stuff of girlhood dreams."

His expression darkened, his eyes so vibrant a green that she shuddered against him. "You fling at me that our marriage isn't real, that it isn't truly legitimate because we haven't consummated it. You don't expect me to docilely agree with such prattle, do you?"

"That wasn't a provocation to maul me!"

"Wasn't it?" His gaze dropped to her dress, to the modest neckline. His voice lowered to a husky whisper. "You know what I think?"

She shook her head.

He pressed his hips into hers, driving his erection into her belly. She gasped. A dull throbbing ache stirred between her legs.

"That all this was your ploy for me to claim you."

"Absurd—"

"You're doing everything in your power to provoke me into it."

"Drivel!"

He smiled a dangerous grin that made her belly clench. "Let us skip these games, Evie, shall we? We've been heading toward this moment from the start."

Her heart thrilled, tripped with treacherous speed. "Never!"

His smile slipped. "Stubborn woman. I'll make it easy for you, then."

Chapter 18

His head swooped down.

Desperation pumped through her blood, and she jerked her head to the side with a whimper. His lips grazed her cheek.

Don't let him kiss you, Evie! Don't be like poor Linnie . . . susceptible and weak to a man's persuasions.

Still, he chased her mouth.

She thrashed her head against the door, avoiding his descending lips. Pins fell loose from her hair until the mass unraveled to her shoulders.

He grabbed her face with both hands, sliding his fingers in her hair, his palms warm on her cheeks, a delicious rasp that made her insides quiver.

His green eyes snapped fire, and she could see how this man commanded soldiers into battle. Right now, she felt like she was engaged in battle with him. And losing.

Nose to nose, his breath mingled with hers. Trapped, she drowned in the intensity of his eyes—the swelling green of a sunlit forest she could not escape.

His head dipped then, mouth crashing over hers in a savage kiss, punishing, devouring—the sole purpose to claim her, mark her. The press of his mouth on hers stunned her. He had never kissed her like this. Not in Little Billings, not at the inn. This tasted of anger and dominance. A man out of control.

Her hands struggled between them, trying to create a wedge. Body writhing, she fought him, fought herself, holding her lips motionless against the searing invasion. The door hard at her back, him harder at her front, she fought until her every nerve wept with exhaustion.

She couldn't surrender, couldn't let him discover her inexperience . . .

As if he read her mind, as if he sensed her anxiety . . . as if he knew that he wasn't going to win her like this, his lips gentled against hers. He kissed her top lip first, nibbling gently, taking it between his warm lips and sucking before laving it with his tongue.

Hunger pooled in her belly, the throb between her legs increasing. Her body softened, melting against him.

His hands dropped to her hips, holding her in better position to his bulging manhood. She rose on her tiptoes and thrust her pelvis forward, the throb near pain now.

She knew what she did . . . knew she played with fire.

"I don't want this," she choked, tearing her mouth from his. Her voice, hoarse with need, marked her a liar. Swallowing, she tried again. "Please."

Those mesmerizing eyes scanned her heat-flushed face. "Don't you?"

She squeezed out between him and the door, holding her hands awkwardly before her. Thankfully, he let her go.

Her hands flew to her hair, but the damage was done. She couldn't hope to tidy it right now. Lacing her fingers tightly over her clenching belly, she tried to forget that she faced him with her hair a wild mess and her lips throbbing from his rough kiss.

His eyes glittered down at her, terrifying in their ice-cold beauty, their desperate hunger. He wanted her. As unbelievable as it seemed, it was true. It couldn't all be about the begetting of an heir. Could it?

Then the thought occurred to her. Perhaps his fierce desire had nothing to do with her specifically . . . and more to do with the woman downstairs. True, he hadn't appeared overly affected by Adara's presence, but Evie was convinced they shared a history that went beyond what was seemly for a brother- and sister-in-law. An altogether different heat swept over Evie as mortification rushed through her.

Her chin lifted a notch. "Why did you marry me?" she demanded, her thoughts churning at a furious pace. "Truly? It wasn't all honor and obligation, was it?"

"I told you. I had a duty to wed and fill my nursery. A duty to provide for you and Nicholas." An angry muscle ticked in his cheek. "Marrying you seemed a convenient arrangement."

She motioned toward the door. "Was it because of her?"

He looked confused. "Who?"

"Lady Adara."

If possible, the ice-green of his eyes grew even colder. "Adara doesn't mean anything to me anymore."

"Anymore," she echoed. That one word knifed her through the heart. Unaccountably. She had no right to feel jealousy over the women of his past. She had no right to feel jealousy over the women of his present.

She swallowed against the tightness in her

throat. "She matters enough to be here now. What was she to you?" Her voice changed, sounded tinny and distant in her ears.

A dull pain pulsed at the center of her chest. She rubbed the spot through her gown as if she could rub it out. This was meant to be a practical arrangement. Why should it hurt?

That muscle ticked in his cheek again, feathering his skin. "Adara married my brother. Not me—"

"But you wanted to marry her?" It shouldn't be so important. It happened long ago.

He hesitated before admitting, "Yes. She agreed to run away with me, then chose my brother instead."

"Apparently she still holds a soft spot for you."

He shrugged. "What she feels is of no consequence to me. I don't even know why we're discussing this."

Because she's here now. "So marrying me so quickly upon returning to England had nothing to do with her?" She crossed her arms tightly.

He looked furious, and she resisted stepping back.

"It was as I said. I needed to wed."

"And just as well me as anyone else, right? A woman too stupid, too desperate to question your motives," she ground out.

He shook his head, his voice cutting. "Why should it matter to you one way or another? You married me for your own reasons." His top lip curled on a sneer.

Indeed. She was behaving like a jealous shrew. Still, she could not stop herself from accusing, "You married me to punish your sister-in-law, to make her jealous."

His eyes narrowed. "You care so much? You can't even bring yourself to let me in your bed because you're in love with a bloody ghost!"

She inhaled sharply as if slapped. He was correct, of course. Not about loving a ghost, naturally, but the rest. There was nothing between them. They had not married for love or affection, so why must she play at the hot-tempered wife desperate for her husband's undivided attentions?

The memory of his hands on her, stroking her most intimate places, heated her body. Well. There was *that*. Desire. Perhaps that had confused her. Rattled her head into thinking there could be more between them. Eventually, she would surrender her body to him. She must. She had agreed. He needed his heirs. If he didn't discover her carefully guarded secret then perhaps they could have something beyond a coldly calculated marriage of convenience. Even with her subterfuge yawning as wide as a chasm between them.

Shame swept through her then. *Her subterfuge.* How could she stand here, haranguing him for misleading her when she had lied about *everything*? Her very name!

Her skin prickled with mortification. She pulled herself as tall as her height would allow. "You're right, of course. I'm acting foolish. You owe me no explanation about your past."

His gaze drilled into her, probing. Strangely, he looked even angrier at these words. His large hands flexed at his sides. "You are the most vexing female."

She looked away, noting his well-appointed chamber, masculine with its elaborate molding of rich walnut.

"Where am I to sleep?" Certainly she would not be expected to share his bed again. Once had been more than she could endure.

"You'll sleep through there." He motioned to an adjoining door, his gaze still fixed on her.

She nodded. Without another word, she strode ahead and opened the door, eager to put a wall between them—desperate for the solitude to regain perspective. Theirs was a marriage of convenience. Somehow she had forgotten that. Somehow she had begun to think they were more than conveniently wedded strangers. A real marriage where one might expect happiness, affection. *Love.*

Just before closing the door, she could not resist another glimpse at his face, at his form standing so stalwart, chest impossibly broad, muscled thighs braced apart, as if he stood at the edge of a battlefield.

Lifting her gaze, her eyes met his where he stood in the center of his room. She wondered at his thoughts. Did she vex him so much that he regretted marrying her?

She shut the door and collapsed back against its length, struggling against her own thoughts, chiefly the matter of her desire for the man one room over.

For the next few days, Spencer remained conspicuously absent. She pretended not to notice, tried not to care, focusing instead on settling into her future home and ignoring pangs of loneliness. She missed home. Her family. Her friends.

And yet even as she struggled to adopt tasks and routines in order to make her new life as Lady Winters more palatable, she strained for the sound of his tread. Especially at night.

Alone in her bed, she would wait, staring at the shadows twisting along the walls, wondering if tonight would be the night he claimed his husbandly rights. Her teeth worried her lip until she tasted blood in her mouth . . . or fell asleep.

On the third morning she was unable to bear it another day. He wished to forget he possessed a wife? Very well. She, however, had a son waiting for her. While he may have forgotten that fact, she had not.

Unable to locate her husband, she tracked down Mrs. Brooks in the kitchens, grumbling unkind words about Lady Adara and her houseguests, who had yet to vacate the premises. Fortunately, Adara and her friends kept to their own amusements and did not seem overly concerned that Evie eschewed their boisterous company. Indeed, they were too amused with themselves and their own diversions to pay her much heed.

At Evie's inquiry on her husband's whereabouts, Mrs. Brooks straightened over a list she was reviewing and angled her head thoughtfully. "His lordship? Hmm?"

Evie smoothed at a wrinkle in her skirt, hoping her question appeared idle, no more than that. With luck, Mrs. Brooks did not know that her husband was avoiding her.

"He was pouring over some ledgers in his study earlier. Right now he's out and about the grounds somewhere."

"I see. Thank you."

Evie felt the housekeeper's pitying gaze on her back as she moved away.

Initially, she convinced herself that Spencer would have a great deal of business to attend to after so long from home. Especially with the added responsibilities of the viscountcy on his shoulders. Certainly he did not avoid her on purpose.

Craving nothing more than the solitude of her chamber, where she could privately nurse her battered spirits, she hastened down the corridor to her bedchamber.

"Ah, Lady Winters!"

She turned at the cheerful, masculine voice. Mr. Gresham approached in that loping saunter she had marked in all three of Adara's gentlemen friends. As if they'd never once had to arrive anywhere at a designated time. As if the world forever waited on them.

"Aren't you in a hurry," he mused, his eyes large and dark, almost too pretty for a man. All of Adara's friends possessed looks that far exceeded the charm of their personalities. Stylish and beautiful, the lot of them—and very aware of that fact.

She motioned lamely behind her. "To my chamber."

"In the middle of the day?" Those dark eyes danced wickedly. "Ah." He held up a hand, displaying an elegant palm as smooth and refined as any lady's. "Say no more. You're meeting your husband for a romantic tryst." He pressed his palm over his chest as if his heart ached. "Ah, newlyweds."

She blinked at his bold language, her cheeks burning. "No," she replied, too stunned to consider her next words. "I don't know where Spencer is."

"No?" As if that information translated into an invitation, he stepped close. Too close. "Such a shame." His gaze scanned her, insolently familiar. "May I be so bold to say—"

Could he possibly be any bolder? She shook her head no, but he continued to speak regardless.

"—if I had free access to such temptation as you, I would never leave your side."

Shocked, she could not speak, could not think to move.

Then, his gaze dropped to her lips.

He couldn't mean to . . .

She broke free of her astonishment and quickly jerked aside of his descending head, narrowly avoiding his lips.

Placing several feet between them, she held one finger aloft. "Stay away from me."

He tsked. "Come now, don't be a bore. Adara told me how neglected you've—"

"Adara!" she bit, her astonishment evaporating. "Did she put you up to this?"

He shrugged. "She thought you might be agreeable to . . ." His voice faded. He arched a brow eloquently.

"Well, I am *not!*"

He stepped back, both palms held out. "No need to take offense. You're not ready yet. I can be patient."

"You'll have a long wait."

"I doubt that." His lip curled in an unattractive smirk. "You don't know Adara like I do. She always gets her way in these things, and unfortunately she has set her sights on your husband, my dear." His expression turned almost pitying. "Her charms can be exceedingly tempting. When you tire of the lonely nights, come and find me."

Unable to stand the sight of his smug face, Evie whirled around and rushed to her room. She took great relish in slamming the door behind her. Leaning against it, she breathed deeply, outrage constricting her lungs.

Pushing off the door, she paced her chamber, a silent scream building deep in her lungs as her legs worked across the carpet, her swishing skirts an angry rush of whispers.

That settled it.

She would find Spencer at once and consummate this marriage—give him no reason to look to another woman for his needs.

Hopefully, she was not too late and he did not already regret marrying her. A painful lump rose in her throat at the thought. Determination burned through her hotter than any hurt she might feel. She would not languish in the neglect of her husband, suffering the insolence of his guests as she fought to deny her desire.

It was high time she became a wife.

Chapter 19

Evie entered the dining room that evening with both dread and determination tightening her chest. She wore her best dress. Again. The faded blue muslin looked a rag compared to the other ladies' vibrant silks. She shoved the thought from her head and reminded herself that she was the lady of the house. No matter how Adara sought to undermine her.

While she did not relish an evening with Adara and her houseguests, she knew Spencer would be present, and she longed to set matters right with him. As soon as dinner ended, she would pull him aside and request a private audience.

As it turned out, disappointment was the first course. Spencer's seat loomed empty at the head of the table for the entire meal. Mr. Gresham sat to her immediate right, his arm brushing hers far too frequently throughout their meal. The dinner was a tiresome affair, full of laughter and gossip about people she did not know. She begged off charades in the drawing room and excused herself as soon as dessert was finished.

She had nearly escaped when the melodic sound of Adara's voice froze her at the base of the stairs. "Are you unwell, Evelyn?"

With a deep breath she turned and faced Adara, a brittle smile pasted to her face. "Nothing of which to concern yourself. I'm afraid dinner did not set well with me." A menu that Adara had been audacious enough to dictate. Evie had yet to beat her to Cook in the mornings.

"Oh, I hope it wasn't the sole." Adara pursed her lips in seeming concern. "I instructed Cook to make certain it was fresh." The ring of sympathy in her voice did not accord with the dark glitter of her gaze. "When I see Spencer this evening, shall I tell him you're not feeling well, then?"

An icy chill chased over Evie's flesh; she did not mistake Adara's intimation. True or not, Adara wanted Evie to believe she would see Spencer first . . . that she saw him frequently. Unlike Evie, who could not catch a moment alone with him.

"If you wish." Unwilling to engage with the viper before her, she lifted her skirts and started up the stairs again, then stopped, unable to hide her claws after all. "Or I can tell him myself when I see him tonight. He usually wakes me when he gets in." A lie, but one which pride demanded. Let Adara think that however much he absented himself from her side during the day, her nights were filled with him.

Adara's face broke out in angry red splotches.

Satisfaction curled through Evie at the sight. And yet it failed to last.

Adara smiled slowly, catlike and knowing. "Indeed. How very . . . *diligent* of Spencer. He does know his duty. Never a chore left undone."

The words struck Evie as effectively as any well-aimed arrow. He'd married her for duty. For heirs. Nothing more. Adara knew that. Everyone knew it. And why not? It was the truth.

Did she really think offering herself like a roast goose on a platter would validate their half marriage? Turn it into something real and abiding?

She didn't even bother ringing for the maid when she reached her bedchamber. Furious and feeling a fool for even thinking seduction would win her Spencer, she undressed herself and slipped her nightrail over her head. As she sank down onto the stool at her vanity, she freed the pins from her hair and shook the gold-brown mass loose.

After vigorously brushing her hair, she paced her room, the soft hem of her nightrail sweeping her ankles. After awhile she stopped and added coals to the grate, appreciating the added warmth, not to mention the added glow of light. It wouldn't do to wake to a darkened room. That was still one aspect of her life she could control. One fear she could fight.

Finished with that task, she sank down onto the chaise, plucking up her book where she had discarded it earlier. Occasionally, a loud burst of raucous laughter carried from downstairs. Apparently the game of charades was still in full swing.

Time crawled as she strained to hear any sound next door. When she realized she'd stared, unseeing, at the same page for well over half an hour, she dropped the book and resumed pacing.

Then she heard it. A slight noise, nearly imperceptible from next door.

Nerves tight as a string, she strode forward and knocked briskly. Inhaling a single deep breath, she opened the door and marched inside.

Spencer stilled for a moment in the armchair where he sat, his green eyes locking with hers. Heat flushed her face at the sight of him, shirtless. The view brought her up hard. Her gaze de-

voured the broad expanse of chest, the flat belly
ridged with muscle. Something tightened in her
belly. Perhaps she should have waited for him to
bid her enter. Although she doubted he would
have adopted modesty and covered himself.

A boot thudded to the floor from his lax fingers. She blinked.

"Yes?" He dropped back against the chair, his
expression coldly unaffected.

"I need to speak with you."

Sighing, he dragged his hand through his hair,
rumpling the dark locks. "It's late, Evie."

"I'm not aware of any other time where we may
speak privately. For days you've avoided me." Her
hands tightened into fists, the nails digging into
her tender palms. "We'll talk now."

His eyes glittered darkly in the shadowed room
before returning his attention to his other boot, dismissing her. "I don't think that's a very good idea."

She charged forward, stopping before his chair.
"Why not?"

"I simply *don't*," he announced, his voice tight,
strained. His gaze lifted, skimmed her before
glancing around the room, almost as if seeing it
for the first time. "We'll do this in the morning. In
my study—"

"Why can't we do this now?" She inhaled
thickly. "Do you have a more pressing engage-

ment?" she demanded, Adara not far from her thoughts.

He unfolded his great length and towered over her, his jaw clenched tight. "Don't push me, Evie. I'm in no mood."

He could not have tossed down a more tempting gauntlet.

She arched her brow and brought her hand to his chest, palm flat, and *pushed*.

He snatched hold of her wrist, squeezing the bones until she felt certain they would snap. She didn't flinch, didn't back down a step. Even as the heat in his gaze scalded her.

She had initiated this. She would hold her ground.

"What do you want from me?" he growled, thrusting his face close. "Must you plague me?"

She shook her head. Moistening her lips, she asked in a quiet voice, "Do you really hate me so much?"

He jerked as though struck. His hand loosened around her wrist. She stepped back.

"*Hate* you? Is that what you think?" he asked.

She rubbed her tender wrist. "What else should I think? You've avoided me for days. Ever since we returned here. Ever since Adara—"

"Adara?" He shook his head. "What does she have to do with anything?"

Did he mock her? She pressed her fingertips to her temples, digging deep against the sudden ache starting there. "It's all gone horribly awry, hasn't it? A marriage of convenience." She snorted, the sound ugly. "It was supposed to be a simple matter, but this is anything but." She flung a hand in the air. "We thought we could exist as polite strangers, without the other ever affecting—"

"I never thought that. You did," he growled.

"Oh, no? You merely want me about for a few months, until we conceive your heir—"

"Hardly a possibility when you won't fulfill *that* particular duty!"

"Duty," she snapped. "Furthering your line. Is that all you think about?"

His nostrils flared. "When it comes to you, I think about a great deal more than that."

"Indeed? And when is that? When you're avoiding me?" Her hand flew wildly on the air. "Attending to countless beyond important tasks—"

"Evie," he snapped, his head cocking at a dangerous angle.

Still she continued, could not stop herself, unaccountably hurt. Had she thought to seduce him and risk exposure so that she might know desire? So that she might taste passion at last? With him?

Adara's face flashed across her mind. *Never a chore left undone.* Bedding her was no more than a chore for him. She stared hard at his angry face. Perhaps a chore he could no longer bring himself to pursue.

She blinked stinging eyes. Her words rushed forth in a scalding burn, "If you cannot abide to be in the same room with me mere days after our vows because I simply require time to acclimate myself to becoming wife and broodmare to a stranger, then how can—"

He grabbed her by the shoulders with both hands, nearly hauling her off her feet. "Would you stop nattering and allow me a word?"

She blinked.

His chest heaved an inch from her, emitting a heat that she felt dangerously drawn to. His furious gaze scoured her face, piercing, intent. She had never seen him this way. For a moment, she feared he would strike her.

Finally, he snarled, "Maybe I do hate you."

She shuddered and closed her eyes against the glittering dislike in the pale green of his gaze.

His words pained her more than she could have expected, killed something inside her that she didn't even know existed. *Hope.*

Somehow, since he'd entered her life, she had begun to hope again—for everything she'd thought lost when she'd given up her future for the sake of her sister and Nicholas.

Eyes still closed, she asked, "Why?"

He shook her, forcing her eyes open again. "Because you've made me hate Ian. My own flesh and blood." He sucked in a ragged breath. "Because he had you first. He has you *still*. I'm glad that he's gone . . . glad that it's my turn with you." He looked at her bleakly. "I don't know who I blame more for that. You or me."

Shock rippled through her. She read the hard glitter in his eyes, understood it for what it was now.

With a strangled groan, he hauled her the last inch separating them and kissed her with feverish desperation. His hands were everywhere all at once. He kissed her like he couldn't get enough, like this would be his last taste of her.

After a shocked moment, she lifted her hands, cupped his face. A day's growth of beard scratched her palms as she kissed him back, arching against him, mewling when even that wasn't enough.

He'd avoided her because he wanted her? Because he felt guilty for wanting her? It had nothing to do with Adara. Elation swelled through her and she kissed him harder, deeper.

Men like him did not fit into her world. She wasn't beautiful or charming or sophisticated . . . nothing about her should drive him to desire.

But somehow . . . she had. *She did.*

Still holding his face, thumbs caressing the hollows of his cheeks in small circles, she angled her head and tasted his tongue with sinuous strokes of her own.

He groaned into her mouth and broke away, holding her back even as she strained against him, panting, eager for his mouth, for the warm press of his body against hers again.

"Ian did this. Put you in my head, my blood. Somehow, listening to him all those years, I grew infatuated with the idea of *you*."

You. Linnie.

Not me.

His words seized hold of her heart and twisted it. The seductive haze he wove on her dissolved in an instant.

"If you don't want me to finish this, then go," he said thickly. "Now."

Breathing raggedly, she choked back a sob.

She wanted him with an intensity that vibrated in her bones. She'd never imagined she would want a man like this. Never thought she could *have* a man of her own. She'd sacrificed all hope for such a future. She'd made that choice the day she'd taken Nicholas into her arms.

Even as she'd never regretted that, she found herself wanting this. Wanting *him*.

Millie had warned her. Told her the wanting could be this . . . *deep*. This intense. Dangerous. Evie had scoffed at the idea, but here she stood, wanting, craving, desperate to have him love her . . .

Only he never would.

Even if by some miraculous occurrence, Spencer Lockhart, Lord Winters, could love his wife, he wouldn't love her.

Because it wouldn't be *her*.

Whatever he felt, he felt for Linnie—the woman he thought he had married.

With a pained blink, she stopped leaning toward him and stepped back—watched with her heart in her throat as his hands dropped limply to his sides. His eyes returned to their cool green, all that glittering heat banked, the stark need for her gone.

"Very well." He continued, his voice strangely thick, "If I can't have you, then stay the hell away. I tire of playing cat and mouse with you."

"Send me home," she blurted, desperate to remove herself from temptation, to keep the house of cards she had constructed from tumbling around her.

He stared at her coldly. "You are home."

"You said I could live wherever I wish—"

"After a period of time," he reminded.

He'd also said he would require an heir before he released her . . . but she had no intention of reminding him of that just now. "I want to see Nicholas—"

"We can send for him."

"Why do you care so much if I remain here?"

A myriad of expressions crossed his face. "I can't let you go."

He couldn't let *Linnie* go.

He was infatuated with her. Perhaps he even loved her. A miserable sob scalded the back of Evie's throat. She whirled around and stalked to the door, feeling ridiculous. She had worried she had to contend with Adara. She was wrong. She only had the ghost of her sister to battle.

"You're making this harder than it has to be."

"Perhaps you are," he countered.

She glanced over her shoulder at him.

He crossed his arms over his impressive chest,

a single dark brow arching in challenge. A sigh of wretched longing shuddered through her at the enticing sight.

If only he was right and it could be simple.

If only she could drop her guard and allow herself to love him. She wished it could be so simple . . . wished she could freely and openly love him.

If only he knew the truth.

And didn't care.

That thought struck terror in her heart. Because he *would* care, of course. He would care that he had married the wrong sister. If he knew the truth, he would never again look at her with desire warm in his eyes. Men hated being made the fool. He could expose her to the world for her lies and take Nicholas away. Such a risk was inconceivable.

Resolve hardening her heart, she opened the door to her room and passed inside, wondering if it would not have been better to have never met him. To never know for herself the yearning a woman could feel for a man.

Secretly, in her heart, she had considered Linnie weak and stupid to ever let a handsome face addle her judgment and leave her compromised. And then she'd thought her sister even more stupid to continue to love the scoundrel after he'd aban-doned her.

But now she knew.

Now she understood how one's heart could overrule logic. Now she knew love.

She'd never been more miserable.

Chapter 20

Spencer watched her go with his heart lodged somewhere in his throat. He'd bared himself, exposed that ugly part of himself and admitted the feelings she roused in him. Feelings that had begun in the Crimea.

The guilt had been there from the start. Wanting her. Resenting a dead man, his cousin, his best friend. Which made him one miserable bastard. Especially because now that he'd met her, *married* her, come to know her, he was more infatuated with her than ever.

Cursing, he dragged a hand through his hair and dropped down on his bed. He should release her. He'd given her the protection of his name, lifelong security. She wasn't his to keep—marriage or no. She wanted to go home. He should just let her return to her rustic little village.

Tossing one hand over his forehead, he stared

at the dark canopy above him, wondering when precisely he had swerved off the honorable path and into lust with a woman he had assured himself would be nothing more than a point of duty to check off his life's list.

When exactly had he fallen in love?

Evie's steps slowed as she neared the kitchen, Adara's peevish tones a grating grind on her ears. She stopped in the threshold, observing Adara wag a paper before Cook, hostility emanating from the gesture.

"Pray explain. I don't understand why we cannot serve the lamb tonight."

"My lady," Cook began, the worn lines of her face looking especially haggard.

Dressed in a purple velvet riding habit trimmed in ermine, Adara looked like something out of a fashion plate.

"Lamb isn't to be had this time of year."

Adara's gold ringlets jiggled above her ears. "I am certain you are just trying to be difficult!"

With a slight clearing of her throat, Evie made her presence known and suggested, "Perhaps I should plan the evening's menu and spare you the upset?"

Adara swerved to face her, her chocolate-brown eyes narrowing. "Evelyn," she murmured silkily.

"That won't be necessary. I have a great deal of experience in such matters—"

"As do I," Evie smoothly inserted. "And the task falls to me as the lady of the house, after all. I have no wish to impose on you. You're our guest. It's been unpardonably rude of me to allow you the chore for this long."

The Cook looked back and forth between them, wide-eyed, lips slightly sagging.

Adara blinked her eyes in seeming innocence. "Oh, but I live to be obliging! And come, Evelyn— you're a newlywed. Surely you have other things to occupy your time." The little witch. She knew Evie had more time on her hands than she knew what to do with, that Spencer left her woefully alone. Evie had scarcely seen him long enough to exchange greetings in the last week.

His startling confession still rang in her head.

Because you've made me hate Ian. My own flesh and blood. Because he had you first. He has you still. *I'm glad that he's gone . . . glad that it's my turn with you.*

He wasn't immune to her, wasn't numb. No matter what Adara would have her think.

And yet, he still avoided her. Following such a confession, she thought he might try his hand at seducing her again. A seduction she might no longer resist.

She didn't know what to think about him. She only knew she did. Constantly. From the moment she woke, to the minute she fell asleep every night.

With a polite smile, she turned her attention to Cook. "The lovely shepherd's pie you prepared my first night here would be tasty on such a frigid day."

Cook bobbed her head. "Yes, m'lady."

Triumph swelled in Evie's chest. A small skirmish to be sure, but she felt she had gained some leverage in her battle to assume her role as lady of the house. For as long as she was here at any rate.

"Shepherd's pie?" Adara's lip curled in scorn. "Peasant fare?"

"It's Spencer's favorite dish."

Adara's face mottled, but she possessed the good sense to hold her tongue.

Evie stepped beside Cook, and together they arrived at the rest of the menu. Adara watched silently. From the corner of her eye, Evie noticed her white-knuckled fist.

"Might I suggest a claret to complement the evening? The cellar boasts a fine assortment." Adara's voice was silk.

Evie blinked at the unexpected kindness, uncertain. Still, it was not an olive branch she could ignore. "That would be lovely."

"Come then." Turning, Adara floated from the kitchen. Evie followed her down the steps and into another corridor, this one narrower and lined with several pantries and closets. A door loomed at the far end.

Adara unlatched it. "I believe the clarets line the right wall." She held the door wide with her body and motioned Evie ahead of her. "Go on. Choose whatever suits you."

Evie peered down the shadowy stairwell. A great clamminess rose up from the deep interior to caress her cheeks. "Perhaps you would like to select—"

"Of course not. As you said, the task falls to the lady of the house."

Evie descended the first stone-slick step. The light from behind her illuminated her path to the bottom of the stairs and the first few racks of wine and large vats. Beyond that, swirling darkness. Her throat thickened. "I really would not mind if you—"

"Don't be silly. I'll wait here. One of us has to prop up the door." An impatient look crossed over her face. "Will you hurry? I'm supposed to meet the others on the back lawn for croquet."

Nodding, Evie lifted her skirts and descended the rest of the steps. She moved quickly, avoided looking into the deep clawing stretch of darkness. She shivered, her skin puckering to gooseflesh as she surveyed the first rack, determined to snatch the first claret she came across. Finding one, she turned and started up the well-lit steps.

The sound of the door slamming shut reverberated on the air, shuddering through her.

She froze, swallowed up in relentless black. "Adara?" She rushed up the steps, telling herself the door had slipped shut accidentally, that she was not lost to darkness.

At the top, she tried the door's latch. "Adara!" Nothing.

She pounded the wood with her fists. Her heart seized in her throat at the door's solid immobility. She pushed harder, rattling the latch.

"Adara!" She beat on the door until she could no longer feel her hands. "Adara!"

Fear closed in, choking her. Spinning around, she flattened herself against the door, breathing hard, staring blind into the swelling darkness.

"It's just a cellar," she muttered, breathing slow, careful sips and sinking down onto the top step, wincing at the terrible creak beneath her. Just a cellar. Not Barbados. No Hiram Stirling lurked, waiting to pounce.

Someone would come. Spencer would come.

A strangled laugh rose up in her throat. Why should he come? He wouldn't miss her. He wouldn't even note her disappearance.

She doubted anyone would notice. Especially her husband. She was stuck here with no salvation in sight.

Spencer strode into the dining room, bracing himself for the sight of Evie and the desire that slammed its fist into him every time he faced her.

Even though he'd managed to avoid her, he had thought of little else but the moment he'd confessed his desire for her, his shame. Her singular reaction—the demand for him to send her home—stuck bitterly in his throat.

Clearly, he had horrified her with his revelation. As he had horrified himself.

Had he actually blamed *her* for wanting her? For his complicated feelings toward Ian? Disgust churned through him.

He would relent and give her what she wanted. She likely read his avoidance as cruel neglect rather than something derived solely for the preservation of his sanity.

He would release her. She had not married him under pretense, after all. Their marriage was not based on love. Or even attraction. That was simply an unfortunate casualty. On his part, it seemed.

In time, he would forget how badly he wanted her, and maybe then they could come together and produce an heir. When he could go about the task objectively.

"Spencer!" Adara straightened to attention in her chair, the motion causing her shockingly red gown to pull dangerously low on her shoulders. "You've decided to join us."

He paused, eyeing the small group gathered at his dining table. He fought to keep his lip from curling as he surveyed the indolent lot. Vaguely, he'd been aware they still remained on, clinging about like a bad rash. One advantage to avoiding Evie was that he'd failed to see them, too. Only gazing at their dissolute faces, it occurred to him that Evie had been forced to suffer their company. He grimaced.

"Winters," Gresham exclaimed, not bothering to stand. "Good of you to join us." He reached for his wineglass and took a healthy swallow, sighing in satisfaction.

Spencer gripped the back of his chair. The man had cheek, sitting at his table and drinking his wine as though it all belonged to him. As a member of Cullen's set, he likely thought he had better claim to all Spencer now possessed.

Glancing around the table, he quickly learned that the one person he wished to see—the only one who mattered to him—was missing. "Where's Evie?"

"Oh." Adara fluttered a hand. "She's probably in her rooms."

"Yes. Likely napping." The female beside his sister-in-law tittered.

Adara drove her elbow into her side.

Cocking his head, he cut the woman—Beatrice, he thought her name—a swift glance. Her lips quickly squashed into a tight line. She reached for her glass of sherry and downed it with a toss of her glossy-dark sausage curls.

"Didn't know you were so interested, ol' boy," Gresham murmured around the rim of his glass.

Spencer snapped his attention back on him. "And why wouldn't I be interested in my wife?"

Gresham splayed his hands before him. "Meant no offense."

Spencer's fingers curled and dug into the back of his chair. "What did you mean, then?"

"I've merely noticed you've been preoccupied with matters other than your lovely wife."

"That so?" Spencer moved from his chair, a dangerous burn starting in his blood. Suddenly he saw Gresham as he'd seen him so many times before. With Cullen. And any number of women. Girls. Father only employed the most attractive of girls. When both Cullen and Frederick had visited from school, they'd brought Gresham. Spencer had spied the three of them up in the loft, engaged in all manner of sexual degeneracy with the household maids. Girls too young and callow to resist the advances of the young bluebloods they held in such awe. "And you've found my *lovely* wife of interest?" His voice was as dangerous as a blade to the throat.

Gresham was just like his brothers. A scoundrel with all the honor of a slave monger. In that moment, Spencer wanted him out of his house.

The bastard leaned back in his chair, his look smug. "How could I not? She is . . . *noteworthy*."

It wasn't his words as much as how he uttered them.

Spencer grabbed him by his heavily flounced cravat and hauled him from his chair. "You best occupy yourself with other matters and keep your attention off my wife."

Gresham squawked and clawed at Spencer's grip on his neck cloth.

Adara rose from her chair. "Gentlemen, come now . . . let's be good children. No fighting at the dining table."

Spencer glanced at each and every vapid face

before settling his gaze on Adara. "Where is Evie?" he repeated, his voice a growl.

"It's hardly my task to keep track of her." Color blossomed in her cheeks. "Really, Spencer, you're being such a bore. Don't tell me you're going to be one of *those* husbands?"

"And what kind would that be?"

She rolled her eyes. "One of the hovering types. Evie cannot want that—"

"Neither can you," Beatrice murmured at her side.

Adara shot daggers at her friend.

Surveying the group, Spencer dropped his hold on Gresham and adjusted his sleeves. Shaking his head, he gave voice to the thought running through his head. "Why are all of you even here?"

All gazes swung to Adara.

Beatrice murmured yet again. "I've been wondering that myself. It has ceased to be even marginally entertaining."

"I've had just about enough of you, Beatrice Summers," Adara hissed. "Why don't you go home and *entertain* your time with that fat, sweating husband of yours."

"Well," Beatrice huffed. "I do have other friends, you know."

"Truly, Dare. Look at the man." Gresham tugged

at his cravat in an attempt to set it to rights. "He's clearly besotted with his wife."

"Clearly. His *wife*. Not you," Beatrice echoed, dropping her napkin to her plate and pushing to her feet. "I want to go back to Town. I've had enough of this dismal place." With that ringing comment, she flounced from the room.

A tense moment passed before the others rose to follow her out.

Spencer and Adara remained, alone in the dining room.

She rose and stepped toward him, her dark eyes wide and supplicating. "Don't let her ruin what we could have together, Spencer. We've been apart for too long."

He stared at her for a long moment, trying to remember what it was he ever saw in her. All he saw now was a shallow, empty creature. A barren shell, the only love in her heart that which she reserved for herself. Not like Evie. Evie was selfless. Evie loved. Loved a man to the grave.

And isn't that what you want for yourself? Evie to love you with that depth?

"It's been a long time, Adara. Whatever we had is over. Now that I think about it, I'm not sure we really ever had anything at all."

Air escaped her lips in an angry hiss. "You don't mean that—"

"Don't embarrass yourself any more than you have. You should go with your friends," he said, not ungently, "and leave." Turning, he started to leave the room.

"Spencer!" Adara cried. "Spencer! Don't walk away from me! Where are you going?"

Without a glance over his shoulder, he forged ahead. "To find my wife."

Chapter 21

Evie shivered and buried her head in her bent knees. The wall at her back felt cold and damp and uncomfortably hard, but she required its support, grateful for something to hold her up and keep her from falling into the swirling blackness around her, consuming her, swallowing her.

A faint scratching sounded on the air. Rats. They scurried among the vats she had glimpsed on the far side of the cellar. Before Adara had locked her in. Before darkness. At least she told herself that—told herself the creatures weren't too close to her.

She couldn't accurately judge how long she'd been down here. It felt like a lifetime since Adara had slammed shut the door. Surely someone would come. Even Adara couldn't be so spiteful— so illogical—as to think she could keep her down here forever. Someone would come. Her fingers turned numb where she clutched her knees. Eventually.

She only had to cling to her sanity until then. A very real challenge. Alone in the dark, only one thing occurred to her—flung her back years. As though she were there again. In that bed. In Barbados.

It happened so long ago that she rarely thought about it anymore. Only trapped in darkness did her will fail her and catapult her back in time . . . force her to live it all again.

The surf roaring gently outside her window.

Warm sea air in her nose as Stirling's sweaty body bore her into the bed.

The salty taste of his flesh as she sank her teeth into his arm.

Then, came his fists. The agonizing pound of knuckles. The burst of pain in her ribs.

She whimpered. Trembling, she drew her knees closer and squeezed herself into the smallest ball possible, as if she could hide and prevent the past from finding her.

But it always did. In the dark, it always could find her.

"Spencer." His name rose, unbidden.

Whatever he was to her, whatever they had, he made her feel safe, protected.

She'd never been able to say that about a man

before. She'd only experienced neglect or cruelty at the hands of men. Her father had abandoned her to Penwich. Master Brocklehurst had been overly fond of applying his strap to her back for the slightest infraction. And then there was Stirling.

Spencer was different. If he were here, she wouldn't be struck cold with terror.

He'd married her for duty, for heirs, but he had yet to claim his husbandly rights. It was almost as though he wanted their physical union to mean something. He wanted it to matter.

"Spencer." She rocked harder, hugging herself until she could hardly draw breath. The next time she saw him she vowed to hold him and kiss him and never let him go. To put her fear aside and cross that threshold into the final intimacy.

She would no longer give him a reason to avoid her. She would give him herself. Completely. Totally. Again and again.

"Find me. Just find me."

"Have you seen Lady Winters?"

The kitchen buzzed with activity, the staff at work on the evening meal. "She was headed to the wine cellar with Lady Adara the last time I saw her." The cook slammed a pot down at that last mention of Adara, her lip curling over her stained and crooked teeth. "That would have been this morning."

This morning? Unease curled through him at this information. He gave a curt nod of thanks. The kitchen staff paused amid their work, watching him with wide eyes as he departed for the cellar.

Dark fury brewed inside him, his pace increasing as he considered that his wife had not been seen since this morning. With Adara. The little witch had lied, then. Not only had she seen Evie, but she had escorted her to the wine cellar. And why would Adara have bothered? She wasn't the solicitous sort. Especially given her attitude toward Evie.

His stride increased until he was running down the length of the corridor. His heart thundered against his ribs.

He flung open the bolt to the cellar and squinted down into unremitting gloom. He winced, hoping Evie wasn't down there.

"Evie!" he called down.

Thick silence answered him.

Digging into his jacket pocket, he pulled forth a handkerchief. Bending, he jammed it between the door and the floor, effectively keeping the heavy door wedged ajar.

He stomped down a few steps, his boots strong cracks on the wood. Peering into the swirling black, he called again, "Evie, are you down there?"

His stomach cramped at the thought of her trapped in the dark. All day. Alone. Although she had denied it, he knew she feared the dark. Remembered her gasping, choking breath when she woke at the inn, the fire dead and cold, the room black.

"Evie?"

Nothing. Silence.

Relieved, at least, that she had not been trapped down here after all, he turned, only to stop on the top step.

A sound. The barest scratch dragged against the rock floor. Then, he heard it. A whimper. *Evie.*

Swinging around, he flew down the rest of the steps. "Evie, where are you?"

Why didn't she answer him? He stalked the cellar floor, knocking into vats, a crate. Then the tip of his boot struck something soft and yielding. His heart clenched. *Evie.*

She jerked away from the contact, scurrying aside. Spencer crouched and stretched out a hand, feeling the air, searching the dark. His fingers brushed something soft. He curled his hand around a fistful of fabric and tugged.

"Evie?" He tugged again, inching closer, pulling her toward him by the hem of her gown. "Evie? Are you—"

A sudden kick to the chest knocked the breath from him. Caught off balance, he fell back onto the floor. He heard her scramble away, moving deeper into the cellar.

He followed, catching hold of her arm. "Evie! Stop! It's me!"

Dropping to his knees, he slid one hand up her arm to her face, cupping her cheek. He lowered his forehead to hers and spoke directly into her face, willing her to hear him, to believe. "It's Spencer. You're safe. I'm here."

She stilled against him, her breath falling fast and hard. For several moments, she said nothing. Not a sound escaped their lips as he held her close, their breaths mingling, lips so close he almost felt the tender swell of her upper lip.

His mouth tingled, remembering the taste of her. He yearned to close that last bit of distance, touch that lip with his mouth.

Bloody hell. Now was not the time to suffer lust toward his wife. She was in the grip of some living nightmare. He refused to let his cravings outweigh her peace and well-being. Especially since the blame for this entire incident could be settled on him. He should have sent Adara home. Instead, he'd left his wife to her sharp claws.

"You're fine," he repeated. "Safe." His thumb trailed small circles over her cheek as he waited for Evie to recover herself.

He sucked in a deep breath and tried not to notice the petal-softness of her cheek beneath his hand. Or the close press of her shuddering body to him.

At last she spoke, her voice small and shaky. She'd climbed back from whatever edge she'd been toeing. "Spencer?"

"Yes."

A sob caught and twisted her voice. "What took you so long?"

Then she was in his arms, the last bit of space between them gone.

He sighed, the sound ragged with relief. "I'm sorry. God, sweetheart, I'm sorry."

She sniffed against his throat, the tip of her nose ice on his skin. "You're cold." He cursed and started to pull back, ready to remove his jacket.

Her fingers tightened their clutch on his arms. "No, don't go."

He shook his head in the dark. "I'm not leaving you."

She slid her fingers from his arms, delving beneath his jacket to wrap her arms around his chest. She shifted, practically sitting in his lap. "I called for you," she whispered. "Knew you would come."

"I'm sorry I didn't find you sooner."

"You're here now." She buried her face into his neck and clung harder, inhaling deeply. The sound clenched his gut. His cock hardened beneath her voluminous skirts.

He cupped the back of her head, noticing her hair had fallen loose, trailed thickly down her back. He couldn't resist. The thick mass felt too soft, like silk in his grasp. He delved his fingers through it.

"I'm so sorry that Adara locked you down here. The fault is mine." And it was. The thought of Evie hurt, in pain, when he could have prevented it, filled him with fury. "Let's get you out of here and warm you up."

He knew of her aversion to the dark. Doubtlessly, she wished to be out of the cloying gloom that had reduced her to such terror.

Her arms squeezed around him, stopping him from moving. She shifted, pressing her breasts into his chest. His breath fell faster, harder.

"Not yet," she purred. The words fanned warmly against his skin.

He looked down, trying to make out her features in the impenetrable black. She moved again, pressed a light, openmouthed kiss to his jaw.

He hissed.

"Spencer," she sighed his name, before flicking her tongue against his lip. Just a lick. A taste that made him tremble like a boy with his first maid.

His grip tightened on her arms. "Evie, you shouldn't—," he broke off, leaving his warning unfinished. *Touch me? Whisper sweetly against my skin?*

Was he a fool? He'd wanted nothing else since the first moment he saw her, muddied pinafore, hair a horrid mess, blue eyes snapping with clear unwelcome.

Her fingertips brushed his cheek. "You make me feel safe. You chase away the fear, Spencer."

Something loosened inside him at her words.

She continued, "When I'm with you, I forget everything except this." She took his hand from her arm and dragged it to her breast.

He sucked in a breath at the feel of her nipple beading through the fabric of her dress. He surged again, his erection a near painful throb.

Bending his head, he crashed his lips over hers.

He shuddered at the first taste of her. Holding

her face, he angled her head for a deeper kiss as hunger exploded hotly between them. Her breast seemed to swell against his hand. He fondled it, found her nipple, delighted in her gasp.

Her palms slid down his chest and then up again, wrapping around his shoulders. He groaned, yearning to strip off their clothes and lose all barriers between them, to feel her hands on his flesh.

Never breaking their kiss, she shifted until her knees slid down his hips, her dress pooling around them.

He grasped her other breast, cupping the sweet little mound. A little mewl escaped her from their fused lips. Desire spiked through him, dark and heavy, sinking heavily in his groin, simmering through his blood. His cock strained against his breeches, hard and aching, ready to plunge into her warmth.

With a gasp, he tore free. He grasped her arms and forced her back. She strained toward him with a frustrated moan, hands still clutching his arms, her sharp little nails digging.

"Evie," he croaked, his arms shaking with restraint. "If we don't stop this now—"

She climbed off him, tugging him to follow. "Don't stop. Don't think."

Unable to deny her, deny himself, he came

over her. Her hands skimmed up his arms, laced behind his neck. She arched beneath him, her face shaking, trembling near his own. Her skin felt incredibly soft against his skin. "Take me, Spencer."

It was everything he'd ever wanted to hear from her. What he'd been waiting for. His desire for her edged close to pain now. He wasn't sure he could stop at this point.

"Spencer," she breathed sweetly against his ear.

"Down here," he reminded her, his voice rough and choking as she dragged her lips down his neck. "In the dark? You are certain?"

"It doesn't frighten me. Not with you."

"I won't stop," he vowed, warned, his voice thick and unnatural.

Her cool fingers splayed over his cheeks, and there was such tenderness in the clasp of her hands that something unraveled inside him.

Her words fanned over his mouth. "I'm counting on that. Make love to me." Her voice choked a little against his ear. "Please. Not because of duty or honor. Not for the purpose of conceiving an heir. Pretend to want me. Even a little."

Pretend? "In all my life, I've never wanted anything more than this. Than you." He sank over her and claimed her lips again. All gentleness fled.

His hands drew her up against him and slid around her, working quickly over the tiny buttons at the back of her gown. He slipped each cloth-covered one free, fumbling and cursing in his eagerness, pausing as she slid his jacket and vest free. He growled impatiently as she pulled his shirt over his head. She laughed lightly, gasping when he gave up and ripped the last few buttons at the back of her gown. They popped and scattered to the ground with light dings.

He yanked her dress down to her waist, pulling her arms free of the sleeves. Her arms felt warm and deliciously bare wrapped around him. Loosening her stays, he pulled her corset down enough to bare her breasts.

In the dark, everything was sensation. Taste. He wished he could see her, but this would have to be enough. For now.

Palming the perfect mounds, he let his hands act as his eyes. She gasped. His thumbs tested the nipples, rolling and stroking the pebbled tips. She arched into his hands, moaning.

"There's no going back now," he growled, kneading the soft flesh. "It won't be like before, Evie." *It will be me. Not Ian. Us. You in my bed every night. No more running.*

Wild whimpers escaped her. He increased the

pressure of his fingers, rubbing the tight buds until she moaned and writhed under his hands. So wonderfully responsive, arching into him, moaning . . . begging.

"Say it. Say *my* name."

"Spencer," she sobbed.

His cock throbbed against his breeches, the erection painful, thick with need. He slid one hand beneath her skirts, skimming her stockings until he located the slit in her drawers. He brushed the soft curls between her legs, a satisfied smile curving his mouth at the wetness he found there.

She jumped, gasped, her fingers clamping around his wrist.

"Easy," he murmured, still touching her, his fingers sliding against her slick folds. "Let me feel you."

She didn't release her grip on his wrist, but her body trembled, quivered. Her legs parted wider for him, and she thrust herself against his hand, ready, eager after the initial shock of his touch.

He glided his fingers over her, sliding toward her little nub. He brushed the spot, lightly at first, teasingly, gradually firmer, harder until she was surging against his hand in a desperate rhythm, crying out.

Unable to wait another moment—he'd waited long enough—he freed himself. Sliding his hands over her slim thighs, he splayed her wide for him. Sweat broke out over his brow as he nudged her entrance, edged inside the delicious, sucking heat of her.

He pushed deeper.

She wiggled free. "Wait!" The sound of her voice, desire-laced and sultry, only made the blood pump harder in his veins.

"Evie," he groaned her name. She couldn't mean for him to stop now!

She urged him back with her hands on his chest and rose to her knees before him. He tried to haul her back, but she pressed a hand to his chest, stopping him. He had a sense of her shaking her head at him. "Not yet."

He strained to see in the dark, heard the slight rustle of her skirts, then gasped as her small hand closed around his cock—stroked him, at first slowly, then harder, each pump of her small hand driving him mindless.

"Evie," he groaned, falling back to the ground. "Please, I need you to—"

He reached up and grasped her arms, determined to end the torment and finish this properly. Before she finished him.

Her hand lifted then, left him . . . replaced by her mouth.

Defeated, his hands dropped from her arms as her lips surrounded him. "Evie," he moaned, "you're killing me."

Chapter 22

Evie prayed she knew what she was doing. Millie's advice was imprinted on her brain. Advice that had seemed bold and impossible at the time, but no longer.

She didn't wonder if she could do it . . . only whether she could do it right. Do it *well*. If she could please him. Drive him wild with desire the way that she not only *wanted* to but *needed* to.

"Evie, stop, please . . ." The rest of his words died as she worked her mouth over him, tasting, savoring.

When Millie had told her about this part of it, she had thought the idea vaguely revolting. She had not guessed at the heady empowerment she would receive from bringing him to his knees, at reducing him to broken pleas.

She laved him with her tongue, enjoying the ripples of pleasure coursing through his body, flowing into her. His groan ripped across the air, shuddering through his body and into her. The sound undid her. Her belly twisted and tightened. If possible, he swelled, grew harder, larger against her lips.

He seized her arms and tried to pull her up. "Evie, please, no more—"

She sucked at the tip of him, resisting the pull of his hands, determined that he take her only when he was overcome, mindless with need, so lost that he wouldn't notice her lack of experience . . . or her maidenhead.

"No more," his voice bit out, pulling her out from between his legs.

In a single move he rolled her beneath him, on top of his discarded clothing. His hands delved beneath her skirts, grasping her hips with a roughness that both thrilled and alarmed her. She had done it . . . driven him to the point of mindlessness.

She stretched her hands into the darkness, searching for his face. Her palms brushed the scratchy texture of his cheeks and she latched on, dragging his face down to hers even as his hands tore at her drawers, ripping the slit in the fabric even wider.

Then he was there.

She gasped against his mouth at the sudden surge of him inside her. He didn't ease in gently.

He was beyond that. She'd made certain of that.

He filled her, stretched her to capacity. Slick and large and alien. She fought the instinctive urge to pull back, to escape the strangeness of his throbbing member buried deep inside her.

She whimpered.

He must have taken the sound for pleasure, because he groaned and repeated the process, clutching her hips for leverage.

Relax. Breathe.

He still kissed her, his lips fierce, bruising as he eased out and drove back inside her again, lodging himself to the hilt with another shuddery groan against her lips. She drank the sound, reveled in it. The sound of his surrender. His passion for her.

Gradually, the strange and uncomfortable sensation of him inside her changed into something else as he began to move, setting a quick pace, pumping in and out of her. Something raw and desperate that made her move faster against him. Without grace or rhythm.

Clenching heat grew at her core, turning to a growing burn. The slick drag of him against her weeping flesh made her fidget, writhe beneath him, reaching, seeking for something close, near, within reach.

The burning twisted into a deep, gnawing

ache. Desperate for more, to increase the delicious friction of him inside her, she tangled her tongue with his and parted her thighs wider, lifting her hips off the ground.

She moved with him, against him. Any way she could. Her hands slid around him, found the taut cheeks of his backside, and reveled in the sensation of his flesh flexing as he worked over her.

She moaned, no longer caring if he was mindless, if he was lost to passion. She was. Her body afire, she thrust her hips to meet his every drive. Her inner muscles clenched around the delicious hardness of him. A ragged cry broke from her lips, the sound shameful and decadent and something she'd never imagined to hear from her lips. A sound she didn't know she *could* make.

And still, he moved harder over her, thrusting deeper. He slid a hand beneath her, lifting her off the hard ground and bringing her even closer for his penetration.

Evie gasped, swallowed, clung to his shoulders. She felt like she was being propelled forward, pushed ahead in a great race, a desperate chase for something elusive . . . just within reach.

She moaned his name, the sound twisting out

from deep in her throat. The pressure grew, built. She bit down on his shoulder, tasted the warm saltiness of his skin as her body exploded, came apart, splintered into a thousand pieces. Spots danced before her eyes, and she was convinced she would never come together again. She would forever be this, changed, never herself again. Shattered.

He collapsed over her, sliding his hand out from the small of her back and bracing his panting length over her.

They lay there for some moments, their bodies rising and falling with heavy breaths. She felt him pulse, still lodged fully inside her.

He lifted his head from the arch of her neck. "Evie?"

"Hmmm." She reached up to touch the ends of his hair lightly, rubbing the silky strands between her fingers, afraid of what his next words would be, if they might somehow possess the power to ruin this.

Had he realized? Did he know?

"Did I hurt you?"

Her chest tightened, painful pinpricks breaking out over her flesh. Because he knew he'd breached her maidenhead?

"N-no."

"I'm usually not so . . . forceful." He made a

rough sound in his throat. "I certainly never imagined our first time together would be like this . . . on the floor of a cellar."

A sigh shivered through her. He didn't know.

She reached a hand for his cheek, enjoying the rasp of his skin against her fingers, feeling both relieved and awful. *Because he didn't know.*

A small part of her wished he had figured it out. Then the truth would be out. For better or worse, subterfuge would no longer hover between them. As long as her secret remained hidden, he didn't know her. He never could. She was no different than his father, gulling him into believing an illusion.

"It was perfect," she murmured, her eyes burning, her voice thick. Perfect as it could be.

His voice rumbled low and deep. "Indeed? Then it shouldn't be difficult to impress you a second time. A bed shall help in that endeavor."

He rose and pulled her to her feet. Her skirts fell around her legs in a whisper.

In the dark, he helped her set her clothes to rights, buttoning the back of her gown with an efficiency that convinced her of his experience in such a task. Legs steady as jam, she swayed for a moment until he steadied her. Her head spun. She clutched his arm for support.

He folded a hand over hers. "Are you unwell?" His voice rang sharply in her ears.

"Just a bit dizzy. I didn't have a chance to take breakfast this morning—"

"You mean you haven't eaten since yesterday?" he demanded.

She nodded, then realized he couldn't see her face. "Yes."

He cursed and swept her up into his arms as if she weighed nothing at all. "Damn fool," he muttered.

"I beg your pardon?" she demanded. "I don't appreciate—"

"Not you. Me," he growled in an angry voice as he stomped toward the shadowy stairs. "I should have known better than to take you down here like a well-seasoned . . ." His voice faded away with a low growl.

"I might have had something to do with that," she inserted, her lips twisting wryly as he carried her up the wood steps with jarring force. She smoothed a palm over his shoulder, the skin warm and smooth beneath her palm. Deliciously bare. "You forgot your clothes."

They cleared the threshold and stepped into the muted glow of the corridor.

She blinked at the sudden emergence from dark and turned to stare at his face, searching the masculine angles and hollows, the deep-set eyes, the well-cut lips as though she'd never seen him before. She brushed a fingertip over the slight dimple in his chin.

She devoured the sight of him, his hair mussed from her fingers, his green eyes bright, staring at her hungrily. The way a man stares at a woman he's only known intimately.

"I'll fetch them later."

Her fingers fanned over his shoulder, enjoying the bunching muscles. "You intend to march through the house half-dressed? What if someone sees—"

"We're married, Evie. They can think what they like. And last time I checked, I was master of this house."

He strode the length of the corridor until he reached the servants' stairs. He passed a footman on the way up. Startled, the callow-faced youth pressed himself against the wall, averting his gaze from their obvious state of dishabille. Evie buried her overly warm face in his chest, hiccupping with laughter, feeling lighter and happier than she had in years.

He did this—made her feel young and free. As though happiness wasn't a sentiment reserved for a lucky few. It was something she could have. With him.

"We'll acquire you some fresh clothes, food—"

"A bath?"

"Of course." He turned his face then and nuzzled her cheek, lips dropping to her neck.

Her belly fluttered at the warm press of his lips on her skin, at his easy familiarity with her. She'd never thought to have this with a man. Never, certainly, with a husband.

She twisted her head around as he passed her bedroom door.

"Where are you taking—"

"I don't really see the purpose of you sleeping in there anymore." His gaze swung to hers, the green clear and probing. "Do you?"

Heat crawled over her cheeks. Indeed not. Her body belonged to him now. She freely relinquished herself to him.

"No. I don't." She didn't want to sleep alone anymore. She wanted Spencer, to be his wife in the truest sense. Only one thing stood between them anymore. One thing killed the lightness sweeping through her.

She hid her face in his neck to hide her frown.

Inside his chamber, he set her on the edge of the vast bed. She forced herself to brighten as he stared down at her with those mesmerizing eyes.

He brushed his thumb down her cheek. "I won't be long."

She nodded, watching breathlessly as he left the room. Once the door clicked shut, she was on her feet and at the basin, determined to wash away any evidence of her virginity.

Her hands shook as she poured water into the porcelain bowl. She told herself it was simply from the day's events. Locked in the dark, forced to face that long-standing fear, and then her other fear—the risk of exposure when she surrendered her body to her husband.

Surely it had nothing to do with the fact that she had fallen in love with her husband. A man that would want nothing to do with her if he learned the secret she harbored. She closed her eyes in a tight blink. *If* no longer seemed to be in question.

It was a matter of when. *When* she told him. Because she couldn't have him until she confessed the truth. She could no longer live with this lie between them.

You don't lie to those you love.

A simple enough tenet.

She could only pray he understood and did not judge her too harshly . . . that he did not toss her into the same category as his father.

After ordering Evie's bath and dinner tray, Spencer set out in pursuit of another matter that required his attention. After several knocks on

Adara's door, he opened it and stepped into an empty bedchamber. Not so surprising.

Smiling grimly, he moved down the corridor and proceeded to beat on the bedchambers of each of her companions. Turning the latches, he flung doors open, heedless to shouts of outrage.

Very few of Adara's guests slept alone. They stumbled from their rooms with words of indignation, hastily knotting their robes. He found Adara in the last chamber. In Gresham's bed.

"Spencer!" she cried, wrapping a coverlet about her ample curves. "It's not what you think!"

He arched a brow. "I have eyes, Adara. Your mistake is in thinking I care."

Gresham visibly relaxed at his declaration. He even had the temerity to wink. "Your brother never bothered to care either—"

"I'm sure," Spencer drawled, imagining that his amoral brother had been too busy chasing the skirts of other women to care who diddled his wife. He issued a fervent prayer of thanks that Evie was nothing like these people, that she knew nothing of the *ton*'s sordid practices. Like him, she likely had no wish to frequent the drawing rooms of London's High Society.

"Spencer, listen to me. I made a mistake when I chose Cullen over you. I'm sorry I lied and said I would run away with you. I was young. Don't punish me for one bad decision. I've suffered enough. The way Cullen died—" She shuddered. "It was mortifying."

He sighed. "I'm not punishing you. I simply don't care."

Rising from the bed, she latched onto his arm. "You cannot mean—"

"You're my sister-in-law, Adara. Nothing more. I'll see to your needs until you've remarried. Something I suggest you do with all haste." He narrowed his gaze on her.

Hurt flashed across her face. She quivered her lips. "You wish me to marry another man?"

"I expect the banns posted within the fortnight. Mind you, I'll bestow a handsome settlement on you." He shot Gresham a significant look. "Something to consider, Gresham, if you're so fond of bedding her."

"Quite so," he murmured.

Adara glared between them. "As if I would marry a mere *mister*."

The crowd that had gathered near the door tittered at this slight.

Gresham's face flushed. "Good enough to tup, just not wed, is that it? And I suppose a woman that's serviced half the *ton* can expect better? You'll be fortunate indeed to attract a husband half as understanding or forgiving."

The crowd tittered again.

A female muttered, "This is the best house party I've ever attended!"

Weary of the lot of them and eager to return to Evie, Spencer snapped, "Until you wed, you'll only be granted the most meager of allowance. Perhaps that will change your mind."

"*Allowance?*" She pressed a hand to the swell of her cleavage above the coverlet.

"Yes," he said tightly, leaning his face close. "And rest assured, that will vanish in a heartbeat if you ever"—his voice dipped darkly—"harm Evie again. The streets would be too good for you."

"Evie!" she screeched, bouncing with rage. "This is all because of that little drudge?"

"Wife," he inserted, teeth clenched. "Have a care, Adara. Evie is my wife."

"Indeed." She narrowed her eyes to slits. "You daft fool," she snarled. "You've fallen in love with her."

Spencer pressed his lips shut . . . letting the words sink in, settling deeply inside himself. Surprisingly, he felt no impulse to deny them. "Perhaps," he allowed.

"Bastard! How dare you prefer her to me?" She charged him, fingers curled to strike.

He caught her wrist, speaking calmly, flatly. "How could I not? I want you gone. Pack your things." He swept his gaze over Gresham and the rest of Adara's friends gawking from the doorway. "All of you."

"Tonight?" Gresham demanded. "Not very hospitable of you, Winters."

"Nor have any of you been very gracious to my wife, *your hostess*. Now get out. You're not welcome here."

Gresham ducked his head. Looking a bit shamefaced, he nodded.

Spencer flung Adara from him. "I will look for your announcement in the *Times*. Don't thwart me on this. You won't find me a forgiving man."

Adara stumbled to the bed and dropped down, her small frame sagging with defeat in a very affected pose. The sight did nothing to move him.

In that moment, Spencer felt spared, relieved. Well and truly saved from the miserable fate that would have been his had he married her all those years ago. He sent forth a small prayer of thanks to Cullen for stealing her away.

Gresham patted her bare shoulder. "Come along, Adara. Let's pack."

She ignored him. Her eyes glittered across the shadowy room at Spencer. "You're a damn fool. A fool! You think you love her? You think she loves *you*?" she sneered.

He held himself still, watching her, listening.

He knew he shouldn't. Knew he should turn away, but he couldn't. He watched, transfixed as she blasted him with her venom.

"Wait and see. Your perfect bride will break your heart. I see it in her. She's the same as everyone else. Out for herself. She doesn't really care about you. Why do you think she married you?" Her pretty lips twisted. "Do you even know each other?" She laughed cruelly. "You're nothing but a title to her. Wealth and security. Not a man! Not anyone she would ever care for!"

"You're wrong." He shook his head slowly. "Your mistake is in thinking Evie is anything like you."

With that parting comment, he turned and left the room, ignoring the ring of her words in his ears, the uneasy feeling they left in his gut.

She was wrong.

He wasn't a fool to permit affection for his wife into his heart. He wasn't a fool to think she might return his affection. She was different. Good and sincere. Why not let himself care for her?

A dark voice whispered across his mind. *Because she's Ian's Linnie.*

He shook his head. Not anymore. She was his now. His Evie. It wasn't a mistake to let hope creep in . . . hope for a marriage based on something more than duty and convenience. Hope for them both.

Chapter 23

Evie woke to warm lips on her neck, her throat, her breast. Opening her eyes, she smiled and laced her fingers through Spencer's thick hair. A predawn gray crept between the damask drapes.

"Hmm, good morning," she murmured, then frowned. "I tried to wait up for you last night. Why didn't you wake me when you came to bed?"

She remembered little after her bath and meal save climbing into his bed. Apparently, replete with food and relaxed from her bath, her body's exhaustion had overcome her.

"You looked so peaceful, I didn't want to wake you." He kissed a spot directly beneath her ear and she shivered. "I decided this could wait for morning."

She surveyed the broad, naked chest spread above her. "It's morning now," she murmured, secretly awed at the wanton she had become.

He grinned. "I'm aware. I waited this long

before waking you." He pulled back slightly to gaze down at her. Even in the shadowy room, his intense gaze penetrated her. He fingered the modest neckline of her nightrail. "I'm going to burn this. All your nightrails."

"What will I wear then?" she teased.

A wicked gleam entered his eyes. "The sheerest, *smallest* satins and laces." His finger slipped inside the high neckline. "More like handkerchiefs, really. They'll cover your most delectable parts for all of five seconds before I remove them with my teeth."

She couldn't help herself. She tossed back her head and laughed. "My, my, you are wicked."

When she looked at him again, he wasn't smiling. He simply stared at her, somber and brooding.

Her laughter faded. "What?"

"I've never seen you like this."

Her chest felt tight, the air frozen in her lungs. "Like how?"

"So easy to be with, so . . . happy and free. I like it when you laugh. When you're not fighting me."

Her chest felt tight, impossibly small. "Me, too." And she suspected he possessed the power to make her laugh often. To make her happy. If she permitted it.

He smiled then. A smile she had never seen on

him before. A smile she felt echo through her. He brushed a strand of hair off her neck, his thumb remaining, lingering over the pulse at her throat as he looked at her in that intense way that melted her bones.

And she knew she had to confess everything to him. If she held any hope of building anything meaningful between them, anything *true*, she must. Somehow. Some way.

She opened her mouth to begin, unsure how to start.

He shifted, pressed his erection against the curve of her hip. The hungry look in his eyes stopped her. Heat pooled low in her belly. She shifted, rolled her thighs apart as much as her gown would allow, inviting him in.

Mouth flattened into a firm line, he reached down and dragged her nightrail up over her hips, her torso, her head. She shivered in the morning air. He came over her again, warming her with his naked body. His skin felt like satin stretched over solid muscle and sinew. Wherever she touched him he rippled and undulated. He made her feel small and delicate.

"Hope you didn't have plans for the day." His calves slid against hers, his coarse leg hair erotic and stimulating. Her insides quivered.

"Why?" she breathed.

"Because we'll be doing this. All day and all night."

"Can we do that?"

He chuckled and lowered his head, kissing her long and deep until she was gasping, clinging to his shoulders and urging him closer. His mouth dragged free from hers, burned a searing trail down her neck. "We can do anything we want."

She sighed and arched against him. "Anything?"

"Everything." He took her nipple in his mouth, sucking deeply. She cried out, arching more sharply against his warm tongue, clutching harder at his head. With each pull of his mouth on her breast, he created a deep pull inside her. A tight ache that throbbed between her legs.

"I'm never leaving this bed," she moaned.

He chuckled, his warm breath fanning her wet nipple. "Not even tomorrow?" He flicked the tip with his tongue, tormenting her.

"What? Why?" she moaned, thrashing her head, beyond understanding as he danced his fingers up her thigh, brushing her wetness.

"We could do this in a carriage, couldn't we?" He paused to blow over the tip of her wet, engorged nipple.

A *carriage*? She shook her head. "Why would we wish to when we have a bed?"

He closed his mouth over her other nipple, biting down lightly. She shrieked and grabbed his hair.

"I thought you might like to take a trip."

"Where?" she panted, tugging him back to her breast.

"Little Billings."

She blinked and propped herself up on her elbows. Her heart tripped at the crooked smile he wore. He really was too handsome. "You're taking me home?"

"You miss your family, don't you?"

She nodded mutely, overcome that he cared enough about her to grant her this. Her heart seized in her chest when he reached out to stroke her cheek. "I want you to be happy, Evie. I've sent Adara and her friends home. We can stay here or in Little Billings. Wherever. I've lived in a tent for years, so anything is an improvement."

Her hand flew to her chest, pressing against her racing heart, hearing only one thing just then. "You sent Adara away?"

His face tightened with a scowl. "You didn't expect me to let her remain after her little stunt."

She touched his face, delighting in the rasp of his cheek against her palm. "This is your home, Spencer. I want it to be mine, too. I want it to be where we raise Nicholas and our children."

She'd clung to The Harbour out of fear and desperation. For so long she had viewed the outside world in the same way she'd perceived the darkness. Something to be feared. Avoided. A place where only bad things happened. Like in Barbados.

"You mean that?"

The Murdochs were long overdue a rest, a reprieve from hard work and the overhanging cloud of poverty. Because of Spencer, she could give them the security and peace to enjoy their last years. Nicholas would adore Ashton Grange and the grand adventure it presented. Amy, too. It would provide them hours of exploration. Her aunt, on the other hand, would likely choose to remain at The Harbour. She'd not wish to leave her home of so many years.

Evie nodded, smiling. Again. "I do."

He smiled back, a deep, contented curve on his lips. He lowered her back down on the bed, his arms twin bands of muscle on either side of her, caging her in. Her belly tightened. His eyes gleamed pale green down at her, devouring. "Then let's fetch Nicholas and bring him home."

Home. Their home. For the first time, she believed it. Believed she could have that with him.

Perhaps she could have everything.

He kissed her then, and her heart thrilled at the taste of him on her lips. She gasped when he entered her, exulted in the hard fullness of him fitting inside her so perfectly. Nothing had ever felt as sublime, as right as his body merging with hers.

He slid his hands under her to cup her bottom and lift her for his every thrust, driving her deeply into the bed. She turned her face, crying out into the pillow beneath her head and hiding her tears.

Tears of joy. Tears of grief that her courage had failed her and the man she had fallen in love with did not yet truly know her. That when he did, she risked losing him forever.

Much later she woke to a darkened room. Her sore and well-used body stiffened for a moment at the swirling black surrounding her until she felt Spencer's chest beneath her cheek.

She sighed. The dark didn't frighten her anymore. Not with Spencer near her. "Hmm." She stretched. "What time is it?"

His hand caressed her arm, the rasp of his callused palms already familiar. "Late."

He slid from the bed, and she shivered, bereft without his warm body against hers. "Spencer?"

"Just a moment."

She heard him add logs to the fire. Sparks popped and a dull glow grew, swelling on the air. Smiling, she settled back on the bed and waited, wondering if she had ever felt so contented, so safe.

In moments, he joined her again. Shivering, he pulled her close to his naked body. A body that had lost some of its decided warmth in his brief visit to the hearth. She squealed at his icy toes on her calves. "Stop!"

He laughed and hugged her tight.

Sobering, she murmured against his skin, "You don't have to do that, you know."

"Do what?"

"Stoke the embers."

"You're not afraid of the dark anymore?"

She didn't bother questioning him on how he knew about her irrational fear: she'd failed to hide it well from him that night at the inn.

Rolling her fingers against his chest, she planted a kiss on his supple flesh, then answered, "I guess it was never the dark that frightened me."

"No? What then?" His hand drew circles over her arm.

"The demons of my past, I suppose. They always seemed to find me in the dark."

"What demons?"

She took a deep, bracing breath. "One night,

long ago, a man broke into my bedroom and attacked me."

His hand stilled on her arm; he went rigid as stone against her. She didn't move, didn't dare look at him, too afraid at what she might see in his face.

"He didn't"—she broke off, moistening her dry lips—"succeed at his foul purpose, but I've never shaken the memory."

"When did this happen? Where?"

Alarm trickled down her spine at his biting voice. She was afraid to give away too much, and rightly so. She had no idea what Ian had told him. He could easily start connecting pieces in her patchwork of lies if she mentioned an employer, if she mentioned Barbados.

She should have said nothing, should keep herself apart from him, but she couldn't. She wanted him too much. Needed intimacy beyond the physical.

Tossing caution aside, she murmured, "This was before Nicholas, before Ian." That much was true, at least.

"I'll have this man's name." His voice rumbled dark and forbidding beneath her ear.

A shiver chased down her arms. She propped up on an elbow to look down at him, apprehension rushing through her blood. "Why?"

A muscle feathered his jaw as his mouth pressed into a hard line. His hand on her arm tightened. "I want his name, Evie."

She shook her head. "Don't bring this back for me. Please. Let it go."

Something in his eyes flickered then. His hand on her arm loosened. "Have you?"

"It's over. Done, Spencer." She moistened her lips and slowly shook her head. "Something changed yesterday in the cellar. I stopped hiding from the dark. I finally faced it. And you came for me." Her voice gained speed, conviction. "Then, I realized good things can happen in the dark, too." Wonderful, splendid things. She spread her hand, splaying her fingers outward over his chest. The strong, steady thump of his heart pulsed against her palm.

Those bad memories didn't plague her anymore. It was as though Spencer had exorcised her ghosts, buried them firmly in the past . . . given her something else, something better on which to focus.

"I still want the man's name, so that I could pay him a visit. You're my wife now. He needs to be held accountable."

Sighing, she settled back against him. "Well, he's far from here. You would have to cross an ocean to mete out your justice, and I'm not keen on you leaving me."

He grunted and wrapped his arms around her. "I never want you hurt again. The thought of something happening to you . . ." He tugged at the ends of her hair draped across his chest.

An unfamiliar pang clenched her heart. She'd never thought a man would care for her this way, that she could find what Fallon had found with her husband. Spencer hadn't declared his love for her, but she knew that he liked her, wanted her. They had affection. Wasn't that enough?

Would it be enough if he learned her secret? If he learned that he hadn't married Linnie? That she wasn't the woman he had developed a tendre for through the battlefields of the Crimea? Would it matter to him? Was she brave enough to find out?

How long could she keep a lie from the man she loved? Her chest tightened at the idea of breaking free of the lies, confessing all to him. Could she bear to do it if it meant losing their newfound closeness? Losing him? Wild desperation burned through her at the prospect.

With her throat tightening, thickening with dread, she knew she had to risk it. She must. Because they could never have anything real, anything genuine otherwise.

"I want you happy, Evie. I would never want you hurt or frightened."

A ragged breath shuddered up through her chest. "I am happy." And that bit of truth frightened her. It didn't seem wise to let herself feel happy. *Happy with him.* When it could all disappear with a few simple words. "Nothing scares you," she teased, eager to change the topic. "You survived war."

"I wouldn't say that. Fear drove me to take the commission."

She propped up on one elbow and looked down at him. "You became a soldier *because* you were scared? You'd rather risk a saber, a *bullet*, than"—she shook her head, bewildered—"than *what*?"

"Becoming my father. My brothers. Reprobates all, drowning themselves in vice until they were shells of men. I watched my father crush my mother, kill her with betrayals and lies and then not shed a tear at her grave."

Lies. Her stomach heaved. Betrayals and lies colored his past—a past he'd entered war to avoid.

Lies and betrayals colored his present, too. He just didn't know it.

He continued, "My father and brothers thought nothing of lying or cheating to get what they wanted in life."

"Adara," Evie couldn't help suggest, too curious to hold her tongue.

"Yes. Adara. She was the catch of the season. A prize for Cullen to lord over all those vying for her hand. Myself included." He caught a strand of her hair, rolled it between his fingers. "Only I'm glad he won her."

"You're not like them, Spencer."

"Am I not?" His gaze ensnared her. "I didn't give you much choice in marrying me. I manipulated the situation. I let Sheffield think I was Nicholas's father. Because I wanted you."

It hurt to hear him say that. He wanted Linnie— he thought he had her. There was never any escaping that in her mind.

She forced a smile and teased, "Well, yes. That was a bit manipulative. Perhaps you're a *little* like them, then."

Spencer smiled, only there was no levity behind it. "My father believed our birthright made us above everyone. The Winterses take what they want and the rest of the world be damned . . . he raised us to be that way."

Her smile vanished, and she shook her head. "You're not that way," she insisted. "You're considerate. Selfless. You married me for Nicholas, for Ian—"

"Did I?" he broke in, his eyes vivid, almost a silvery green. "Looking at you right now, feeling the way I do, it's hard to imagine that."

She swallowed.

Still holding her hair, he tugged her face closer. His lips singed hers as he spoke. "I'll be honest."

Because honesty was so important to him.

"I married you out of the basest, most selfish of impulses."

And then he kissed her like a man denied food and water for far too long. Like a man returned from war, hungry for the woman of his heart. Anything else to say was lost in the hot press of his lips over hers.

He didn't need to explain himself. She understood perfectly. Understood the slide of his tongue against hers . . . the hand tangling fiercely in her hair, the roll of his body over hers. As if he could never get enough of her. As if he wouldn't be whole until he found a way to fuse their bodies together.

She understood.

Just as she understood her desperate love for him swelling in her heart. *Damn.*

Chapter 24

Evie fidgeted in her seat as they clattered through Little Billings and neared home. Spencer watched her, warmth constantly glowing in his green gaze. The look made her *feel* warm, made her remember what he could do to her . . . what he had done all the previous day. And still, she longed for more. Longed for him again and again.

"You look like a little girl bouncing on your seat," he teased, leaning forward to adjust the heavy blanket over her lap.

"I've never been apart from Nicholas this long before," she replied.

Her heart raced as they stopped before the house. Spencer didn't wait for the driver to open their door. He descended and helped her down. She surveyed with fresh eyes the whitewashed cottage that had been her solace during the last years.

The Harbour looked different. Smaller, not nearly so . . . *essential* to her existence. She missed the people within, but not the house, not the sanctuary she had clung to through the last five years. She slid a glance at the strong profile of her husband. He had done that. Had wrought change in her.

He offered his arm and she placed her hand in the crook of his elbow. The front door groaned open, and she turned her head at the familiar sound, smiling widely as Nicholas tore free from Amy and barreled down the snow-dusted steps. His small arms locked around her legs and nearly knocked her down.

Laughing frothy clouds of white, she disentangled his arms from around her and knelt down, nearly toppling over when he flung his sturdy little arms around her neck.

"See, Momma," he cried, as if needing to assert something to her, "I knew you would return! I knew it!"

"Of course I would. Did you think I would not?"

"Grandmama told me you probably wouldn't never come back now that you're married."

Her blood chilled in her veins. *Grandmama.*

Her stepmother was here?

Holding Nicholas firmly by the arms, Evie pulled him back to stare starkly into his face. "I will never leave you, Nicholas. Never. Wherever I go, you shall, too."

A beatific smile broke out over his face. Her heart swelled at how easy he was to please . . . how easy to love.

"Are we going somewhere?" the boy asked.

She glanced at Spencer. He arched a brow. "Perhaps." That was a topic better reserved for later. Right now, she needed to pursue this matter of Georgianna lurking about The Harbour.

"Evie! You've returned." Apparently, she didn't have long to wait.

Her stepmother crossed the threshold, nudging Amy aside. Papa stood just beyond her, looking a bit apologetic, but helpless. As customary. Other than supporting Evie's decision to keep Nicholas, he rarely ever stepped out from his wife's shadow.

Georgianna's deeply set eyes rested on Spencer, narrowing until they disappeared to mere slits. Clearly, she wondered whether Evie had told him that she wasn't Linnie.

"Mr. Lockhart, so nice to see you again. Imagine our surprise when we called upon our Evie here and learned you two had eloped to Scotland. How very . . . audacious."

A trickle of unease ran down Evie's neck. Georgianna and Papa had not visited The Harbour in all her time here. Whatever motivated this visit could not bode well.

"Yes," Spencer murmured. "It must have come as a surprise."

Georgianna rattled on, "I certainly did not expect for you to return to this little . . . *cottage*, Evie. Not after you've wed."

She might as well have uttered the word *hovel*.

Evie flexed her hand around Nicholas's chubby one. "Of course I would return. Would you expect me to leave my son?"

Georgianna angled her head to the side. "Your son?" Her gaze dropped to Nicholas. She stared at him flatly, nothing in her eyes. Nothing to show she even saw her grandchild when she looked at him.

"Did you think I would forget him now that I've wed? I *am* his mother."

Georgianna fluttered a hand in the air and laughed gaily. "Who's to say?" She looked back and forth between Evie and Spencer with great interest.

Evie narrowed her gaze, attempting to convey a warning for Georgianna to hold her tongue.

Georgianna continued blithely, "Then you still intend to live here? I was certain you would move into your husband's residence . . . wherever that may be."

Her tone indicated that she suspected Spencer to be a man of little to no means, without home or property. And she would just love that—would relish watching Evie's husband squeeze into their already cramped dwelling. She would enjoy even more watching him join their struggle to subsist.

"It's been a long day," Evie said tightly. "Let us come out of this cold and warm ourselves by the fire."

"Oh, of course, of course, silly me." Georgianna stepped aside, following them into the tiny foyer. Evie pressed her chilled cheek to Papa's in empty greeting.

"Evie." He smiled wobbily.

"Hello, Papa," she returned.

They once had a strong relationship. Before he married Georgianna. He'd at least been fond of her. But that had been a long time ago. She could scarcely remember those days.

"Come, Nicholas." Amy took his hand and guided him from Evie. "You'll visit with your mother and Mr. Lockhart more later. Let them settle in."

"Thank you, Amy."

"Yes," Georgianna waved them away. "Off with you." Turning, she motioned Evie and Spencer toward the parlor. "I'm sure you would like some refreshments. Tea. Biscuits. I'll just send Mrs. Murdoch—"

"Actually, I would prefer a rest." Spencer's hand fell on the small of Evie's back, gently pushing her toward the stairs.

"Yes," she hastily agreed, eager to escape her parents. "I agree."

Georgianna's eyebrows winged high. "Indeed." Her tone dripped disapproval.

At the top of the stairs, Evie glanced over her shoulder. A shiver skated down her spine at the undisguised animosity in her stepmother's stare.

At every point in her life, Evie had suffered either her stepmother's cold indifference or endured the sting of her viciousness. If not for her, Evie never would have been sent to Penwich. The idea would never have entered Papa's head without his wife putting it there.

Upstairs, Spencer squared off in front of her. "What was that about?"

Rather than answer questions she wasn't clear on how to answer, at least until she spoke to Georgianna and figured out her game, she circled her hand around his neck and pulled him in for a kiss. He hesitated only a heartbeat before kissing her back, lifting her so that the toes of her shoes skimmed the floor as he carried her toward the bed.

He broke their feverish kiss, pulling away only long enough to undress her. Then his mouth was back on hers, frenzied as his hands roamed her body.

Soon she forgot that she had begun this as a ploy, a distraction to keep him from asking difficult questions.

She forgot the sense of impending doom that had washed over her the moment she'd seen her stepmother standing in her house.

Lying back on the bed, she watched, her breath trapped in her chest as Spencer hurriedly cast off his clothes, revealing his beautifully sculpted body to her hungry gaze.

After all, what could Georgianna possibly do? Exposing Evie exposed herself as a wretched mother and grandmother. She was the one who'd effectively buried her daughter's pregnancy and then married her off to a rich, unsuspecting old man. She wouldn't want her role in that sordid business revealed. Image and position were everything to Georgianna. She wouldn't risk what little she possessed to cause problems for Evie and her new husband.

Nor would Evie let her.

She had Spencer now. She wouldn't let anything ruin that.

* * *

Evie dressed herself quietly as Spencer slept soundly on her bed, the fading rays of sunlight limning the beautiful expanse of his back. Stepping softly, she crept from the room, determined to find Georgianna and Papa and learn the true purpose behind this visit.

Walking the upstairs corridor, she was struck again with the humbleness of her home. The passageway was dim and narrow.

Her lips curved in a smile at the thought of Nicholas tromping through Ashton Grange's vast halls, exploring the large rooms full of light and interesting things. And perhaps, someday soon he would have playmates to run the halls with him.

Her hand curved against her stomach. Certainly it was a likelihood, given recent activities. Her smile slipped. All the more reason for her to confess the truth to Spencer. She closed her eyes in a pained blink. Now. Today. After she spoke with her parents.

She could put it off no longer.

Descending the worn steps, she spotted a harried-looking Mrs. Murdoch leaving the parlor pushing a service of cluttered, dirty dishes. Georgianna's voice carried from within, calling out orders for the housekeeper to return posthaste with a stack of only the most current fashion plates.

Evie squeezed the housekeeper's arm in gratitude. "You're a saint, Mrs. Murdoch."

She shook her graying head. "Aye, that's for certain. Anyone else would have strangled her long ago."

"Where's Aunt Gertie?"

"Where she's been the whole time since they arrived. Hiding in her room."

Evie nodded. "Wise woman."

Mrs. Murdoch snorted. "Coward, if you ask me."

Evie's lips twitched, but her smile quickly faded as she entered the parlor to find her stepmother pacing a hard line before the window and dressing down Papa with a waspish tone.

"Hello," Evie flexed her hands at her sides and braced herself.

Georgianna swung around.

Papa looked relieved to have the attention shift from him.

"Oh, you've deigned to grace us with your presence, have you? Where is your husband?"

"Resting. I thought it better if we speak privately."

"Indeed. Perhaps you would now care to explain how you possessed the temerity to marry this—this—" Her lip curled. "I don't know *what* he is. But it's clear he comes from poor stock if he's any relation to the blackguard who misused Linnie so—"

"If you will allow me to explain, it's simple, really—"

"Does he know? Have you dared to tell him that you're not Linnie?"

"Not yet—"

Georgianna's eyes flashed. "You vowed never to tell!"

"I'm certain when he learns the truth, he won't denounce me. He wouldn't do that to Nicholas, no matter how angered he is over being tricked."

Georgianna sniffed, seemingly gratified. "Perhaps. But why did you marry him in the first place?"

"The opportunity presented itself to give Nicholas a father. To save us from penury, hunger." She shrugged with a lightness she did not feel in the face of her stepmother's ugly glower. "I could not ignore the opportunity to give Nicholas a future. A future he could never have otherwise."

"And you found that justification to bind yourself in marriage to this *Mr. Lockhart*, kin to the very scoundrel who ravished my daughter."

"First of all, Linnie was not ravished. You know that. And secondly, Spencer is not a mister," she bit out, unable to stand her scathing references to Spencer another moment.

Georgianna froze. "*Not* a mister?" she echoed, her face paling. The alternatives clearly raced across her mind.

Evie sighed and lowered herself onto the worn chintz sofa. "He failed to mention it on introducing himself." Or even later. "Both his brothers died while he was away in the Crimea."

"What is he? Knighted? Titled?" Georgianna sank down across from her, her hands whiteknuckled fists in her lap.

"A viscount."

Georgianna's deep-set blue eyes, usually so small, bulged almost to a normal size. "You married a bloody *viscount*?"

Papa made a hissing sound between his teeth. "By God, Evie. You're a viscountess. You did it, girl. What we always hoped for in the family—"

"For Evangeline," Georgianna bit out, glaring at Papa. "Not Evie! Our plans were always for Linnie. It was supposed to be my daughter."

Papa turned his head, looking out the window as if he suddenly found something of vast interest on the lawn.

"A viscountess?" Georgianna continued, shaking her head. "You?" Her gaze skimmed Evie, none of her aversion hidden in her small blue eyes. "Oh, that's brilliant . . . and vastly fair. Linnie's dead, but you marry a viscount. Life is full of surprising delights, is it not?"

Evie's hands tightened in her lap. Foolish tears burned the backs of her eyes. "I've sacrificed my good name, my freedom, my *life*, for this family. I protected all of us from the scandal that would have fallen had Linnie's indiscretion been exposed." Heat filled her cheeks. "Can I do nothing right?" She'd long given up on the notion of Papa or Georgianna loving her, but she had hoped for basic consideration. She would have even been glad for their gratitude.

"Oh, Evie." Georgianna propped her elbow on the arm of her chair and flicked out her hand. "You really are the most selfish creature. You wanted to keep Nicholas. I tried to stop you. It would have been just as easy to get rid of him."

Evie sucked a breath through her teeth. "You really are a monster." In that moment, she no longer cared. No longer wanted to win her over. She didn't want this woman's consideration or love or gratitude. She wanted nothing from her at all. "You should leave."

Georgianna's nostrils flared, her cheeks spotting red. "Oh! You little brat! Everything is always about you, isn't it? You've just landed yourself a gold mine . . . and now you think you can toss me out of your life while you reap the benefits."

Evie stared at her, stupidly shocked.

"Oh, no, you don't," Georgianna continued. "Since you've come into such good fortune, I expect you shall move us into a more suitable residence and introduce us into the circles your husband—"

"No."

Georgianna stopped. "No?"

Evie nodded.

If possible, Georgianna's face grew redder. Then her gaze flickered, drifted beyond Evie's shoulder. Something crossed her features, a calculating expression Evie had never seen before. Pulling herself straighter in her chair, she spoke in jarringly clear tones. "I'm sure you will reconsider." Her voice grew louder in an odd, theatrical way as she fixated on that spot over Evie's shoulder. "After all, you wouldn't have fallen into such good fortune if not for Linnie . . . if *she* had not disgraced herself with that wretched soldier. What was his name? Ian? If your sister had not let that stupid boy slip beneath her skirts, then you would never have been able to dupe this viscount into marrying you."

Evie was speechless, outraged.

Then she heard it.

The slight shifting of a foot in the threshold.

Her fingers tightened in her lap, twisting until

they were bloodless, numb. Her gaze lifted, catching on her stepmother's gaze. Her stomach cramped at the cold triumph there. And she knew.

Georgianna had spoken her every word on purpose. So Spencer could hear.

She stood slowly, a loud roaring filling her ears.

Papa, as usual, sat silent. Only this time, his eyes bulged as he leaned to the side of his seat, peering around her on the sofa to the man who stood in the threshold.

She shoved to her feet on trembling legs. With a deep breath, she quickly turned around and faced her husband.

A stranger stared at her.

It was Spencer, to be certain, but not as she had ever seen him. He stood rock-still, as stoic as he'd been on that first day, the first time she'd ever seen him, in this very room. He held himself still, his face impassive. All except for his eyes.

They looked wild as they stared at her. Coldly enraged.

"Spencer," she murmured, edging forward one step. "Let me—"

"What?" he bit out. "Let you explain? That would be a neat trick, wouldn't it? But then you're full of tricks. I already know how affecting you can be." His gaze slid over her in an insulting manner. "In every way."

She flinched. "Please."

His hands flexed open and shut beside him. He continued as if she had not spoken. "But perhaps you can accomplish it. Convince me I am not the greatest idiot. You're such an accomplished little actress, after all. You belong in Vauxhall."

She withered inside at his words. This was the moment she had feared. Only worse. Nothing in her imagination could have prepared her for the way he looked at her now.

"Oh, come now." Georgianna stepped forward and placed a hand on Evie's shoulder. "Don't be too harsh. Husbands and wives always have these secrets between them."

Evie shrugged free of her hateful hand and took another step in Spencer's direction. Again, she said the only thing she could think to say in this terrible moment. "Please."

"No." The word bit into her. He held up a wide palm as if he would ward her off. "I don't want to hear you. I don't even want to *look* at you."

"Now, now. You mustn't be that way," Georgianna reprimanded. "She's your wife now. For better or worse."

Evie's fingers curled inward, her nails cutting into her palms, yearning to gouge into her stepmother's eyes. "Georgianna, you've done enough. Be quiet."

"So you told a few lies." Georgianna fluttered her hand. "Well. Several." She focused a coldly cheerful gaze on Spencer. "You must move on and accept that she is nothing at all like my beautiful Linnie. She is flawed. Imperfect." Georgianna closed her hands around Evie's arms again and pushed her toward Spencer. "Your wife."

Evie held her breath and suffered Spencer's blistering stare. She felt waves of loathing radiate from him. At last, he turned without a word and left her standing in the parlor with her stepmother still holding onto her arms.

The moment he passed through the door, Evie called out his name.

"Don't beg, dear, it's most unbecoming."

Evie shrugged free and whirled around. "Are you not happy unless you are hurting someone?"

Georgianna shrugged. "So he found out the truth. You couldn't have expected to lie to him forever."

Evie pressed a hand to her heart. "*I* was going to tell him. He didn't need to hear it from you." Especially in such a horrible fashion."

"Well, thank me, then. I saved you the trouble."

"You're truly wretched." She pointed to the door. "And I don't have to abide you anymore. Pack your things and get out."

"Surely you jest—"

"No jest. I want you out. If you don't leave, I'll have Mr. Murdoch throw you out." She slid a glance to her ever silent father. He could have spoken up on her behalf. "Both of you."

Georgianna gaped, her expression almost comical. Evie might have enjoyed the sight on any other occasion; instead, she lifted her skirts and ran from the room, determined to find her husband and explain. Whether he wanted to hear her or not, she'd tell him her side, make him understand, convince him not to hate her. If need be, she would grovel.

Anything to keep him in her life.

Chapter 25

Spencer strode outside, his boots biting into the snow-covered earth. He didn't have a destination in mind, only escape. He could not stomach another minute in Evie's house. *Evie.* He laughed harshly, the sound ugly on the cold wind. Her name alone made him feel sick. Bile rose up in his throat. Now he understood why she didn't wish to be called Linnie. Why it was such a point of contention for her.

She wasn't Linnie.

And he was a fool.

She was another woman entirely—a female of whom he knew nothing. Questions whirled in his head. How had she carried off the deception of raising Nicholas as her own?

Why would she have wished to?

He stormed past the garden, past the spot where he'd taken an arrow in the back. That afternoon seemed long ago. He should have taken that as an omen. He should have crawled atop his mount, arrow still in his back, and ridden away and never looked back.

Instead, like a besotted fool, he'd remained and let her weave her spell on him.

He spied Nicholas, bundled from ankles to chin, with his nanny at the pond's edge. The boy waved excitedly at him. Spencer returned the wave, unwilling to take out his bad temper on the lad. He was Ian's son. At least, he believed so. Unless that had been a lie, too. The sour taste in his mouth intensified.

Nicholas was the spitting image of Ian. Still, Spencer could not sort anything from the jumble of thoughts careening through his head. Only one thought eclipsed all others.

She had lied to him.

From the start, she had looked at him with her fathomless blue eyes and lied. She had duped him during their every moment together. When he'd made love to her, he'd felt there had been something there, something that had run deep, deeper than anything he'd found before.

He should've stuck to his initial plan—married her for convenience, duty, heirs. He shouldn't have started hoping for more. If he'd expected nothing, his chest wouldn't have this abominable ache at its center. He should have known better.

Unbidden, Adara's voice came to him then, her cold prediction ringing in his ears.

Your perfect bride will break your heart. I see it in her. She's the same as everyone else. Out for herself. She doesn't really care about you. Why do you think she married you? Did you even know each other? You're nothing but a title to her. Wealth and security. Not a man! Not anyone she would ever care for!

It killed him that Adara had been right.

He veered off the path, away from the pond, detouring through the wood. At that moment, he craved solitude and perhaps a tree to beat his fist against. Then, later . . . later he would return to the house and deal with his wife. *Wife.* The mere word turned his stomach. He'd accepted the notion of marrying Ian's paramour. He'd even accepted that he had come to care for her and wanted a real marriage with her. But that was before he'd known she wasn't *real*. Before she'd betrayed him.

He might not know who she was, but he had a fairly good idea that she was not anyone with whom he could spend his life.

Unfortunately, he was saddled with the lying, manipulative little viper.

He walked deeper into the woods, his feet tromping out his fury. At the snap of a twig, he spun around, a growl erupting at the willowy shadow emerging from the trees behind him.

"You followed me," he accused. "That's unwise."

She nodded jerkily, her wide eyes fastened on him as she approached, either unaware or unconcerned of the danger. Foolish female.

"You should not be here," he bit out. "Go."

Her bottom lip quivered in her wan, narrow face, and he felt his fury all the more keenly.

"Spencer, I want to—"

"No! I'm in no . . . *condition* for your company."

She blinked and considered him for a moment in the lengthening shadows. She looked so solemn and young, the winter wind nipping her cheeks red. Like a child caught at mischief—the very picture of regret. The sight fed his dangerously swirling anger.

"The sight of you makes me . . ." His fist curled at his side, and he swallowed against the thickness of his throat. "Just go."

She glanced from that fisted hand to his face, her blue eyes impossibly wide. So bloody innocent. But he knew that was an act.

After some moments, she murmured, "We need to talk." She inhaled, her chest lifting. "You're an honorable man. I don't believe you'll hurt me."

"Then you're a fool. Because what I'm feeling toward you right now is decidedly . . . unsafe."

Her slight jaw locked at a stubborn angle. With her stare unwavering on his face, she took several more steps, her slippers crunching over packed snow. "If you would please hear me out—you must understand. I loved my sister."

"Linnie," he could not stop from snapping.

She nodded. "Yes. Half sister. She was so scared when she had Nicholas . . . I only wanted to help her. To stop my parents from tossing Nicholas out like he was rubbish."

She was close now. Close enough for him to see the tiny flecks of gold in her blue eyes. Had he never noticed that before? Her lashes fanned her eyes in ink-dark webs.

He grabbed her by the arms and pulled her against him. His fingers flexed against her slim arms. She winced but did not move, did not struggle, simply continued to stare at him with that damned solemn look, as if she were a bloody martyr and he the grand inquisitor, unfairly meting out punishment.

"How do you do that?" he growled, frustration bubbling up deep in his chest.

"What?"

"Look so innocent when you're not?"

She closed her eyes in a slow blink. When she opened them again, she stared at him through a shimmer of tears. He bit back a curse. "I know I was wrong not to tell you. I was going to tell you everything. I had already decided—"

"When?" he snapped. "In ten years? Fifty? On our golden anniversary? You've had plenty of opportunities. In the carriage ride here. Could you not tell me then?" He gestured wildly. "Or how about upstairs? In your bedchamber?"

She nodded. "You are right. I could have told you. Any of those times." She shook her head. A honey-brown strand of hair fell, brushing her pale cheek. "I was scared of this!"

His chest tightened, the air in his lungs trapped. "Did you even know Ian? Did you ever meet him?"

She hesitated before answering. "No."

He cursed and flung away from her. "I thought I was marrying Linnie—"

"She's dead, Spencer!" She stomped after him, pulling him around by the arm to face her. Her breath puffed from her lips like clouds of smoke. "You needed something to cling to during the war because you didn't have anything . . . no one back home gave a damn whether you survived or not."

Her words hit their mark as effectively as a well-aimed arrow. "You don't know what you're saying."

"You fell in love with a fantasy of Linnie," she accused, nodding doggedly. "You would still rather love that fantasy than the reality of me."

He inhaled deeply, feeling as if he had been flayed alive, as though her words stripped him bare, leaving him raw and bleeding before her in the cold kiss of winter.

"You're right about one point at least," he snarled. "I don't love you."

Moisture gleamed suspiciously in her eyes, but she blinked until her eyes looked normal again. "Only because you won't let yourself."

"No. Simply because I *don't*. Is that so difficult to believe? That you are undesirable to my heart?"

She shook her head fiercely. "Who's lying now?"

He laughed, the sound hollow. "I married you because I believed you were Linnie. Because I thought I was correcting my cousin's mistake."

"You married her because *she* was Ian's," she snapped, and God help her if she didn't sound angry. With *him*. The gall! "I'm not." Her chest heaved with rapid breaths. "But I could be yours."

It took him awhile to respond, to sort through the burn of emotions. He found the one that still stung hottest. Betrayal. "You're not, though."

She flinched, dropping her hand from his arm. "That's it, then?"

"I don't know you at all."

She nodded. "Why don't you admit what really troubles you in all of this."

He cocked his head, lips curling back from his teeth. "Why don't you tell me?"

"You fell in love with Linnie. With all of Ian's stories about her. With the idea of her. You put her up on some grand pedestal and now you're angry to find out that I'm not her. That your cousin's death did not grant you your opportunity after all."

He seized her with both hands and brought them nose to nose. "You go too far."

She winced and took a deep, shuddering breath, her chest lifting high as though she drew the words from someplace deep inside her. "You've practically said so yourself."

"I think your deception is more than enough to *trouble* me," he ground out. "Nothing out of your lips has been true."

"What I felt for you is true. Real. What we have—"

"What we have . . ." He snorted, dropping his hands from her. He dragged a hand through his hair and released a hissing breath. He stared up at the settling night, at the tangled latticework of branches canopying them. After a moment, he looked down at her, at her blue gaze, her lush mouth. His stomach tightened. "I don't know that we have anything."

"We do." She moistened her lips.

He watched the smooth glide of her tongue over her bottom lip . . . felt the familiar pull. Apparently she could still rouse him.

"We have something," she insisted. "Something special. Don't let this ruin it."

"I won't. You already did that." With an inward curse, he advanced on her and backed her against a tree. "Tell me this . . . since we're finally being honest with each other."

She nodded once, her eyes scanning his face, wide and wild as a moth dancing near flame.

"That night in the cellar . . ." He paused, his jaw clenched so tightly that it ached. A nagging thought had been there since he'd overheard her stepmother in the parlor. One of the many thoughts tangling inside his head. "Were you a virgin?"

Her lips parted on a small, breathy gasp. She dropped her gaze and he knew. She didn't need to admit it.

"Yes," she replied.

He supposed a small part of himself delighted in this—the primitive in him that thrilled in knowing he was her first. And yet she had lied, faked knowledge, let him use her as though she'd been a more experienced woman, accustomed to a man between her thighs.

"So was the whole purpose in getting locked in

the cellar a ploy? The darkness a way to distract me from noticing your maidenhead?"

She sucked in a breath. "You know I had no part in that. I wouldn't have wished myself down there for anything. I spent the entire day down there, terrified."

"Yes. A convenient fear, that."

Hurt flashed across her face. "Will you believe nothing I say anymore?" A certain bleakness entered her voice. "You won't let me make this right, will you?"

"Make it right?" he sneered, hating the ugly feeling coiling through him but unable to suppress it. "You want to make it right?"

She nodded slowly, her eyes uncertain, afraid. As she should be.

His gaze dropped, assessing her slender form shivering against the tree. "And what will you do to make it right? You've already shown how far you'll go to cover your lies." His blood thickened as he remembered those moments in the cellar. He ran his thumb over her bottom lip and felt a curl of satisfaction when the flesh quivered against his touch. "You took me between these pretty lips to distract me, didn't you? Drive me wild so that I wouldn't even notice the rending of your maidenhead. Did it hurt?"

Fire filled her pale cheeks.

"Hmm. I think it did." He slipped his thumb inside her mouth, touched it to the tip of her tongue. "Yes, indeed. You'll go far," he murmured. "So what shall you do to make amends?"

She said nothing, merely watched him with those wide, wounded eyes. He found that he hated that particular expression. He preferred her mad and fighting.

Her tongue started to move against his thumb, her moist lips pulling, sucking. "Will you beg?" he asked hoarsely.

She released his thumb. Her blue eyes glittered as her chin firmed, tilting at that proud, obstinate angle he was coming to recognize as distinctively Evie. "Is that what I must do?"

He angled his head, still assessing her. He pushed his body flush with hers, savoring the sensation of her every line and soft curve that he had come to worship these last few days. It was more than he could take.

"Begging isn't necessary. I much prefer action to words."

She arched a brow.

Stepping back from her, he crossed his arms and commanded in a cold voice, "Take off your clothes."

Chapter 26

In the shadow of the woods, her face paled. She glanced around them, her gaze darting wildly over their surroundings. "Here? It's cold. Anyone could come upon—"

"I thought you wanted to make everything right," he challenged. A voice whispered across his mind, telling him he was being harsh, cruel even. But he couldn't stop himself. His sense of betrayal ran too strong. He had thought that, of all things, Evie was a woman he could trust. Sweet. Honorable.

His jaw tightened, teeth aching where they clenched together. Perhaps honor did not exist among women. God knew he'd seen little evidence of it in the females to cross his path. "Prove it."

For an interminable moment, she didn't move. Cold wind stirred the branches in the trees, whipping a loose strand across her cheek. In the gloom of the woods, it looked almost black against her pale skin.

Then, her hands moved to the front of her dress. She unfastened the ties of her cloak. It fell in a hush to the snow-dusted ground. He watched, his breath coming harder as her fingers crawled over each of the tiny buttons. She shrugged free of the dress, letting it drop in a whisper at her feet. Her shoulders gleamed in the twilight like glistening marble, and his mouth watered.

She loosened the strings of her petticoat until it, too, dropped. The rest of her clothes followed: corset, drawers, garters, stockings. Until she stood naked before him. Her gaze held his, defiant and proud. "I trust you will warm me?" She cocked a brow in challenge.

In the deepening dusk, he noticed the burn in her cheeks. Her hands shook at her sides, her body shivering against the bite of cold.

With a curse, he stepped forward. Even in his fury with her, he hated to see her tremble from cold and would stop her suffering if he could. His anger turned on himself.

He crowded her. Shrugging out of his jacket, he forced her into it. Next he shielded her from the wind with his body, backing her into the tree again.

She said nothing, offered no protest as he took

her shoulders in his hands and stared down at her.

Her gaze remained fastened on his face as his hands dropped, slid inside his jacket to circle her waist. His palms brushed up her ribs—took each breast in his hand.

A sharp little gasp escaped her. He grasped the mounds firmly, his thumbs stroking her pebbled nipples, stroking the cold tips into burning peaks.

As her breath fell faster, so did his movements, until he plucked rapidly at the turgid little crests. A satisfied growl erupted from his chest as her expression altered. Her eyelids dropped to half-mast. She watched him through those partially closed eyes, her arousal a lush, palpable thing.

He released her breasts and jerked her pelvis against him, loving the feel of her naked body. Vulnerable and exposed. Ready for him.

He ground his arousal into her in fierce, angry thrusts that made her head arch back against the tree. She moaned. All his anger spiraled then, swung into a dark desire to have her, to dominate and possess . . . punish her with his body. Make her want him.

He nudged her legs apart with his knee.

A quick hand between her thighs found her ready, wet for him.

Her cry ripped sharply in his ear, the wild sound merging and vanishing into the woods. Her fingers curled around his arms, digging into his biceps through his jacket, drawing him closer.

With a growl, he grabbed her hands, positioned them back against the tree. "You don't touch."

She blinked, nodding.

He moved his hands to his trousers, gazing starkly into her face, hating this need for her, this want that coursed through him like a spreading poison.

Hiking one of her thighs up around his hip, he penetrated her in one hard thrust.

Her gurgled cry filled his ear.

Clutching her bottom in both hands, he lifted her higher, spread her wide for his every driving plunge.

She dipped her head, her mouth seeking his.

He dodged her lips, not allowing her that pleasure. Or himself.

He pumped harder, reveling in her clinging heat. He pounded her against the tree, seeking his release, taking his pleasure and crying out his deep satisfaction when it arrived.

The night swallowed up his guttural shout as he spent himself inside her warmth.

He collapsed against her, pushing her deeper into the tree. The wind rustled the leaves, and he

grew aware of the cold again, aware of the shivering woman against him.

Aware of what he had done.

As another moment ticked by, his actions sank
in all the deeper, and he felt like a wretch. He had
never treated a woman so roughly. With so little
concern for her comfort. But then, never had he
found himself in the grips of such savage need.
And he had reveled in it—in her. Which only
made him all the more disgusted with himself.

Deep within him, her betrayal still stung.
Worse than his father's betrayals. Worse than
when Adara had lied to him and chosen Cullen.
The pain went deeper.

Because he loved Evie. Despite everything.

He cursed beneath his breath. For once, he
could not gather his usual cloak of reserve.

He lifted a hand, let it hover, drift near her face,
over the hair he knew felt like silk against his
palm. She watched him, her eyes so stark, hungry,
and intent, the purest of blues.

Shaking his head, he dropped his hand.

He pulled away, slid his body from hers.

She sagged against the tree, her hands turning,
curling into the bark as if she would fall to the
ground otherwise.

Most of her pins had fallen loose, and her hair
flowed around her like a cloud of shimmering

bronze. She reminded him of some sort of wood nymph, naked and feral, as natural to her surroundings as the air itself.

He forced his gaze away, refusing to let the sight affect him. She'd affected him enough. He could let her affect him no more.

He gazed off into the woods, staring blindly where the trees thickened and nothing but murk and shadows dwelled.

"I'm leaving," he announced, setting his clothes to rights.

"Leaving?" She crouched and snatched up her clothes, pressing them close to her body. "Back to the house—"

"No. Back to Ashton Grange."

"What about . . ." Her voice faded. Thick emotion flickered over her face. Squatting, she stared.

He shrugged. "We haven't anything, you and I."

"Merely marriage," she shot back, rising.

He grimaced. "Unfortunate, that. But nothing too dire. Plenty of spouses live apart. It was our original plan, was it not?"

"But I don't want to. Not anymore." There was no mistaking the tight emotion in her voice.

He ignored it. "Our original agreement still stands. I will see that you are provided for."

"What of Nicholas? Have you forgotten him?"

"Of course not. He'll have all he needs."

She came off the tree then, eyes sparking blue fire. "Except a father."

Perhaps because it mattered so much to her, because he wanted to hurt her as she'd hurt him, he pushed, zeroed in on that most vulnerable spot. "His father is gone. Face it. Just like you can't be Linnie, I can't be Ian."

"Bastard," she whispered.

The dislike gleaming in her eyes gratified him in that moment. An easier sight than when she looked at him with her eyes warm and soft, compelling him to forgive her, to forget her betrayal, to believe in the promise he read in her face. To believe in love.

"The boy stays with you for now."

"For now?"

"He's a child, still. A babe really. He believes you to be his mother—"

"I am!"

"Eventually, he'll need a man's influence."

"You'll not take him from me," she hissed, slipping into her clothes with angry movements, her blue eyes flashing. "Ever."

He angled his head. "Think you can fight me on this? And win? You're in no position to make demands."

"You're vile." She shrugged out of his jacket and flung it at him with great force. "How could I have let myself feel anything for you?"

"Indeed. I'm asking myself that same question." Turning, he strode away, cutting a hard line through the trees. No turning around. No looking back.

It was easier for him to leave that way. And stay away.

Evie remained still for several moments, shaking in the chilled night, but not from cold. Cold fury washed through her as she stared at his retreating back.

How could she have imagined herself in love with such a heartless man? He had narrowed in on her greatest fear, the core reason she had agreed to marry him, and attacked with all the viciousness of a predator.

Was that who Spencer Lockhart really was?

She swallowed against the lump rising in her throat at the notion of losing Nicholas. If this was Spencer's reaction, she was right to have feared telling him the truth at the very beginning.

With trembling hands, she finished dressing. Tears burned the backs of her eyes. She still felt him in the dull throb between her thighs, a mortifying reminder. Heat licked her cheeks. That had been the height of weakness—surrendering herself to him, letting him seduce her and then walk away after saying such cruel things.

Did her betrayal justify such treatment from him? She shook her head, rubbing her fingers against her suddenly aching temples. She didn't think so, but she vowed never to become so close that he could hurt her again.

Dressed, she stomped through the woods, imagining countless different ways to stop him should he ever try to take Nicholas from her. She was a fool to have dropped her guard, to have let him in so quickly. Her stride quickened. She skirted the pond, eager to see her son.

A dull pain spread throughout her chest. Amy would have taken Nicholas inside for dinner by now. They were probably wondering why she had not joined them yet. Of course, she wanted to—she had been gone for so long. She only hoped they did not read her misery.

Her cottage loomed near. The whitewashed walls and brown thatched roof suddenly felt dear and familiar.

She inhaled deeply. Lesson learned. She would reclaim the life she'd had before Spencer ever burst into her world. Yes. She'd take that life back. And pretend it was all she ever wanted.

She would pretend it was enough.

Chapter 27

Spencer sipped from his cup and glanced at Mrs. Brooks, lifting his brow. Cold coffee. Again.

She arched a brow back at him in familiar defiance, daring him to complain. He knew better. Pressing his lips into a mutinous line, he sipped a second time.

"Something wrong, my lord?" she asked with decided cheek.

"Slightly . . ." He chose his words carefully, fully aware that his staff had tired of his foul mood over the last fortnight and was in a state of mutiny. A fate worse than cold coffee awaited him if he did not watch his words.

Ever since his return home, he'd been the veritable lion with a sore paw. In the beginning, he had convinced himself it was merely his lingering anger. Fury over Evie's betrayal. Over being made a fool. However, as days rolled past, he'd realized it might be something more. Something far more serious.

He missed Evie.

Whoever, whatever she was, she had infiltrated his life. In a very short time, he'd become accustomed to her. He had come to crave her, need her as his lungs required air. Logic didn't apply. Otherwise, he would simply shut down that weak part of himself that still wanted her—even after her betrayal—and go about his life.

"*Slightly* what?" Mrs. Brooks asked with a challenging glint to her eyes.

"Tepid," he answered, arriving at a suitable word that wouldn't put her nose too badly out of joint. Especially considering how greatly he missed her scones. She had not made any of his favorite foods since he'd returned without his bride.

"Is it?" she asked with mock innocence. As though she were not fully aware she had been serving him cold coffee the last several mornings. As well as substandard food at each meal. Nor was he too dense to conclude the reason why.

Not after Mrs. Brooks had declared him a fool for leaving Evie behind in Little Billings. He had said nothing. He tolerated her impertinence. What else could he do? Reveal Evie's subterfuge to the world so everyone would understand why he'd deserted her?

Mrs. Brooks left the room with a sniff, leaving him alone with his thoughts. Seated behind his desk, he turned in his chair and stared out at the gardens. The weeks had not eased the bitter ache in his chest. Evie's betrayal still stung. It stuck in his throat to know that the first woman to fill his heart in . . . well, ever . . . had not trusted him enough with the truth of her very identity.

Mrs. Brooks returned then, clearing her throat. "You've a caller."

"Who is it?"

Her nose lifted a notch and her eyes glinted with accusation. "Your father-in-law, Mr. Cosgrove." The relish in which she uttered his name implied that she thought Evie's father was here to upbraid him. Unlikely. He recalled her father clearly. The spineless fellow lived in the shadow of his formidable wife. He'd more than likely come to beg for funds now that he'd learned Evie was wed to a viscount. A new relation with deep pockets was a singular opportunity.

"Show him in."

Moments later, Evie's weak-chinned father stood before him, hat in hand.

After a moment, Spencer rose to properly greet

the man, even if he wasn't feeling kindly disposed to visitors, especially the related-to-Evie variation. In particular this fool. What kind of man permitted his daughter to sacrifice her good name and engage in fraud? Even to benefit his other daughter.

"I'll be brief," Henry Cosgrove began, stepping forward.

Spencer rounded the desk, reluctant to offer his hand, but supposing he would. He was midstride when the smaller man dropped his hat, swung back his arm, and planted his fist in Spencer's face.

Spencer staggered from the unexpected blow, the desk behind him catching him. Holding one hand over his eye, he glared at his father-in-law. "What the hell was that for?"

"A father is supposed to protect his daughter." Cosgrove tugged on his jack, his face red and twitchy. "I confess I've done a poor job of it over the years, but I figured it's not too late to start."

"Your daughter doesn't need protecting," Spencer sneered. "She manages quite well on her own."

Cosgrove nodded grimly. "Yes, well, I've given her little choice. She had to do the things she did."

"We all have choices."

"And you're so perfect? You fought with the Light Brigade, for God's sake! That alone makes you guilty of stupidity, at the very least. Your regiment practically committed suicide."

Spencer's hands clenched at his sides. Through gritted teeth, he spat, "Careful, or you'll be picking your teeth off the floor. You know nothing of what you speak. Clearly. What you did to your daughter reveals your own lack of honor."

Cosgrove paled. "I admit I've made mistakes with my family. Let me say what I've come to say, and then I'll be on my way." He sucked in a deep breath. "You shouldn't fault Evie."

"No? And why is that? Because she's been so honest and open with me? Because she let me believe she was someone else?"

Cosgrove shrugged and tossed out a hand. "You and the rest of the world. You shouldn't take it so personally."

"I'm her husband. I think that makes it a fairly personal matter."

"She did it for Linnie. For the child." He winced. "She sacrificed her future to save all of us the shame. I was wrong to encourage her to do it, but Linnie was my daughter."

"Evie was your daughter, too."

The older man continued as though Spencer had not uttered the reminder. "Evie had just returned from Barbados, and was quite . . . shaken from the experience. Since she was sacked without letters, she didn't have too many options."

"So you threw Evie to the wolves and let her take Linnie's place?"

For the first time, Spencer began to wonder if he would have even liked Linnie . . . a chit too scared to stand on her own feet, a female who gave away her child and let her sister bear the burden.

"She wanted to do it."

Spencer shook his head, envisioning Evie in his mind. "Why?"

At that moment, he realized he should have let Evie answer that question. He should have listened to her that day at The Harbour when she'd tried to explain. Instead, he had been intent only on hurting her . . . on fleeing.

"Because she loved her sister. One glimpse at Nicholas, and she loved him, too." For a long moment, Henry Cosgrove stared intently into Spencer's face. "She's that kind of person. Kind, good. The very best of souls." He laughed weakly, without humor. "You know, she's never said a cross word to me, and God knows I deserve it. Perhaps my coming here will remedy some of my mistakes."

"You are not remedying anything," Spencer growled, hardening his heart. He would not relent, not release his anger.

Cosgrove moved to the door. "You're a fool to let her go. Evie will make you a loyal wife. She knows how to love with her whole heart. How many can say that? You could have done much worse." He sighed heartily. "Believe me on that account." Setting his hat on his head, he moved to the threshold. "I'll show myself to the door."

Fingers tapping on the edge of the desk, Spencer studied the empty door through which Cosgrove had departed. Several moments passed. The eye Cosgrove had struck throbbed, the vision a bit blurred. Despite the utter silence of the room, blood rushed loudly in Spencer's ears, his thoughts racing.

His fingers tightened around a crystal paperweight, its heavy hardness cutting into his palm. He tossed it once. Twice. A third time.

Evie's face flashed through his mind. He recalled his last sight of her at the end, after he had taken her so savagely against the tree. The dead look in her eyes.

He had done that. Killed whatever she'd felt for him.

Without deliberation, his hand moved, flew, launching the crystal across the room, crashing it through the glass of the French door.

The ruptured silence, the shatter of glass satisfied him for an instant. Then the moment faded, and he was left in silence again.

Alone. Only the dizzying rush of his thoughts for company.

"Evie. I think you should come see this."

The sound of Mrs. Murdoch's anxious voice sent a bolt of alarm through Evie. She lowered her quill, heedless of the large ink blot forming on the parchment. "It's not Nicholas?"

"No, no, come." The housekeeper fluttered her hand and hastened back out the parlor's doors.

Somewhat mollified to know her son had not broken a limb, Evie rose from her writing desk where she labored over a letter to Fallon. Marguerite's letter sat to the side, already written and ready for posting.

She'd delayed writing them, her heart too heavy to take quill in hand and explain everything. It was no small feat to impart the details of her hasty marriage and subsequent abandonment. News like that, she discovered, read terribly on paper. As terrible as it felt upon her heart.

It had taken her this long to collect herself and pen the missives. Sighing, Evie rubbed at her ink-stained fingertips as she departed the room.

Given the hasty notes she'd dispatched before

leaving with Spencer for Ashton Grange, her friends were aware of her marriage and no doubt on tenterhooks for the particulars. Since Penwich, the three of them knew everything about each other. The years had not changed that. Evie needed to tell them. Besides, they would see with their own eyes soon enough that her husband had abandoned her.

A shudder passed over her as she realized she had become that very popular *tonnish* lady Fallon had told her about—the kind who did not even reside in the same house as her husband. Years could pass without speaking or seeing one another.

Evie inhaled deeply as she descended the stairs. So she was married to a man who could not stand the sight of her. Who thought her the worst sort of female. She exhaled through her nose. She was working hard to believe that whatever happened was for the best, but she found her current reality difficult to stomach. She had vowed to reclaim her old life, but it was quickly apparent she did not want her old life. She wanted a new one. With Spencer—the man she had fallen in love with. Who curled her toes into her slippers with a look and filled her lonely nights with kisses and tender whispers.

Was that gone? Never to be had again?

Fallon had survived the debacles in her life to find love. Despite the tumultuous beginning to their relationship, she and Dominic were happily wed. Absurdly happy. And while Evie did not expect such joy for herself, for a few days at Ashton Grange, she had thought she'd found something special in Spencer's arms, that she and he might have a future together with some measure of happiness and affection.

Nicholas's happy shrieks could be heard from some far-off location. At least Nicholas would benefit from their marriage. There was still that.

With another sigh, she smoothed her palms over her skirt, determined to no longer mourn a man whose heart she had never truly possessed. No sense in that. And she had always prided herself on being sensible.

Once in the small foyer, she spied Mrs. Murdoch at the front door.

Evie inched closer, peering around the housekeeper. "Mrs. Murdoch, what—"

The rest of her words died on her lips.

Mr. Murdoch and several footmen marched up the steps, unwieldy luggage in tow. Beyond them, Fallon and Marguerite stood, framed before two carriages bearing the Duke of Damon's family crest. Fallon's daughter ran in wild little circles, chased by a harried-looking nanny.

"Jillian," Fallon commanded, "stop at once or you can forget about the treat you were promised."

With an impish grin, the toddler stopped and dutifully trotted to her mother's side. The girl's long hair, gathered in velvet ribbons at the sides of her head, gleamed blue-black in the sun. She was a gorgeous girl, bearing a striking resemblance to her father.

Sighing, Fallon looked away from her daughter and faced the house. "Evie!"

Tugging her daughter behind her, she hastened forward in her confident gait, elegant and beautiful in a crimson traveling gown. Most redheads couldn't accomplish such an ensemble, but she managed it with success.

Marguerite moved at a sedate pace, tiny and lovely in her brown wool gown that should have made her appear a drab little mouse—the perfect nurse to the ailing dames of London. Nothing, however, could detract from her unusual beauty. Her catlike eyes glowed a golden topaz, a striking contrast to her ebony hair.

Marguerite and Fallon. They were here. And Evie felt like that Penwich girl all over again . . . sad and trapped, dreaming of a different life. A lump formed in her throat.

She met them halfway down the steps. Their

faces, so full of joy at the sight of her, broke something loose inside her. Perhaps because she knew she could keep nothing from them. Perhaps she hadn't realized how much she hurt inside until this moment.

Fallon folded her into her arms, her hug tight and strong, comforting. Like she could save Evie from all pain.

Evie burst into tears.

"Oh, love! What did he do to you?"

Marguerite's hand smoothed soft circles over Evie's back. "What happened, Evie?"

Evie lifted her face from Fallon's shoulder to stare at the blurry images of her friends—and spoke the words that destroyed her heart bit by slow agonizing bit, no matter how she tried to pretend otherwise. "He didn't love me enough."

Chapter 28

They tucked Evie into bed that night like she was a child in need of cosseting. Then they crowded around her on the bed, knees tucked beneath their nightrails, faces scrubbed and glowing. It reminded Evie of nights at Penwich. Whenever one of them suffered a bad day, either at the hands of Master Brocklehurst or bullying pupils, the other two would crowd on her cot and whisper encouraging words and silly stories late into the night. Anything to distract. Sometimes they fell asleep like that—the three of them curled on a cot that could scarcely hold one, hands clasped together.

"Here now, hold still." Marguerite worked to tie off another scrap of linen in Evie's damp hair so that she might have something resembling curls in the morning. Evie didn't bother reminding them that her hair couldn't hold a curl.

"You know." Fallon rose from the bed and dropped down on the chaise. "You could be wrong. He might simply need time to adjust to the notion that you're not your sister."

Evie shook her head, which earned her a growl from Marguerite. "Hold still."

"You did not see his face." *Or hear how he spoke to me.*

"I've been there, Evie," Fallon murmured. "Sometimes men are slow to realize—"

"Men," Marguerite snorted. "Who needs one blundering about your life? They all seem a bit useless to me." She darted Fallon a glance. "No offense. Yours seems the exception, Fallon."

Fallon grinned, her amber eyes dancing with light. "Not all are useless." She leaned back, stroking a hand over her nightrail, brushing her belly. "Some are quite *good* . . . at certain things, at least."

Marguerite's delicate cheeks colored. "Tart," she accused without any real heat. "You're shameless."

Evie couldn't stop a small laugh from escaping.

Fallon sat up higher, stabbing a finger in the air. "I'll remind you of this conversation after you've met a man who twists your stomach into knots."

Marguerite shook her head in firm denial, then

returned her attention to Evie. "Truly, if your husband possessed an ounce of sense, he'd see that he landed himself something far better than an imaginary female," Marguerite interjected. "Just look at the sacrifices you've made all in the name of love! He would find no more loyal a wife."

"Spencer doesn't see it that way." Evie plucked at the hem of her nightrail. "I can't really blame him, I suppose. I had plenty of opportunities to reveal the truth, only I . . ."

"What?" Marguerite prompted.

Evie inhaled. "I was convinced he was in love with Linnie. Daft, I know. And selfish. I couldn't hide the truth forever." Evie shook her head. "I was too enamored with the notion of him being in love with me . . . even if it wasn't *me* he loved."

"It's his loss," Marguerite uttered, her topaz eyes gleaming.

"He sounds like an idiot," Fallon interjected with her usual candor. Color rode high in her cheeks. She crossed her arms over her chest. "I should pay him a call."

"All men can't be as perfect as your husband," Marguerite inserted pertly, tying off another ribbon in Evie's hair.

"True." Fallon nodded before her amber eyes turned serious. "But Dominic wasn't in the beginning. There were moments when he behaved the perfect ass." She angled her head and considered Evie. "Perhaps your Spencer will come around, too."

Evie shook her head. "I don't think so . . . and he did say some terrible things."

"And you can never forgive him those things?" Marguerite surmised.

"I can forgive," Evie replied even as the ache in her chest still burned deeply, ceaseless. "I just can never forget."

And that was the heart of the matter. Even if Spencer softened toward her, they could never go back to the tenderness they'd shared before. Not after that day in the woods. Not after everything that occurred.

He would never look at her the same way.

"But what if he forgave you? And asked for your forgiveness in turn?" Marguerite prodded. "Would that not make it right?"

"Asked? He should beg," Fallon inserted.

"I don't know." Evie shook her head. "I don't think it could happen."

Because she would forever remember this hurt. She would remember the look in his eyes when he'd turned from her, the dread he'd placed in her heart when he'd intimated that he would take her son from her.

Her eyes burned and she blinked fiercely. She

couldn't risk it. Couldn't endure that again. If this was love, she wanted nothing to do with it.

Not that she had anything to worry about.

He would never come back for her.

She would learn to live as before. Without him.

Spencer awoke in a cold sweat, his bare chest rising and falling with each gasping breath. A scream trapped in his throat, choking him. Dragging both hands through his hair, he pulled at the ends as if he would rip the strands out by the roots. After a moment, he managed to gulp down air and slow his breathing.

Flinging back the covers, he rose from the bed. It had not been the first nightmare of the war he'd endured. He'd dreamed of blood and death many times. During the war. Since the war.

Only less since Evie had entered his life. Somehow she had given him something else upon which to concentrate. Cursing, he paced a hard line in his vast bedchamber.

The nightmare had started out like so many others. The stinging smoke. Thick, suffocating. Ian was there, as he had been at the end, spitting out his final words, demanding Spencer's pledge.

And there were the others. Faces Spencer knew, remembered. Others he did not. Anonymous soldiers whose eyes were always frozen with shock.

Even among unremitting death, no one ever expected he would be the next to fall. They always looked shocked, cruelly surprised.

Then Ian vanished into the smoke.

In every dream Spencer climbed over the fallen, crawled over the dead, shouting for Ian, searching, scouring the razed field. Before, in the past, he always found Ian at the top of a hill, hidden in wildflowers that reached to Spencer's knees. Buried in lush grasses and vibrant flowers, he always looked so peaceful, so calm. As if he weren't dead but merely lost to slumber.

Of course, Ian never woke, never roused no matter how loud Spencer shouted his name, no matter how hard he shook him.

"Christ." He pulled back the drapes and stared out at the night, his heart beating a wild tempo in his chest, his hand shaking against the wall.

But this time the dream had been different.

It had changed.

It wasn't Ian on that hill waiting for him amid wildflowers.

The figure he found, still as death and lost to all his shouts, the body lifeless, unreachable, dead to all his pleas, had been Evie. His wife.

A shuddery breath tripped past his lips. He didn't know what it meant, but he couldn't stop shivering at the memory.

The sight of her narrow face, so still and lovely, pale as cream but marble to his touch, sent a pain deep and penetrating into his heart. Her gold-brown hair surrounded her like a spill of undulating honey.

That's when he awoke, a scream silent on his lips.

The lawn glinted up at him, the snow winking, as if it had been dusted with diamonds. He looked over his shoulder at his great bed, the coverlet rumpled, the mattress a great barren stretch. Void of Evie.

He told himself she was fine. Alive and well miles away at The Harbour.

But she might as well be dead for all that you've chased her from your life, banished her from your heart, exorcised her from your presence.

Her father's words played over and over in his head. As they had all day. Spencer flattened his hand against the cool glass of the mullioned window, pressing hard, as if he could break through the pane. As if truth awaited him on the other side. An answer, a cure for the feelings swimming like venom through his veins. *Regret.*

He'd fought it. Resisted acknowledging the reality of his feelings before.

He wished he could go back. He wished he could travel back weeks ago, to when he'd first walked into the parlor and overheard Evie's step-mother flaunting the sordid truth so recklessly.

He wished he had reacted differently to her betrayal, perhaps seen it for more, tried to understand her reasons. If he could take back his words and actions, he would.

He had allowed rage to get in the way—a resurgence of the feelings he had suffered years ago, standing witness to his father's deceit, watching as Adara and Cullen had merrily announced their engagement even when she had promised to elope with him. The familiar sense that he wasn't worth enough to be told the truth, that he deserved lies and betrayal, had surged through him, a vitriolic burn in his blood that had blocked out anything else.

Linnie was dead. The very female around whom he had woven impossible dreams. But Evie was alive. His wife. He swallowed against the tightness in his throat. And suddenly, he knew.

He wanted no other.

Chapter 29

The day dawned bright and golden, warming the late winter nip in the air. The snow had begun to melt. It was a perfect day for the outdoors. Mr. Murdoch swept clean the small lakeside dock and double-layered it with blankets.

Evie felt as happy as she could given the numbness encasing her heart. Her friends worked hard to cheer her, distracting her with their conversation and antics, exclaiming delightedly over Mrs. Murdoch's cucumber sandwiches spread out before them. Everyone in the world who mattered to her surrounded her. She steered her thoughts from Spencer, deliberately refusing to lump him into such a category. She would not think about him. Soon, he would fail to matter. Soon, she wouldn't think of him at all.

She need only continue telling herself this for it to become true.

She had a full life. Plenty. *Enough*. People who

loved her. Nicholas, the Murdochs, Amy, Fallon, Marguerite. Even Aunt Gertie, lucid and fairly good-spirited, had emerged from her room with the departure of Georgianna. Nicholas and Jillian chased each other over the lawn, Amy in close pursuit, warning them not to fall on the slushy ground.

It was a fine day.

Mr. Murdoch set up a target for the ladies. Given what had happened last time Aunt Gertie held a bow and arrow in her hands, she was not permitted to shoot. Marguerite took turns with Fallon.

At that moment, Mrs. Murdoch arrived with another tray of food.

Fallon patted her stomach. "I'll need to let my dresses out."

"Nothing wrong with that," the housekeeper replied, grinning her apple cheeks. "Find myself doing the same once a year or so. Mr. Murdoch simply claims I give him a bit more to love that way."

"Your Mr. Murdoch sounds a splendid man." Smiling, Fallon reached for another sandwich. "I can hear Dominic saying the same thing." The two women shared a knowing glance, the kind only two women completely confident in the love of their men could share. It made Evie feel a little lonely. She dropped her gaze and played with the hem of her dress.

"What's *he* doing here?" Evie's gaze snapped up at the sound of Mrs. Murdoch's biting voice. "Oh, the absolute cheek!"

Evie followed her housekeeper's gaze across the lawn.

Spencer strode in her direction with long, purposeful strides, Mr. Murdoch close on his heels, his face red with anger.

Evie rose unsteadily to her feet, her pulse spiking against her throat at the sight of him. Even from this distance, those green eyes of his looked brighter, more vivid than she remembered within his handsome face. His hair blew about his head as he walked. He looked haggard, severe. Lips hard and unsmiling. Still, her heart beat faster as he cut a swift path down the incline to where they picnicked.

Fallon swept to her feet and thrust Evie behind her towering person. "Spencer, I presume? I shall handle this, Evie."

"Fallon, that's not necessary—"

"You've no business here," Fallon announced as he drew near.

He blinked, eyeing her Amazon of a friend. The Murdochs joined Fallon, standing on either side of her, forming a wall before Evie. She peered over

Fallon's shoulder, her heart thundering loudly in her ears.

Fallon waved a hand, gesturing for him to leave in the direction he'd come from. "You can't break her heart and then stroll back in here like nothing happened."

He stared hard at Evie where she peered over Fallon's shoulder, his green eyes startlingly intent. "Did I break your heart?"

The deep sound of his voice—the question he asked—sent a ripple through her.

Fallon and the Murdochs glanced back at her, waiting for her to respond.

Tension weighed the air. She stared back at Spencer, unnerved by his stare.

"Evie?" he pressed, pushing for her answer.

She wet her lips. "Go home, Spencer."

He said nothing; he merely stared. And stared.

"Stop looking at me that way," she snapped.

"What way?"

"As if what I feel . . . what I *say* . . . suddenly matters to you," she choked.

"It does matter," he declared.

Fallon snorted.

Evie crossed her arms tightly, defiantly over her chest and looked away, unable to bear the earnest expression on his face.

"I have to know," he demanded, his voice desperate in a way that made her tremble. "Did you love me?"

The question jolted her. *Why did he care?*

She shook her head, unable to answer.

"*Do* you love me, Evie?" he repeated, spacing each word.

"That's a fine thing for you to ask now," Marguerite called indignantly from where she stood close to Aunt Gertie.

"The better question is how you feel about her," Fallon inserted.

Heat crawled over her cheeks. "I can speak for myself. You two don't need to protect me."

"What are you doing here?" Aunt Gertie demanded, stalking forward to stand beside Marguerite. "You're not welcome here."

Amy and the children joined the growing crowd, too. Voices ran over each other, irate and indignant on her behalf, flogging Spencer as effectively as a whip.

Evie's head began to spin. She longed to simply run away. Disappear from a situation that was quickly spiraling out of her control.

Spencer scanned the small army before him before settling his glittering gaze back on her. "Evie."

She couldn't hear him above the din, but she read her name on his lips and her heart lurched.

The pale green of his gaze searched her face. "Please. I need to talk to you," he said.

She shook her head and inched back a step, unwilling to let herself melt, to soften at the mere sight of him. He'd destroyed her when he'd left. She had just begun to believe she would survive losing him. She couldn't risk letting him back in again.

"Just go, Spencer," she pleaded.

He stared hard at her before shaking his head. He lifted his voice above the others'. "You don't want that, Evie. You want me to stay."

She closed her eyes in a pained blink.

I do. I do.

"You heard her," Aunt Gertie growled, one reed-thin arm waving. "She wants you to go. Now off with you."

Eyes still locked on Evie, his jaw hardened as he announced, "I'm not leaving until I've said what I came to say."

"You're not lord of the manor here," Mr. Murdoch proclaimed as he began pushing him back toward the house. Spencer struggled to break past the burly man, his face tight with frustration.

Something twisted inside her at the sight.

After several yards, he broke free.

It all happened very quickly then, descending from bad to worse.

"Off with you now, or I'll shoot!" Aunt Gertie threatened, snatching the bow from Marguerite's hand and hastening forward.

"Gertie, no!" Evie gasped, struggling past the barricade of bodies. "Don't!"

"Go ahead," Spencer flung out, still advancing, his glittering eyes locked and hungry on Evie. "It wouldn't be the first time."

Marguerite lunged after Aunt Gertie, reaching her the precise moment she let her arrow fly.

Helpless, Evie watched, her heart a wild bird fluttering in her chest as the arrow curved in a whistling arc through the air toward Spencer.

The arrow struck him—grazed his arm and then skipped across the lawn until it landed, imbedding itself weakly in the earth.

Hissing from the burst of fiery pain in his arm, Spencer clutched the flesh wound with one hand. Blood blossomed over his right sleeve. He pulled back his hand and examined the crimson staining his fingers.

He felt his features slacken with surprise. "You actually shot me." He looked up, staring at Evie's aunt with incredulity. "*Again*," he repeated.

"My aim was off," Aunt Gertie huffed.

"What were you aiming for?" he called.

Gertie's chin lifted. "The heart, of course."

"Enough!" Evie pushed through the throng. Her voice sounded strangely choked, like she was weeping. He saw at a glance that she was. Tears streamed down her face as she arrived at his side.

Scowling, she gingerly touched his arm, muttering, "I can't believe she shot you again."

His gaze devoured her, absorbing everything as she peered through his torn sleeve at the wound. She gasped when he stroked a tear from her cheek. "I would suffer an arrow a third time if it meant I could keep you."

She sucked in a deep breath. "Don't be daft."

Despite her words, he saw that she shivered, and against logic, hope blossomed in his heart.

"I'm sorry, Evie. I've been a hardheaded fool."

She motioned to his arm with a shaking hand. "We need to get you inside and tend to this."

"I'm sorry," he repeated, ducking his head to peer into her eyes, his voice starkly intense, desperate and hungry He leaned close enough for his forehead to brush hers. His hand lifted to circle her neck and hold her close.

As she stared at him, her chest rose and fell with rapid breaths. "Don't. It hurts to breathe when you look at me like that."

"I'm sorry," he repeated, happy to keep saying it. As long as it took for her to believe him, to forgive him, he would say it.

"Why?" she asked in a breathless voice. "What are you sorry for?"

"I should have listened to you. I should have understood."

"But I was the one who lied to you. Like everyone else in your life—"

"And I was the stubborn fool."

A small smile played on her lips. She glanced down at his bloodied arm. "Well, a man who would agree to being shot with an arrow a third time could well be called a fool."

He didn't smile, only stared at her in that starkly intent way. "I don't want to live without you."

Her eyes held his, the light in the blue depths glowing fiercely.

He sucked in a deep breath. "I love you, Evie. I love *you*, Evelyn Lockhart. I've never loved anyone before you. I'll never love anyone after."

She released a strangled sob, giving her head a small shake. "You—"

"I said I love you. Nothing else matters."

With a happy sob, she nodded, smiling hugely, as if words escaped her.

Then he was kissing her, hauling her into his arms, indifferent to his wound, to their rapt audience.

Dimly, over the intoxicating taste of her mouth,

he heard her friend Marguerite mutter, "I suppose this means we're supposed to like him now?"

The redheaded Amazon laughed. "Oh, Marguerite."

"Should I shoot him again?" Aunt Gertie shouted.

"Miss Gertie, don't you dare—give me that thing!"

Evie smiled against his lips. He didn't need to look to know they were confiscating her aunt's bow and arrow. At least he hoped so.

"I think I've some ground to cover with your friends," he murmured.

"They'll love you."

"Indeed." He nibbled her plump bottom lip. "How can you be so certain?"

She curled her hand against his cheek. "Simple. Because I do."

He pulled back, drowning in her blue eyes. "Say it."

"I love you, Spencer. I love you." She kissed him again, pulling away when her friends and family broke out in an embarrassing display of applause. "Perhaps we should retire inside where I can patch you up—"

"And we can be alone."

She smiled saucily. "Precisely."

* * *

Hours later, Evie finally found herself alone with her husband. She exhaled, both relieved and eager for their solitude.

The bedchamber hummed in the silent wake of noise and activity. Everyone had taken it upon themselves to trip into their chamber, one after the other, and verify that Spencer was comfortably ensconced and well on the mend. Nicholas had been the last to leave, carried away asleep in Amy's arms. He had snuggled close to Spencer's side, content as Spencer assured him he would not leave anytime soon and he would most certainly be up and about to take him fishing.

Her heart expanded even further at the memory of Spencer's deep voice asking Nicholas to call him Papa. The only thing sweeter had been the look on her son's face. She felt that same joy in her heart still. She doubted anything would ever rob her of it.

"Alone at last," he murmured.

"You do not mind, I hope. Solitude may be hard won, especially with Nicholas about."

"He's my son now. I want him around."

Her heart squeezed. That was enough. Enough that he loved her son. Could she be so greedy to hope he loved her? *Truly* loved *her*? By the pond, he had claimed to, but she still grappled with the reality of it all.

Lifting her nightrail to her knees, she crawled in bed beside him and pressed her lips to a spot on his flat belly, delighting in the way his tight flesh quivered beneath her lips. "Does it hurt here?"

At his groan, she looked up to where he splayed so deliciously upon her bed, his dressing robe parted wide, the sheets loosely bunched at his waist.

"Everywhere," he sighed. "It hurts everywhere."

She smiled, propping her chin on his chest. "Then I suppose I must kiss you everywhere."

He tangled a hand through her hair, his green eyes hard with a desire she remembered . . . felt echo in the melting of her bones. "I suppose you must."

"And you won't tire of such treatment?" she queried between nibbling and lingering kisses.

"Tire of this? Kisses from the wife I love? Adore?" His green eyes darkened. "Never."

His words made her flesh tremble, her heart shudder.

She eased away, sitting back on her knees, hovering over the glorious stretch of him. "Why, Spencer?" she shook her head, felt her hair toss against her shoulders. "I lied to you—"

"Only because you were caught in the tangled web you created to save Linnie, your family . . . Nicholas. It was a great sacrifice, Evie. A noble thing. I see that now." He swallowed, the tendons of his throat working, his eyes suspiciously moist. "You're one of the strongest women I've ever known, and I am the luckiest of men to have such a woman for my wife."

"Oh, my," she sighed, her hand lowering, shaking, to his chest, directly above his heart.

He grinned. "Does that answer your question, then?"

She started to nod, then stopped. Biting her lip, she glanced away.

There was still one thing . . .

"Evie?" he prodded. "If there is more on your mind, then speak of it. I want nothing more between us."

"Linnie." She said her sister's name solemnly, as if afraid to mention her. "I'm not her, you know. Not the one you dreamed of throughout the war. Not the—"

He sat up on his elbows, wincing at the movement of his injured arm but not dropping back down.

Her hand flew to his bandage and the fresh spot of blood staining the stark white. "Spencer! Down with you—"

"Let us be clear." He gripped her face with his hand, his large palm chafing her cheek as he held her stare with his glittering one. "You are more than I ever dreamed. More than I deserve. That's why I came back. Why I couldn't stay away. I shall spend the rest of our lives loving you so fiercely that you shall not breathe a single moment without knowing you are loved, adored, and valued above anything else in my life."

Shattered, astonished, she stared at him.

And then they were kissing, heedless of his wound, of anything save each other.

She knew he spoke the truth—felt the truth of his words resonate deep in her soul.

She knew *him*. He was her heart. And she, his.

"Spencer," she sighed, her eyes drifting shut into sweet, peaceful dark . . . where only wonderful things awaited her.

At Avon Books, we know your passion for romance—once you finish one of our novels, you find yourself wanting more.

May we tempt you with . . .

- **Excerpts** from our upcoming releases.

- Entertaining **extras**, including authors' personal photo albums and book lists.

- Behind-the-scenes **scoop** on your favorite characters and series.

- **Sweepstakes** for the chance to win free books, romantic getaways, and other fun prizes.

- Writing **tips** from our authors and editors.

- **Blog** with our authors and find out why they love to write romance.

- **Exclusive content** that's not contained within the pages of our novels.

Join us at
www.avonbooks.com

An Imprint of HarperCollins*Publishers*
www.avonromance.com

Available wherever books are sold or please call 1-800-331-3761 to order.

FTH 0708